Father Winter
A Yule Story

ERIC TANAFON

Copyright © 2017 Eric Tanafon
All rights reserved.

Cover art © Mythja Dreamstime.com 27851737
ISBN: 1939697026
ISBN-13: 978-1939697028

To my daughter Rowan, gentlest of readers.

And thanks to Colette for the original idea, and for making sure I kept writing.

Contents

One - 1
Nothing Was Stirring ~ Making a List ~ Hide and Seek ~ It Just Had to Be ~ Not Sugar Plums ~ Made to be Broken ~ Fairies vs. Aliens

Two - 27
The North Pole ~ I'll Be Back Soon ~ Blown Away ~ Lost ~ A Well Wind ~ Brownie Points ~ Hard, and Cold, and Far

Three - 54
Just Make a Wish ~ The Right Stuff ~ You'd Never Been That High in Your Life ~ Where Were the Reindeer Then? ~ Good Boys

Four - 74
Thirty Below Zero ~ Chase Me ~ Three Ghosts and One Walrus ~ The Marine Mammal's Ball ~ A Shapechanger ~ Running With the Pack ~ Out of Their Element ~ A Strange Time

Five - 103
The Night Before Solstice ~ People Forget ~ What Good Is It Being Good? ~ One, Two, Three, Howl! ~ Hungry ~ A Frozen Sea ~ The Snow Fox

Six - 122
Shadow-of-Birds ~ The Moon is Cooler in the Summer ~ The Old Man's Herd ~ A Cozy Den ~ First Course ~ Pure as the Driven Snow ~ Never Grow Up ~ Winter Wonderland ~ Some Things Even You Can't Do

Contents, continued

Seven – 161
For Other People ~ Still Night ~ You Have To Decide ~ Back Door ~ I Don't Feel Any Different

Eight – 180
Impossibly Green ~ May the Spirits Protect You ~ Almost Home ~ Dreaming ~ Invisible ~ We Have Time ~ On, Dancer! ~ On, Blitzen!

Nine – 205
Bridge of Light ~ Stronger Than You Can Imagine ~ Snowflakes ~ A Broken Dream ~ Too Late ~ You Don't Have to Believe ~ One Small Step ~ Nightmares

Ten – 232
Where My Tears Won't Freeze ~ Lumps of Coal ~ See What She's Seeing ~ Dance of the Nutcrackers ~ Going to Pieces ~ Not Too Late ~ 100% Magic ~ One Persistent Dream ~ Look Out

Eleven – 263
A Known Associate ~ Another Door ~ Checking the List ~ The High Seat ~ I Hate Rule Four ~ Now You Believe Too ~ Just Don't ~ The Hall of Rejected Toys ~ Swordplay

Twelve - 301
Mother Winter ~ Milk and Cookies ~ The Old Man Himself ~ Tell Me What You Want ~ Not an Accident ~ The List Is Finished ~ Something About the Dawn

Contents, continued

Thirteen – 336
Let It Snow ~ All the Colors of the Rainbow ~ Sometimes…

One

It was just two days before the Winter Solstice in Seattle.

In other words, it was raining.

Nothing Was Stirring

Connor splashed around the street corner, ducked down into a crouch behind the dripping mailbox, and looked up and down his block. It was only three-thirty or so, but already dark. Nothing was stirring. The houses sat dim and quiet behind their rainbow-haloed lights.

Looks like I made a clean getaway, he thought.

He stood up and started wading down the street. Just as he reached the fifth house on the right, and was about to cut though the unfenced side yard, a police car swung down the street from the far end. It cruised slowly down the street with its spotlight on.

Okay, he thought. *I'm not about to climb into my bedroom window with the cops watching. Time for Plan B.*

He veered toward the front of the house, careful to walk slowly. *Just out for a casual stroll in the pouring rain, officer—is there a problem?* He went up the porch stairs softly as the police car went by. Was it his imagination, or did they slow down a touch more, maybe so they could check out the address?

He eased the door open and shut it behind him as quietly as he could. He stood just inside without moving, listening to the sound of the car engine fading in the distance. For a second everything seemed still, but then he heard his mom putting dishes away in the kitchen. For once, his little sister Holly wasn't lurking around.

Tiptoeing through the living room, he glanced at the tree. It was still bare, of course—Connor's family waited until the Eve to trim—but the pile of presents beneath shone with color, like pieces of a broken rainbow.

Next step, his foot came down wrong and he nearly tripped over something lying on the floor. It was a small notebook. He picked it up and made to toss it against the wall, then hesitated. Holly wouldn't have left it there, so it must be his mom's. Maybe if he checked it out, he'd find something he could use.

On impulse he also picked up the fur-trimmed red cap he found lying nearby. If his mom caught him, he could say he was just straightening up the place—good PR. He stuck the book and the cap into his pocket.

He made it past the kitchen and into the hall. He could hear Holly's voice coming from her room, further down. *Talking to her dolls again?* He shook his head. But before he reached his bedroom, her door opened. She peeked out, saw him, and then came out into the hall, stopping to close her own door first. She had curly red hair, and was wearing leggings with a short skirt, and a T-shirt with a picture of a teddy bear on skis that said "Let it Snow."

"Connor, were you out getting into trouble?" she demanded.

Connor muttered something under his breath, and her eyes widened. "You shouldn't use words like that," she said reproachfully.

"I'll talk how I want. You're not Mom. And if you even *think* about telling her anything…"

Holly sighed. "You know I won't. But Connor, you don't have to *steal* things." She looked as impossibly understanding and grown-up as only an seven-year-old could. "Father Winter will bring you what you want, if you ask him."

"I won't hold my breath."

He turned away, but she followed him, tugging at his death metal t-shirt until he looked down at her. "You don't believe, do you?"

"You've got it." Connor felt a touch of guilt about talking like this to his little sister, and it made him more sarcastic than he would have been otherwise. "Do I look like a baby? There's no Father Winter, kid. No Santa Claus. Nobody will ever give you anything for free in this life. If you want something, you have to take it."

She shook her head, still looking into his eyes. "You are *so* wrong. But don't worry. I'll just ask *for* you."

He waved a hand at her, and walked into his own room. He slammed the door, not bothering any more about being quiet. He pulled the cap and book out of his pocket and tossed them onto his nightstand, then dropped his shoes in the corner, just missing a pile of discarded clothes.

First things first, he thought. He picked up his phone and texted one of his friends, Gil. *RUOK?*

In a minute or so the reply arrived, to the sound of a fuzzed guitar chord. *NP. SEE U 2MRW?*

Connor put down the phone and thought. No problem? That wasn't how it felt to him. It had been a close one today. He and Gil and Jason had cut down an alley, with the store detective on their heels. Connor had only just managed to ditch the stuff they'd stolen, without breaking stride or losing speed. At the other end of the alley, another cop car—or maybe the same one he'd just seen—had eased out into traffic just as they passed, like an alligator sliding into a lagoon after prey, and cruised by them at a speed not much faster than a walk. But they'd just kept on down the street, glancing casually in shop windows, and they hadn't been followed.

At least, he thought they hadn't.

He frowned at the phone, hesitating. Maybe, for a change, he should try something on his own. Probably he could do better without those guys—hadn't he been the one who planned this job, only to have Gil mess everything up? If he hadn't dropped that tablet going out the door, they would have gotten clean away and kept all the stuff.

Still, Connor liked hanging with Gil and Jason. They weren't the brightest bulbs on the string, of course, but that was kind of the point. That meant that they looked up to him, and usually went along with his plans without complaining too much. So he decided he'd keep his options open.

CM, he texted back. *Call me.* After a few seconds, the chord crashed again and he read Gil's response, *OK. WLF PAK RULZ.* Then he dropped the phone on the nightstand and fell back onto his bed. He punched in one of his horrorcore mixes—he'd O.D.'d on Muzak-style Christmas carols, hanging around the mall most of the day—and put his earbuds on. He tried to relax as the music raged inside his head.

Wolf Pack, he thought. He was the one who'd come up with that name. A little dumb, maybe, but better than nothing. And nothing was what he had, otherwise. School was a joke, and home was boring.

When his dad was around, he didn't have much to say to Connor. Usually he was gone, anyway. He'd been in the Air Force for years, flying missions just about anywhere, as long as it was far away from home. Then when he retired, a few months ago, he'd joined the Civil Air Patrol, which meant that not much changed.

Of course, his mom was home more, though her nursing job sometimes kept her late. But she made the most of the time they had together, scolding Connor enough to make up for his dad never saying anything.

He pushed up off the bed and looked at himself in the mirror. Man of the house. That was a laugh. Though he did look a lot like his father—the same dark hair and eyes, the same stubborn chin.

Their smiles were alike, too, quick and shy as gleams of sunlight though the Northwest cloud cover. But Connor didn't know that, because when he and his dad were together, neither of them smiled much.

He made a face at his reflection. For a second he felt like throwing something at the glass, but he stopped himself. It would just be another mess he'd have to clean up. Vampires had the right idea. They didn't show up in mirrors at all. That would be cool, never having to look at yourself. Why couldn't he be like that?

Or have the power to turn invisible, better yet. How sick would *that* be? He'd be able to get away with anything. And his mom wouldn't be able to give him those reproachful looks any more. Holly couldn't catch him sneaking in, either, and waste his time talking about Father Winter—which was the family name for the guy everybody else in the entire world called Santa Claus. That was because his mom was some kind of witch and his dad believed in an old one-eyed god called Odin. That was also why his family celebrated Yule, which fell on the Winter Solstice—the shortest day of the year—instead of Christmas, and Connor and Holly got their presents four days sooner than any of his friends did.

But whatever you called the holiday, hadn't even most of the kids Holly's age given up believing in...that fat guy in the red suit? She still seemed so weirdly certain about it.

His mom and Holly...what did that make him think of? He frowned, looking around his room. Oh, right—there was that stuff he'd nearly fallen over as he came in, trying to tiptoe past the kitchen.

Making a List

He picked up the book and turned it over in his hands. It was small and bound in red leather. There was a design of a stylized Christmas tree—*Yule tree*, he corrected himself automatically—in green, on the cover. He opened it and began to leaf through. Most of the pages looked blank. Flipping more quickly, he found some writing near the end. His own name jumped out at him. He turned back to the place. The writing was spidery and a little cramped, but not that hard to read.

Connor Morrison. His name was centered at the top of the page like a title, followed by *Prognosis: Naughty.* That part was underlined. Some lines beginning with numbers followed, like somebody had started making a list.

1) Sneaks out at night and cuts classes.

2) Tells lies.

He frowned. What kind of joke was this? This notebook couldn't be his mother's, it wasn't her handwriting. Holly didn't even know cursive yet. It was more like some petty older sibling he'd never had was checking up on him and making creepy, obsessive notes.

3) Takes things that don't belong to him, the list continued. *Even stole some of this sister's toys.*

I stopped that *years* ago, he thought. But he felt a twinge when he read the next line.

3a) Only stopped because he thought it wasn't cool to play with castles and unicorns any more.

4) Stole a book that he found lying on the floor.

5) Reads other people's private notes...

Connor rubbed his eyes. It seemed like those last two entries had only just appeared on the page. There was more writing, but he didn't want to read any more. He flung the book down and turned his attention to the hat. It was one of those 'Santa's helper' types, a long red cap trimmed with white fur. It looked about the right size for Holly.

He tried to remember if she had some kind of Yule outfit to match, then decided it didn't matter. For sure it isn't *mine*, he told himself, and *I* don't take toys from babies. He turned to stare challengingly at the little book, as if it might argue with him, but it stayed shut up. *Okay, then,* he thought. *To Holly it goes.*

He picked the hat up again, and for a split second he thought he saw some kind of light flicker over its surface. He blinked his eyes, and it went away. His hand suddenly began to tingle, like it had gone to sleep and was just starting to wake back up.

Ignoring that, he yanked out his earbuds and stepped out into the hall. As he got close to Holly's room, though, he heard a strange voice coming from inside. He stopped, confused. Had she just gotten a new talking doll? No way, not before Yule Eve even. And anyway, the other voice didn't sound like any doll he'd ever heard of. Holly didn't have a phone or a tablet, either—their mom didn't believe in technology, or something. So what was going on?

Connor moved closer, noiselessly, and put his ear to the door to listen. He frowned in concentration. There was no doubt about it. He could hear two voices coming from Holly's room, and he didn't recognize one of them at all.

"...what your mother will think," the second voice was saying. The voice was a little on the high-pitched side, but definitely not a girl's.

"I'll leave a note." Holly's voice.

"Oh, okay. *That* will make everything all right." The other voice sighed. "Well, the sooner we start, the sooner you'll be back."

Connor gulped, and his heart began to hammer. Was this some kind of pervert, getting ready to kidnap his sister? He pushed the door open just a crack, prepared to yell or maybe even explode into action, as the voice went on, "So if you can see your way to getting all these *bandages* off me now..."

Bandages? Connor stopped dead, his brain unable to process what he was seeing. Or *not* seeing. Holly stood with his back to him. She looked as if she was unwrapping an invisible mummy. Somehow the bandages held the shape of a body, but as she unwound them, there was nothing underneath.

And then he heard the voice again, seeming to come from the chair itself. No, from whatever was *in* the chair—some impossible pint-sized version of the Invisible Man.

Hide and Seek

After her argument with Connor, Holly had slipped back into her own room, shutting the door softly behind her.

"Umm...a little help, here?"

The elf she'd dragged into her room was conscious now, and looking a bit wild-eyed. Holly had 'made him comfortable' in one of her chairs, which was luckily just the right size for him, after she had bandaged up both arms and most of his body, up to his neck. She'd made the bandages by cutting one of Belinda's second-best dresses into strips. Belinda was Holly's favorite doll, and she hadn't exactly been happy about it.

She was sitting on Holly's bed now, still looking indignant. From shelves lining the walls an assortment of other dolls looked on wide-eyed, like a crowd of people gathered at the scene of an accident. A large black cat crouched in front of the chair, its tail twitching ominously as it stared unblinking at the elf.

"It's okay, Grimalkin," Holly said to the cat. "I'll watch the elf now. Thanks for taking a turn so I could talk to Connor."

Grimalkin arched his back and purred as Holly stroked his fur, before yawning elaborately in the elf's direction. He jumped down and waited at the door until Holly opened it a crack, then sauntered off towards the kitchen.

"Well," she said, with her best bedside manner. "How are we feeling now?"

"How am I *feeling*?" the elf asked, raising his eyebrows. "Couldn't be better. When I knock off work for the night I *always* slam my head against the wall a few times, get somebody to wrap me up in bandages, and find a savage cat to keep me company. The baleful stare, the sinister growling...I just can't tell you how soothing it all is. By the way, what makes you think I'm an elf? Actually I just came into your yard to read the meter."

Holly sat back on her heels and looked at her patient thoughtfully. He was dressed in a red suit, trimmed with white fur. His head was bare, though—his cap had fallen off when Grimalkin scared him—and in fact he was nearly bald. His ears were large, and pointed, as she'd expected. He had a round, chubby face like a boy's, but something told her that he was *old. He might be thirty,* she thought. *Maybe even* forty.

"You can't fool me," she told him. "You're one of Father Winter's elves, all right."

The elf sighed. "Well, I guess I should have known when you saw me and dragged me in here. We're pretty much invisible to people who don't believe. But even most children don't, these days."

Holly nodded. "I'm the only one in my class. Except for my teacher. But mom says you should never stop believing in magic."

"Your mother is a wise woman. Unfortunately. Five hundred years of active duty, and you're the first kid who's ever gotten close enough to talk to me."

Holly whistled. "Five hundred! What are you doing out walking around? Shouldn't you be...well...resting? In a home or something?"

"On the average, elves live to be well over a thousand," the elf said stiffly. "I'm still in the first half of a long and productive career. But as far as field work goes, you've got a point. I'm overdue for a promotion. I'd like to get into R&D. Design is my real forte. I've had just about enough of toy assembly and List duty."

"List duty? Now we're getting somewhere," said Holly with satisfaction. "So you *weren't* just playing hide and seek. You were spying on us."

She'd glimpsed the elf through the front window earlier that day, when dusk had just begun to fall. He'd been lurking in the shrubbery, carrying a little book that he held open while peering in the window. As soon as he saw Holly looking at him, he'd disappeared, only to pop up again a few minutes later in the living room. When she made a move toward him, he'd darted behind the Yule tree to hide.

Or tried to. Unfortunately for him, that was one of Grimalkin's favorite spots. He liked to curl up back there between the tree and the window. Holly always thought he pretended it was his cave and he was a sabre tooth tiger.

The elf couldn't have been more scared if Grimalkin had been a real tiger. Holly heard a snarl and a hiss, then a sort of strangled yelp from the elf, and then a *thunk* that shook the whole tree. She'd dove in after him, brushing past the stiff needles, to find Grimalkin standing over the elf's motionless body. He was still lashing his tail, and was dabbing at the elf's neck with one paw in a questioning kind of way, like he did with one of his cat toys when it had stopped moving.

Holly had checked the elf's pulse, the way her mother had taught her. He was definitely still alive, but he'd knocked himself out. That *thunk* she heard must have been his head hitting the window, she thought. Whatever magic the elf had, it apparently didn't let him walk though things.

Or keep him from losing his hat. It had fallen off and must be lying somewhere under the tree. She was just starting to hunt for it when her mother called from the kitchen.

"Holly? Don't play around the tree, okay? It might tip over. We'll decorate it..." There was a catch in her voice. "A little later. Umm...when your dad comes home."

"Okay, Mom," she called back cheerfully. For a moment she wondered why her mom sounded like that. *But whatever it is,* she thought, *finding an elf knocked out in the living room sure wouldn't make her feel any better.*

The elf was still out cold, but she had to act fast. She grabbed him and half carried him back into her room as quickly as she could, his heels dragging on the carpet.

Grimalkin followed her, stopping just long enough to pick up the elf's hat in his mouth. But after a few seconds he got tired of carrying it and let it fall on the floor.

Holly remembered times her mom had talked about patients with concussions and broken bones. She decided to bandage the elf and keep him from moving around, in case he might hurt himself more.

As she finished winding the last bandage, and the elf's eyelids began to flutter, she suddenly realized that this was it. She had finally gotten the chance she'd been waiting for.

Holly had been worried about Connor since last Yule. Already, she could tell that he didn't really believe any more. But she didn't know what to do.

It Just Had to Be

She'd asked her mother to take her to see Father Winter at the department store, but once again, he'd turned out to be an impostor. They always were. People called this man Santa, and he looked like somebody had stuck a big blob of cotton wool to his face. His breath smelled of some nasty grownup drink—brandy, she'd decided, mostly because she knew Saint Bernards rescued people who got buried by avalanches in the mountains in wintertime, and they always carried a keg of brandy around their necks.

The real Father Winter, she knew, had a beard that was white and soft as clouds. And his breath would smell of nutmeg and cinnamon. And when she asked him to make her brother be good, he wouldn't chuckle and say, "Hey, kid, there are some things even Santa can't do. How about a nice doll?"

But the real Father Winter had never answered her letters. And Connor was still being all stupid and angry and grown-up, even though she'd asked for him to get better. But now she had one of Father Winter's actual elves in her own room. *He* would have to listen to her, and he could get her in to see Father Winter, the *real* one, and then...*well, then everything will be all right,* she thought. It just had to be.

Not Sugar Plums

"...not really spying," the elf was saying now.

"What?"

"I said, I wouldn't exactly call it *spying*. It's my job. It's for the List. We have to know who's naughty and who's nice. What you do during the day, what you're dreaming about, that kind of thing."

"You can look into our *dreams*?"

"Of course. But let me tell you, your mom's dreams are on the boring side. Yours are a little better—you've got some potential, anyway. As for your brother ..." The elf shook his head.

"What does Connor dream of?"

"Not sugar plums, I'll tell you that for free," he said darkly.

"So," Holly said, folding her arms, "what are you going to tell Father Winter about him?"

The elf stared at her. "You've *got* to be kidding. That kid has 'Naughty' written all over him—forwards, backwards, and upside down." Something in Holly's eyes made him add hastily, "There's nothing I can do about it—it's mostly automated these days, you know."

"This," said Holly impressively, "is *two* years in a row now that I've asked for him to be good. I need Father Winter to make him better."

"You mean, you asked for that for a Yule present? Look, little girl, it doesn't work that way. There are some things—"

Holly held up her hand. "Don't say 'there are some things even Father Winter can't do.' And don't call me 'little girl'. My name is Holly."

"Okay, okay. I'm Snowthorn, by the way. And while we're on the subject of names, we don't call *him*...what you called him."

"What *do* you call him?" Holly asked, getting interested in spite of herself.

"He's been around for a long time, and people all over the world have given him hundreds of names," the elf explained. "So we just call him the Old Man. Anyway, I was going to say, if you asked...the Old Man to help *you* be good, he'd probably do it."

"But I *am* good. My mom and dad always say so."

"That goes without saying," Snowthorn said, though he looked as if he had second thoughts about it. "But look, even if you *are* good, you don't get to ask for somebody else. That goes against Rule Three."

"Rule Three? What's Rule Three?"

"Let's take them in order." Snowthorn sighed. "Rule One, be nice. That's my personal favorite, by the way. Rule Two, know what you want. What you *really* want. Rule Three, you need to ask for yourself."

He paused. "Is that all?" Holly asked.

"Well, I'm not sure if I should tell you, but...Rule Four is, there are no guarantees."

Made to Be Broken

Holly looked blank. "I don't get that one."

"Oh, you will," the elf assured her. "When you're a bit older, you will." He squirmed uncomfortably in the chair. "I'm feeling a lot better. How about taking off these bandages now?" he asked, hopefully.

"Not until you swear to help me."

"Help you? Didn't I just tell you there's nothing I can do? Nice is nice. Naughty is naughty. I don't make the Rules."

"My dad told me once that rules are made to be broken," said Holly, with the air of delivering an unanswerable argument. "You *have* to take me to Fath—to the Old Man. My mom says she can't do *anything* with Connor, and I want him to be good before Dad comes home, or he'll get into trouble. Again. So it's up to me. And Father Winter, too, of course."

"And just *how* are you planning to do this?"

"When I ask Father Winter face to face, and I explain everything to him, he'll cross out the Naughty next to Connor's name on the List, and write down Nice. Then he'll bring Connor what he wants for Yule, and Connor won't feel like he needs to steal things."

For a second, Snowthorn looked like he was going to wriggle right out of the chair. He might have been trying to throw up his hands. "You can't go, little girl. Holly. It's not allowed. Look, I have a better idea. Why don't you...umm...write a nice letter to the Old Man? You can write, yes? And then just let me go and I'll take it straight to him, right away. I promise." The elf did his best to look wide-eyed and sincere.

Holly was having none of it. "Whatever little girls you've met before can't be very bright. Can you promise that Fa—sorry, the Old Man—will read my letter right away?" The elf looked crestfallen. Holly nodded with satisfaction. "I thought not. Things get pretty busy this time of year, don't they? My mom's always complaining about it. And besides, the letter might get dropped somewhere, or your dog might eat it, if you have dogs." ("Not really. Just wolves and polar bears," the elf said meekly.) "No way. You're taking me with you."

Snowthorn sighed. "Holly, it just won't work. The Old Man won't change the List just because somebody asks him. It would be a waste of your time, your mother would worry herself sick, and you'd get *me* in trouble, all for nothing."

Holly stared into the elf's eyes. She could tell that he was telling the truth. This was a complication she hadn't foreseen. But she'd come too far to turn back. She turned away from Snowthorn and rearranged Belinda's tea set while she thought.

Then she whirled back to face the elf. "All right, then. We'll sneak into...I guess the Old Man's workshop, wherever that is...and I'll change the List *myself.* So when the Old Man goes to check the List, it will say that Connor has been good. Then he'll *have* to give Connor whatever he wants, and once Connor gets what he wants, he'll be good again."

Snowthorn opened his mouth, then shut it again. "You're right," he managed finally. "I'm not used to dealing with little girls like you. I've never heard of anything like this in my life. My *grandfather* used to tell stories about how crazy human children get this time of year, and *he'd* never heard of anything like this."

"Swear," Holly demanded.

"It will never work," the elf said doggedly.

"Swear! Or I'll..." Holly tried to think of some dark threat she could use, but nothing came to mind. "I'll just have to keep you here forever."

To her own surprise, it worked. "But I've *got* to be back by the Eve, or I'll get sacked!" Snowthorn said wildly. "And you know what happens to unemployed elves? They go into hock, start hanging out with trolls, and things go downhill from there."

"Forever," Holly repeated firmly.

"All right, all right," the elf groaned. "I swear. It won't work anyway, and they'll understand I had no choice...I think."

"That's great!" Holly closed the door and clapped her hands. "When do we start?"

Fairies vs. Aliens

"Ah, that feels better," Connor heard the invisible creature say. "The blood's beginning to flow again."

Connor reeled back a step into the hall. *I've walked into some kind of movie,* he thought. *My little sister landed a role in a movie, without telling me, or Mom...and they're in the middle of shooting one of the special effects scenes. Sure, that's it.*

He tried to believe that for about two seconds, then gave it up and started to grope around for another explanation. He'd grown up hearing stories about otherworldly beings from both his mom, who was Irish, and his dad, whose people had come over from Scotland just a generation ago.

On dark autumn nights by a smoldering peat fire, she'd told Connor and Holly tales of children who were taken by the fairies, stolen away to dance in the hollow hills for years, without ever growing up. And his dad had scared them talking about the Redcaps who live in ruined castles and have to keep killing people, because they stain their caps red with their victims' blood, and if the blood ever dried out they would die themselves. Those stories had made Connor glance uneasily into the flickering shadows, before his father carried them off to bed.

Connor felt himself sweating. No, there had to be a more rational take on all this. *Aliens,* he thought. Yes! That must be it. A little green man...an *invisible* little green man, who was using hypnosis, or mind control, or some kind of super-advanced technology.

Though that idea didn't make him feel much better, since those space people were always kidnapping Earthlings and using them for weird experiments.

He became aware of the voices again. "So if you can go out and take a look around for my cap..."

"What do you need your cap for?" Holly asked.

"It's a wishing cap," the alien said. "When I wish to be back at the North Pole, it will take us there."

"Oh. Okay," said Holly brightly. She turned and opened the door, just as Connor retreated into the bathroom. She ran past without looking in.

Okay, he thought. *Maybe it's more like fairies, after all.* Aliens didn't have wishing caps, did they? But the North Pole—what was up with that? That part sounded more like they were talking about a secret UFO base.

He became aware that he was still clutching the cap he'd picked up outside. *Of course,* he thought. *This must be it. This is what he's looking for. Well, he won't get it. Then we'll see how far he gets kidnapping my sister. Sure, she can be bratty at times, but still...*

He ducked quickly back through his own door, just in time. He heard Holly run by again, and a moment later her voice sounded inside the room. He crouched with his ear to the wall, his heart pounding so loudly he had a hard time hearing anything.

Two

"The cap's not there. I looked all around. *Everywhere*." Holly flung her arms wide to show just how far she'd searched.

Snowthorn groaned. "You're kidding me. We only have a few of those, and we're only allowed to use them this time of year—and then, just those of us who happen to pull List duty. Do you know what will happen to me if I waltz into the Old Man's palace and tell them I lost a wishing cap?"

Holly nodded. "Sure, I remember. You'll get into heck and start hanging out with trolls."

"Hock. Not heck, hock." The elf scowled. "Not to mention, how am I going to get back now?"

"We," Holly reminded him.

"Okay, how are *we* going to do it?"

"Walk?" she suggested, furrowing her brow.

Snowthorn raised his eyebrows. "Do you know how far it is to the North Pole?"

"No...but Pooh and Christopher Robin discovered it once. So it can't be *too* far," she said, hopefully.

For a second, Snowthorn looked like he was stumped for an answer. Then he brightened up. "Oh, sure, but they were over in *England* somewhere. From Seattle, it's almost three thousand miles. That's three. Thousand. *Miles.*"

"So let's drive," Holly suggested, practically.

"We'd still never make it back by the Eve—that's only tomorrow night. Besides, do you have a car? No, I mean a *real* one? I didn't think so. Even if you did, I couldn't reach the pedals, anyway. And if we got stopped—don't even go there. No...think, Snowthorn..."

The elf slapped his head several times, to aid the thinking process. Holly stayed quiet. After a minute, he sighed.

"That might work," he muttered. "She does owe us a favor or two."

"Who does?"

"The South Wind," the elf said matter-of-factly. "See, sometimes her big sister, the North Wind, gets a tad unreasonable—she can be a bully at times, but you didn't hear that from me. When that happens, the Old Man has to step in. Winter's his favorite season, that goes without saying, but if it was cold all the time, people wouldn't look forward to Yule so much. So I'm sure the South Wind will be glad to help us."

Holly's brow wrinkled again. "Wouldn't we want to ask the North Wind instead?"

"We want to *go* north," Snowthorn explained, patiently. "The North Wind blows *from* the north, so if we hitched a ride with her, she'd blow us down to Puerto Vallarta, or someplace like that. Sun and sand," he went on dreamily, "palm trees. Those drinks with little umbrellas in them. I wouldn't mind that, come to think of it, so if you ..."

"I get it," Holly broke in. "Speaking of umbrellas, should I bring mine?"

"Your umbrella? What for?"

"Well, if we're going to fly—that's how Mary Poppins does it."

Snowthorn stood up and stretched. "Listen, I hate to tell you this, but Mary Poppins isn't actually...well, real."

"Are you *sure*?" Holly asked, shocked.

"Trust me. Come on, let's get out of here if we're going."

"Just a minute." Holly rummaged in her closet, pulling out a sweater and her rain boots. She put them on, and stood looking at Belinda, hesitating.

"Come *on*," Snowthorn urged.

Holly kissed Belinda and patted her cheek. "Be good," she told her.

I'll Be Back Soon

They went out into the hall. Snowthorn's red coat stood out against the beige walls like a sore thumb. It was hard to believe he was invisible, but when Holly walked into the kitchen with the elf right behind her, and her mother looked up from whatever papers she was working on, she didn't act surprised.

Holly's mom, Megan, was the one who had given her her red hair. That's what she always said, but of course she still had her own hair. She was still pretty, and didn't look nearly as old as Snowthorn. She seemed tired, though, and like she really didn't want to hear whatever Holly was about to say.

"Mom..." Holly hesitated. "I think it stopped raining," she pushed on. "I'm going to go out and play for a few minutes, okay?"

Her mom frowned. "I don't know, Holly. I know it's early, but it's pretty dark out there. And I'm so worried already..."

"*Pleeease?*" Holly let her lip quiver just a bit. This was usually her last resort, but these were desperate times. "I won't walk outside of the yard..." Which was true, she told herself.

Instead of answering right away, her mom leaned down and gathered Holly in her arms in a tight hug. She let go after a second. "Okay," she said, blinking a little. "But remember, just for a *few* minutes."

Holly nodded. "I'll be back soon. I promise." She stood on tiptoe to kiss her mother's cheek. While she was kissing her, she noticed that what her mom was looking at was a map. She thought it showed some kind of mountain.

Then Holly ran down the hall and opened the front door. She'd just been *saying* that the rain had stopped, but now she saw that it actually had. The sky was still full of dark, smoky clouds, but a mild, steady wind was blowing and helping to dry everything off.

"Here she is, right on cue," Snowthorn said, as they stood on the porch together. "The South Wind." He dragged his sleeve across his face, and Holly saw that he was wiping away tears.

"Why are you sad?" she asked.

"You have to ask? A little girl saying goodbye to her mother like that...look, we elves spend most of our time making toys and singing corny songs. Okay, maybe we compensate by getting a little cynical now and then, but we're not made of stone. Besides, you said 'I'll be back soon'. Nobody can guarantee that. We're going to the top of the world. Who knows what's going to happen?"

"It will be fine," Holly said firmly. "You'll help me sneak into the palace, and I'll just make a little *tiny* change to Father Win—to the Old Man's list. Piece of cake."

"Yeah. Sure," Snowthorn shook his head, as if trying to clear it. He sighed, wet one of his fingers, and stuck it up in the air. "Well. Looks like we should go around to your back yard. Coming?"

Holly nodded brightly, and they walked together around the side of the house. Snowthorn stopped at the side gate, knocked, and waited. Holly reached past him to unlatch the gate, after she realized he was ready to wait there forever until the gate opened by itself.

"That's what they do where *I* come from," he said sulkily. "If they decide to let you through at all, that is."

The gate banged shut behind them, blown by the wind. As they walked toward the back fence, the wind kept on blowing, getting stronger and stronger. Holly found she had to lean back against it, just to keep herself standing still.

In a moment, even that wasn't enough.

"Here we go," Snowthorn said softly.

Blown Away

Connor crept silently down the hall after Holly, giving a quick glance sideways as he passed the kitchen door. His mom was sitting down now, but she wasn't working, just staring at something on the table. He wondered what was going on. Anyway, she didn't even look up as he tiptoed by.

In the living room, he moved aside one of the window curtains, just enough so he could see what Holly and the alien—or whatever it was—were doing outside. He still held the creature's cap, and his hand was still tingling. *Could be some kind of radiation,* he thought suddenly. Maybe it wasn't safe to touch. He balled it up and stuffed it in his pocket instead.

He saw Holly on the porch. She was in her pink sweater and boots. Now he could see the thing standing beside her—it was like a shadow, almost exactly her size, but moving by itself. They did some more talking. Then she started to walk around the house, the shadow moving with her.

Connor rushed back to Holly's room, forgetting to be cautious. His mother's voice followed him. "Connor, is that you?" She was using that sharp, worried tone that always drove him crazy.

His only answer was to slam the door. She wouldn't actually come after him—she'd given that up a while ago—and he needed a minute to think. He felt crazy enough himself without trying to explain to his mom what was going on.

He raised the blinds on Holly's window and saw her standing out in the wet grass, between the tool shed and the plum tree that was bare and black now, but would be covered with pink flowers when February came. She was facing away from him, looking toward the back fence. The child-sized shadow that wasn't her shadow stood with her.

Then *another* thing happened that he couldn't believe. A wind hit the house—he could hear the rafters creaking, and the windows rattling in their frames—and at the same time, Holly spread her arms wide and the wind lifted her up into the air, along with the shadow. They rose fast, soaring over the fence with feet to spare.

Connor tore open the window and stuck his head out, straining to keep sight of his sister and the strange thing that was taking her away. They dwindled in the distance, mounting up into the twilight sky. Another moment, and they vanished into the dark clouds above like stones falling into deep water.

Just then the wind gave one last sigh, and everything grew still.

Connor clutched his head, feeling like it might explode. He closed the window and fell back into Holly's room, then walked unsteadily back to his, and sat on the edge of his bed, shaking. What could he do?

He gulped in deep breaths, trying to slow his pounding heart. He'd wished often enough, when Holly was being bratty or just annoying, that he had been an only child. Now, it turned out that he hadn't really meant it. Who knew?

Why couldn't that thing take me? he thought. *So it wants to eat kids, or do experiments on them, or make them dance until their feet fall off. I could have handled that. Not too much worse than middle school.*

But Holly, she was just a spoiled young kid. She couldn't even settle down to sleep if her *pillow* was crooked.

He remembered the cap and dragged it out of his pocket again, staring at it as if it was responsible for all the weirdness. That sensation in his hand came back, like a mild electric shock. A wishing cap, the creature had called it. Well, it should know. Maybe it would work for Connor, too. In the fairy tales, you just made a wish out loud. That was it. How hard could it be?

The more he thought about it, the more excited he got. He could go after Holly, and save her. She'd be so grateful she would never bother him again. Or if she wasn't, he could wish that she was, and *then* she would be. It would be an adventure. Rescuing his sister from bug-eyed monsters with alien technology! Even his dad wouldn't be able to match that one!

He shrugged on his leather jacket, took a quick look around, and moved by a sudden impulse, picked up the little book he'd found and shoved it in his inner pocket.

Moving slowly now, he left his room, closing the door quietly this time. But that didn't make any difference. No way was his mom going to let him get by her twice. She stood at the door of the kitchen, her arms folded.

"Well?" she said, icily.

Connor stared at her. The job he'd pulled with the gang seemed, at this point, like it had happened a million years ago. He actually had to think for a moment to remember what she was probably upset about.

"Um, Mom..." he muttered. "Listen, I have to go out for a little while."

"Again? You just got here, according to Charlie. I got off the phone with him a minute ago."

Charlie was a cop who lived down the street, a friend of his mom and dad's who was also into witchcraft. One of the cops in the patrol car must have told him about Connor. Just his luck. You might think it was sort of cool to have a mom who got together with other witches and cast spells, but in real life, it turned out to be a lot more like the PTA than you'd expect.

He found it hard to meet his mom's eyes. "Look..." He fumbled for words. "A lot is going on, right now. More than you know."

That was the wrong thing to say, it turned out. "How would I know anything? You never talk to me anymore, Connor."

He sighed. "This isn't the time..."

"No, of course not." Her voice was sarcastic, but he saw her blinking back tears. "When you pulled that fire alarm at the assembly—that wasn't the time, either. Or when you started sneaking out of school to try to impress those loser guys—"

"Hey," Connor protested. "They *were* impressed."

"Or when you and your—*friends*—got into shoplifting. When will it be the time, Connor? When? What are we waiting for—for your father to deal with you, when he comes home?"

Connor stared at his mother. There was something in her voice he'd never heard before. "Mom," he asked, "what is it? When *is* Dad coming home?"

Suddenly his mother crumpled. She turned away blindly and sank back into the kitchen chair, sobbing, her whole body shaking. If Connor had let himself feel anything, it would have been scary. As it was, he stood by helplessly until she pulled herself together and lifted her tear-stained face to him again.

"I don't know," she whispered. "A climber got lost today on Mount Rainier. Then the storm started. Your father heard about it on his way back home, and he decided to fly over the mountain and have a look for him. But then something..." She swallowed. "Something went wrong. The storm turned into a blizzard, and they lost communication with Dad's plane. He's up there, nobody knows where, and nobody else can get through this weather to find him."

Connor saw now that the map spread out on the table showed Mount Rainier. A crystal pendulum lay on top of it, the chain all twisted up. She'd been dowsing to try to find where he was. He didn't bother to ask his mom if that had worked—the way she'd let it fall and lie there told him the answer.

"But they'll send somebody out to look for him as soon as it's safe, right?" Even Connor's lips felt numb. He had trouble getting the words out.

She nodded. "But…there's a huge area to search. And even if they can start tomorrow, it will already be almost…a whole day. You know the rule."

He did. His dad had told him often enough. If you're lost in the wilderness, there's a three-day window. The searchers had that long to find people and rescue them, if they could be rescued at all. After that, the survival rates plummeted.

But on the slopes of Mount Rainier, in the wintertime, you would be really lucky to get even three days…

"Did you tell Holly?" he heard himself asking.

His mom teared up again. "Just...just that Dad's a little late because he had to stop to help somebody. And there was a chance...just a chance he might not be home for Yule."

"Okay," he said. "Okay."

But it wasn't okay. What could he tell her? That Holly was gone, too? She'd lose it completely. Plus, there would be no way she'd ever let him out of her sight.

But if he could figure out the alien technology or magic or whatever it was, and get after Holly quickly, there was a chance he could have her back by dinnertime.

"Okay," he said one more time. *Come on, Connor,* he told himself. *Just one more lie, and this time, it's a little white one!* "Mom, I'm sure it's going to be all right. Listen, I have to do something right now. Nothing bad," he added quickly, as her eyes flashed again. "I promise. And when I get back...we'll talk some more."

His mother sighed and seemed to give up. "All right, Connor. I just want us all...to stay together. To be a family. You know that, don't you?"

"Sure, sure," he agreed nervously. "I know that, Mom. So I'll be back...in a little while, okay?"

"Connor," she said as he turned away, "what's that you're carrying?"

"Oh." He eyed the cap as if he'd never seen it before. "Something of Holly's, I think. She dropped it in the hall. I was going to give it to her. On my way out."

"Okay," his mother said. "I'll make some dinner. And when you get back, we'll sit down together."

"That will be great," Connor said without conviction.

He walked to the front door slowly and stepped out. When he pulled the door shut, it made a sound like a somebody closing a big, heavy book.

Outside, he followed the path Holly had taken, around the side of the house. He wanted to stand where she had stood. *Not that it should really matter,* he thought. Actually, he probably could have stayed in his room and used the cap there. Then he wouldn't have had to talk to his mom at all. Oh well, too late for that.

But then he wouldn't have found out that his dad had crashed on the mountain. Connor tried to get his head around the thought that if his dad was still alive, he might be buried in snow somewhere, with no help coming.

But he couldn't really hold onto that idea. It was too big, it made him feel hollow inside.

He came to a halt and held the cap in both hands, staring at the backyard fence and beyond, house after house, roof after roof, rolling away towards the north. Lights were starting to come on all over the city, as if the rain had washed all the stars down out of the sky. But the sky itself was still blank and forbidding, shrouded by dark clouds.

Suddenly he felt a sharp pain in his stomach. As much as he had problems with his life here, it was predictable. Safe. But once he made his first wish, there were no guarantees. Anything might happen.

Still, he knew that if he backed down now, it wouldn't matter if nobody else knew about it. He would always be a coward. How could he face even his own gang, let alone his mom, then?

There's no safe life for me, he realized. *Not any more. I already left all that behind, when I took those few steps out to my own back yard.*

So he pushed the fear down, deep inside, and lifted his face to the sky. He forced himself to put on the cap—it was small for him, so he had to stretch it out a bit. *I hope,* he thought, *that doesn't like, void the warranty or anything.*

Then, in a voice that shook only a little bit, he said, "Listen, wishing cap. Listen to me. I wish…" He hesitated, then finished all in a rush. "I wish for you to take me to wherever my sister Holly is going."

As soon as he said the last word, *something* tore the clouds open, reached down to grab him, and hurled him bodily up into the sky. He didn't even have time to cry out or take a breath.

Then he stopped as if he'd hit an invisible wall. He stood knee-deep in snow, shivering, looking up into a deep black sky full of icy stars. Rising right before him, not a hundred yards away, was a sharp-edged hill, and still more snow came rushing down its slope toward him, with a noise like thunder.

A Well Wind

The South Wind kept on growing stronger, until Holly could imagine it uprooting trees. But at the same time, somehow, it still felt warm and gentle.

"Yes, that's her way," said Snowthorn, as if he knew what she was thinking. "You've heard the saying 'It's an ill wind that blows nobody any good?'"

"Uh huh."

"There you go," Snowthorn said. "South Wind is a *well* wind."

That made sense to Holly. Closing her eyes, she thought about where the wind was born, and she began to smell wonderful things.

"It's like topical flowers..." she murmured.

"Tropical," Snowthorn corrected automatically, but she knew from his voice that he was smiling, too. "Suntan lotion. That's what *I* smell."

"Cotton candy!" Holly cried as the wind grew warmer and stronger still.

"Hot buttered rum..." said Snowthorn dreamily.

Then the wind took them and lifted them up into the air, as if they were stray leaves left over from the fall.

Like every child, Holly had always wanted to fly, and like most children, she had sometimes dreamed of flying. She found that being blown by the South Wind was a little bit different. She couldn't steer, or decide when she was going to climb or dive. But it was still exciting, and yet comfortable at the same time.

She felt as if a large, warm hand lifted her up and carried her along.

It was like being a baby and having someone you love, who you know would never, ever let you fall, pick you up and hold you high. You get to see, for just a little while, how the world looks to someone taller than you can imagine.

When she looked down, the houses and streets were already growing smaller, starting to look like doll houses and doll streets. If there was such a thing as doll streets. She guessed there must be, the dolls had to get around somehow.

Holly saw a little girl come out the back door of one of the houses, wearing a yellow slicker and carrying an umbrella. The other girl put her hand out, felt that it wasn't raining, and folded her umbrella while looking up at the clouds. She saw Holly and dropped her umbrella, shrieking excitedly and pointing up at the sky.

Holly waved to her, but regretted it when the girl's mother came out to see what all the commotion was about. She looked up and saw Holly, and even from that height, Holly could see that her eyes were wide and her mouth was open.

Snowthorn, who was floating slightly ahead of her, noticed them too. He sighed. "My fault. I shouldn't have let that happen. Wait a minute—" He mumbled something under his breath. "There. You're invisible now, like me."

"I don't feel invisible," Holly said. But the girl and her mother were looking all over now—it must seem to them as if she'd just winked out of sight, like a falling star.

"How did you do that?" she asked the elf.

"Magic," Snowthorn said, matter-of-factly. "We elves are tops at spellcraft, if I say so myself. Well, we're not bad with technology, either, but that's really just for making toys. We don't use it for the really important stuff."

"Oh." Holly remembered her father had told her about some ancient people who had known about wheels but only used them for children's toys. "Like the Mayans," she hazarded.

Snowthorn pursed his lips. "Well, sure, we're a lot like the Maya—except we're shorter, we have pointed ears, and we live at the North Pole. Oh, by the way, are you getting a bit cold now?"

They were still rising higher—the ground below looked more like a night sky now, a scattering of lights against deeper darkness—and Holly realized that she was shivering. South Wind's warmth was ebbing as they climbed into the upper air.

"Uh-huhhh," she nodded, her teeth chattering a bit.

Snowthorn muttered another charm, and suddenly Holly felt as if she was wrapped in a cocoon of warmth. "Thank you," she said.

"No problem." Snowthorn sighed. "Except, there go another few elf points."

"Elf points?"

Snowthorn nodded. He pulled something out of his pocket and held it up for her to see. "It's my 'Elf Help' card," he said.

It was a little square of plastic that looked a lot like the credit cards Holly's mom carried. But it said 'Elf Help' on it where the bank's name would be, and showed a picture of a smiling elf holding up a stocking and putting something into it. A legend in smaller type at the bottom read 'Sock it Away!'

Snowthorn flipped the card over. It had a strip on it like the magnetic strip credit cards have, but this one was mostly white, showing just a little bit of red on the left. It looked like a thermometer turned on its side, on a really cold day.

"What does that red part mean?" Holly asked.

"It means I don't have many elf points left," Snowthorn said ruefully, as he slipped the card back in his pocket. "Every time we do some magic—unless we can draw on the power of a wishing cap, or some talisman like that—we use some points."

"Oh. So how do you get *more* brownie points, then?"

"Elf points. Oh, good deeds, helping to fill the sleigh, getting your toy quota done ahead of time. The kind of stuff I've never been all that good at."

"Well, you're doing a good deed for me now," said Holly, trying to be comforting.

"You forced me to promise," Snowthorn pointed out. "So I'm not sure it really counts. But thanks for the thought." He shook his head. "I've got to face it. It'll take a miracle for me to get into R&D. You need a lot of magic to do a good job at high-level design. Most elves, by the time they're my age, have pretty well-lined stockings. But if you're this old and your card's three quarters empty, it's a different story."

"Which story?" Holly asked, a little confused.

"The one where retired elves wind up in rocking chairs, playing gin rummy with old trolls who've lost all their teeth." Snowthorn sighed. "You know how it is, you're young and you think you've got all the time in the world and a thousand elf points—everybody starts out with that many—so you take a shortcut here, show off for some cute little pixy there, and before you know it, you're on List duty."

"But the List is *important*," said Holly.

"Sure it is. But it's not hard work. The List really writes itself, as long as you just bring it close to the people you want to check out. We're really just along for quality control, to make sure the List is working right. Which it always is. You know what Silverfrost told me when they sent me out? 'Finally, Snowthorn, an assignment even you can't screw up.'"

"You did, though," Holly said, before she could stop herself.

"Yeah, don't remind me. How about if we change the subject?"

"Okay. How long will it take us to get there? To the North Pole?"

"Anybody's guess," said Snowthorn. "She says—"

"Who says?"

"South Wind, of course. She says it will take a few hours to get us as far as she can, which is at least inside the Arctic Circle."

"Why can't she take us all the way?"

"She doesn't have the power. Up here it's the North Wind's country, and the further we go, the weaker South Wind gets. If she took us to the Pole, she might not be able to leave again. That would be bad, take my word for it."

"Hmmm." Holly thought a moment. "Well, it was getting late when we left, so I guess it'll be pretty dark when we get there..."

Snowthorn chuckled. "This time of the year, it's *always* dark up there. You don't get any daylight until spring. And around the Pole itself—well, let's just say that we elves usually go to sleep right after the Eve, and we wake up in the morning, around—oh, April or so. In May we eat a *seriously* big breakfast, then we start getting into high gear with the toymaking about half past June. So sure, when we get there, it will be dark."

"I just meant, it will be my bedtime soon. Oh..." Holly got a sinking feeling. "And I forgot my teddy bear. And my pillow. Where are we going to stay?"

Snowthorn slowed down slightly, until he was floating right beside her. He gave her a look of disbelief. "Stay? Do you think I have this all planned out? I'm improvising, here."

"But...I can't walk all night." Holly thought of toiling through snow and darkness for hours, and for the first time, she realized how *big* it all was, this land, this task she'd undertaken. She had imagined floating down to earth in front of Father Winter's workshop. The windows would all be blazing with light, and when the door opened, the scent of woodsmoke and fresh pine and candy canes would surround her...

But it turned out that everything was going to be hard, and cold, and far. *Real.* It was like when grownups spoke darkly about the "real world" and what it would teach you—mostly boring, hateful things, as far as Holly could tell. Tears started in her eyes, and she gave a sniff.

"*Don't* do that," Snowthorn pleaded. "Elves can't stand it when children cry. Look, if all goes well, we should be able to hitch a ride on a reindeer. The South Wind thinks she might know where the herd is. Well, within a couple of hundred miles, anyway."

Since Holly didn't have any clear idea of how far a hundred miles might be, this cheered her up a little. Also, at that moment they began passing through some clouds that were different from the dark, rainy ones that had covered the sky over Seattle. These were fluffy and white, seen from a distance, and when she was inside, it felt as if she were flying through a snowstorm. It made her think of the real Father Winter's beard.

"So," she said, "tell me. What is *he* like?"

"The Old Man? Oh, I can't complain. He's a good boss. But a bit of a perfectionist. That jolly act is for you human children—*we* don't see much of it, I can tell you."

"But isn't he good? And kind?"

"Of course he's good. Kind? Mostly, I guess. Good and kind aren't always the same things, you know."

"No," Holly said. "I don't know."

"Think it over for a minute," Snowthorn said. "The man lives at the North Pole, and only leaves once a year. That alone should give you an idea of how sociable he is."

"I never thought of it that way," she admitted.

"I've only seen him from a distance, myself," Snowthorn said. "When the tree was being lighted, or the sleigh filled. The times when the other elves are earning points. Maybe someday..."

A silence fell, lasting for a few minutes before Holly asked, "Are we there yet?"

Snowthorn sighed. "I never believed it, but it's true—kids *do* always ask that. No, Holly, it's going to be a while. You should try to get some sleep."

Holly turned over in the air, and snuggled up in the warmth that cocooned her. "Okay," she said. Then, after a moment, she added, "Thank you, Snowthorn."

"Yeah, well...don't thank me yet," Snowthorn said, gruffly. "Wait 'til you see what's waiting for us, up there at the Pole."

"I'm not afraid of anything," Holly said sleepily, and she was telling the truth—at least right then, at that moment.

"That's because you're just a kid. You don't *know* anything," Snowthorn said, under his breath.

But Holly didn't hear him, because she was listening to the South Wind singing her to sleep.

Three

Just Make a Wish

As the snow thundered down the slope toward him, Connor suddenly remembered the wishing cap. "I wish for the snow to miss me!" he blurted out, and the avalanche divided around him, piling up to shoulder height on either side, as if he were surrounded by an invisible wall. After a minute or two, the rumbling subsided, and he gingerly backed away until he stood only ankle-deep in snow, looking at the drifts that now buried the foot of the hill.

Hey, he thought, *this wishing thing is all right.* He smiled with half-frozen lips. Then he remembered what he'd been doing here in the first place. He looked around. There was an icy breeze, but the snow wasn't blowing around much. He could see for what seemed like miles, despite the darkness. The moon was nearly full, with more stars scattered over the sky than he'd ever seen in his life, and the snow cover seemed to glow. But there was no sign of Holly or her pint-sized kidnapper.

Connor frowned as a thought hit him. He'd wished to be taken where Holly was going...but he hadn't said anything about *when*. Since they presumably weren't flying at super speed, they wouldn't be here yet. Maybe not for a while. In the meantime, he'd have to wait—in the open, in this skin-cracking cold, in the middle of nowhere.

He took off the cap and held it up. Energy still tingled around it, making his hand feel almost warm. "But I've still got *you*," he said, out loud. "Let's get down to business."

Half an hour later, Connor was sitting in a lawn chair at the entryway of his heated tent. Under bright floodlights, a cherry-red snowmobile glittered. Not that he had a use for it right away, but hey, there was lots of snow around, so why not? He stood up, putting his hands in the pockets of his new goosedown parka, and took a look around.

The moon had climbed a bit farther up the sky, and he could see another range of hills in the direction his compass told him was north. But there was still no sign of Holly or her kidnapper.

That's good, he told himself. *More time to get ready.* But what should he wish for? He thought of his dad telling stories about some tough spots he'd been in when he was flying.

What was it he'd said? *All you need is the right stuff.* And for fighting aliens, according to all the movies he'd ever seen, the right stuff was...

"Okay," he said aloud. "I wish for a ray gun."

Suddenly he was holding something that looked like a laser blaster, though it was green, with a red handle, and had stencils of holly on the barrel.

So far, so good. But how would he know when the alien was coming? It was invisible, right? So to take care of *that*...

"I wish for an alien detection system, too."

A big radar dish appeared out on the snow in front of the tent, and a second later a console stood next to him. It had a display with an arm sweeping around a circle, blipping once in a while. There was a picture on the console of a green-skinned creature that looked a lot like ET, only it was wearing a Santa's helper cap.

Connor stashed the ray gun in one of his chair's cup holders. He felt a lot more prepared now. And he still had the wishing cap, if he needed more stuff when the alien finally showed up.

In the meantime, he had to have something to keep him from getting bored. "I wish for an MP3 player, stocked with all kinds of tunes," he said.

The player he found himself holding looked kind of weird. The case was white, with diagonal red stripes, like a candy cane. Connor had a sinking feeling. What kind of tunes would come with a player as stylistically challenged as this one was?

Anyway, he touched the screen and it lit up, showing him the built-in playlist. There was music on there, all right—but it was all holiday carols. His dismay grew as he scrolled through the list. *Jolly Old St. Nicholas. Santa Claus is Coming to Town.* This was 'all kinds of tunes'? *Here We Come A-Wassailing. Up on the Rooftop. Jingle Bells. Deck the Halls...*

He stopped, remembering his father singing that song. It used to be one of Holly's favorites. Even Connor's, when he was younger.

Where was his dad now? He had to be still alive—Connor refused to think about the other possibility. But did he have any survival gear with him? Did he have food, water?

For sure, he didn't have a wishing cap.

As long as Connor could remember, his dad had never needed help. He always knew what to do. But Connor got the feeling now, just like when he'd followed Holly, that he had to try. So he closed his eyes and wished aloud.

"I wish...I wish my dad will be all right. That he comes back home soon."

He opened his eyes. He didn't know what he'd expected—a flash of light, a voice saying 'As you command', *something*—but there was no feedback at all. Just the low moan of the wind blowing across the tundra.

It made him feel lonely all of a sudden. It occurred to him that what he really wanted was some company. And since he had the power of the cap, why not? "I could bring the gang up here to check out all the stuff I have," he said aloud, as an experiment. Nothing. Except the wind, rising now. Okay, it was safe to talk to himself as long as he didn't start with 'I wish.' He'd have to remember that.

Wait, though. How could he explain to Jason and Gil everything that had happened? They wouldn't believe him. Or maybe they would—they'd have to, when they saw where they were. But what kind of trouble would they make later? Connor didn't want everybody talking about what he could do.

"I can tell the cap to make them forget," he muttered. "When I send them back."

That seemed like it would work. He started by wishing up two more chairs. *Better have some more Arctic gear on hand,* he thought. *Who knows how they'll be dressed,*

Jason just goes around in muscle shirts all the time. So, a couple parkas and two more pairs of boots. Check.

"Okay," he told the wishing cap. "Now I wish that you bring Gil and Jason to me here, right away."

Nothing happened. Well, almost nothing. The cold wind shifted around and blew straight toward him, and Connor had to grab the cap to keep it from blowing off his head.

What's up? he wondered. *Maybe the cap only gives you a certain number of wishes, and then it runs out of charge? Nice if they told you that in the manual.*

At random, he wished for a pizza. A second later he was holding one, steaming hot, with pepperonis arranged to make a sort of smiley face with branching lines on top that looked like antlers—he guessed it was supposed to be a reindeer.

He tossed the pizza into a snowbank and wished again.

"My friends from Seattle, Gil Stevens and Jason Kozinski," he said loudly, as if the wishing cap might be deaf, or not too bright. "I wish for them to be here with me. Now."

Nothing happened, again, except that the wind picked up. It was really blowing a gale now. Connor clutched the cap with one hand, resisting the impulse to kick something. Even through his parka, he felt the wind, so cold it burned.

A moment's work with the cap, and he was holding hot chocolate in a cup with a cover. That made him feel better. True, the cup was, for some reason, decorated with a tacky design of Yule trees and snowflakes. But the drink itself was hot, creamy, and darkly sweet, without any of those silly floating marshmallows that Holly and his mom liked.

Okay, he told himself, *think*. The wind had died down again now, and he was a little calmer. What was he missing? Maybe the cap didn't work on people? But no, he'd been able to wish himself what, a thousand miles away, in less time than it took to think about it.

Then inspiration hit him. Maybe it didn't work on just *anybody*. Maybe you had to be close to the person for the wish to work. So even if he couldn't wish up Gil or Jason, he might be able to bring *Holly* here. And if he could do *that*...

If I can do that, he thought, then all I need to do is wish that she and I were together, back in Seattle. And then there wouldn't even need to be an adventure. Everything would be over before it started. It would be like one of those stories where in the end, you couldn't really be sure if it was all a dream or not.

It was perfect. Except that he suddenly had a strong feeling that he would be doing something wrong. But he pushed that feeling away. It wasn't the sort of thing that mattered to *him,* Connor told himself. Not him, the mastermind, the guy who could outsmart anybody. Besides, what was the worst that could happen?

He put the hot chocolate down and settled the cap more firmly on his head. Everything was quiet, as if the whole black-and-white Arctic world waited breathlessly to hear what he was going to ask.

"I wish," he said, "that Holly—" and then suddenly the wind was back, blowing a gale now, a howl building in the air far away and rushing toward him, so that he had to shout to hear himself over it—"I wish that Holly and I were back in Seattle together and that none of this ever happened!"

Holly didn't appear. Instead the wind hit him like some kind of invisible ninja, whirling around him, striking first from one direction, then another. He lost his grip on the cap. The wind seized it and the cap sailed off, end over end, only to catch on top of a snowdrift maybe fifty yards away. The wind made the tip of the cap stir around as it sat there, looking like a bird that had just found a perch, but might take off again anytime.

Connor muttered a few choice words, then rushed toward the snowdrift. Just as he neared it, the wind twitched the cap up in the air again, and it blew farther away, just out of his reach. Diving for it, Connor wound up with a face full of snow. Sputtering, he struggled up again, in time to see the cap make a swooping turn and go flying back in the opposite direction.

Down on his hands and knees in the snow, Connor stared after it. Then he remembered his earlier thought—*all you need is the right stuff*—and grinned wolfishly. Keeping the hat in sight as it swirled and danced above him, Connor sprinted back to his tent, where the snowmobile was waiting.

He jumped into the seat. The cap had shifted west again, soaring high as a runaway balloon, then coming back down and almost skimming the snow.

Connor's heart sunk as he realized he had no idea how to start the snowmobile. He hadn't wished for a manual, and there was no time to read one anyway. Feverishly, he looked over the controls. Okay, he'd used a lawnmower, and this didn't look that different. There was a switch to set, a key to turn, and a pull cord with a handle shaped like a little reindeer's head, complete with a red nose.

He grabbed it and gave a heave. The engine coughed, and then roared into life. So far, so good. There was a handlebar, just like a bike, so steering was no problem. He found another lever on the handlebar that seemed to be the throttle—when he pushed it, the snowmobile lurched forward. On the opposite side was the brake—when he pulled that lever, he stopped.

All right, he thought. *Bring it on.*

He looked around, then up. The cap was swirling around a few feet overhead, like it was in a holding pattern, waiting for him. He waited, his thumb on the throttle, until another gust caught it and it went flying to the west again.

He pushed the throttle and then he was speeding over the snow after the hat. The ground was level, and he had no trouble keeping up with it. Squinting up, he could see it beginning to lose altitude. If it kept on the same trajectory, it would be low enough that he could grab it just as he topped the rise that lay a hundred yards or so ahead.

The wind rushed past him as he speeded up. The hat was drifting down softly, ready to fall right into his outstretched hand as he leaned over the handlebars...

Then, as he crested the ridge, he saw the cliff edge right in front of him, the land falling away to blue-shadowed depths below.

No time to brake. Connor threw himself backward and sideways, jack-knifing off the snowmobile as it roared on. He hit the ground hard, jarring his teeth, and rolled over several times, winding up on his back. He looked up, just in time to see the hat and snowmobile both dropping off the cliff into empty space.

He lay there for a minute, gulping air and listening. He didn't hear anything. Why didn't the snowmobile explode? In the movies, cars always exploded when you drove them off cliffs. He crawled to the edge of the cliff and looked over.

Then he clutched the earth tightly as stars swam before his eyes like some kind of cheap special effect.

Connor's problem with heights went way back. He remembered the family trip to Seattle Center when he'd first found out about his fear, or it found him. They'd  gone up in the Space Needle, and Connor had felt dizzy and sick looking down at the city from above. It felt like the floor was tilting outward, and he would get thrown off in a minute, like a squirrel from one of those spinning bird feeders his mom was always thinking about buying.

His dad had wound up having to carry Connor back down in the elevator. They'd planned to have dinner at the rotating restaurant, a special treat to wind up the trip. So Connor hadn't only disgraced himself, but ruined everybody else's day too.

It was much later, only a little more than a year ago, when his dad had taken him up in a small plane. Connor suspected it was his mom's idea, a way for him and his dad to do some male bonding, or something. But his dad had gone along with it, probably figuring that if Connor had any problems before, he'd outgrown them all by himself—wasn't that what boys did? Real boys, at least.

"And if you like it," his dad had said on the way there, "someday it will be you at the controls."

The truth was, he was a little afraid even before they'd begun to taxi down the runway. By the time the little plane lifted into the air, his heart was pounding and his hands trembled.

To hide his fear, he'd talked loudly about the weather. He'd hoped that by the time he looked down, all he'd see below would be cloud cover, like a comfortable gray carpet rolling away beneath him. Boring, but safe.

But he couldn't keep from looking down before then. And all of a sudden, it was like something grabbed his chest, and he couldn't breathe.

Afterwards, he'd thought that his dad should have made the Guinness Book for shortest flight, fastest landing, or something. Once back on the ground, Connor had refused to go flying any more that day—or, as it turned out, ever again.

They'd made their way back home in silence. Almost. His dad had said just one thing to him. "Connor, you just decided you'd never been that high in your life. And you didn't like it."

Well, duh, Connor thought. *That was supposed to be helpful?* At the time, he'd almost wished that his father would yell at him instead, tell him what a disappointment he was, how he'd ordered a macho fly guy for a son, and somehow things had gotten mixed up and Odin, or whoever else was in charge of babies and destinies, had shipped him this loser instead.

That wasn't his dad's style, though. Connor knew that. But he still would have felt better if his dad had pushed it, told him he needed to try again, pointed out how all Connor's acting out since then, cutting school and stealing stuff with his gang, was just a reaction to wimping out that time.

Didn't fathers use to do things like that?

But he never said anything about it, and never even mentioned going up in the plane again. For sure, Connor wasn't about to bring it up.

Things are different for Holly, he thought with a touch of jealousy. *She just needs to be cute, and everything's okay.*

Back to the present, Connor.

So here he was now, peering over the edge, confronting his fears, and there was nobody to see. There wasn't much for *him* to see, either—only a dark, irregular shape that he guessed was the snowmobile, like you could imagine ink blots were different things when a shrink showed them to you. The hat was gone, blowing on over the tundra toward the North Pole, or wherever.

Connor slid backwards, away from the cliff edge, got to his feet, and limped painfully back to his camp. *So much for the right stuff,* he thought. *At least I've still got the radar. And the ray gun. And some music, I guess...*

This time, he scrolled the whole way through the playlist. Mostly the same childish junk. Finally he settled on 'Christmas in Sarajevo' by the Trans-Siberian Orchestra, turned it up until the bass notes made his skull shiver, and put it on endless repeat.

Where Were The Reindeer Then?

There was enough warm air coming out of the tent to make Connor feel drowsy, and even the loud music couldn't keep him from dozing off. So he didn't notice when the alien detector started beeping frantically, and Holly and Snowthorn, blown by the tiring South Wind, appeared above him. But when a snowball fell out of the sky, almost hitting his head, he roused sharply and looked up, just in time to see his sister disappearing over the peak.

They were getting away. Without stopping to think, he grabbed his ray gun and blundered off in the same direction, cursing himself for not telling the cap to take him to the *exact* spot and time that Holly would land. Within a minute or two, he was bogged down in deep snow. With every step, he punched through the crust, floundering in snow up to his knees.

He stopped and forced himself to take a deep breath. *Think, Connor. Snowshoes would have been great, but guess what, you're out of wishes. So, you'll have to go around the hill.* It looked like heading westward might be a good idea—the snow seemed to taper off in that direction.

Once free of the drift he was able to walk more quickly, his boots sinking into snow only ankle deep. He looked back for a second at the tent, cursing silently. With the snowmobile a twisted ruin at the bottom of the cliff, he had no way of bringing any of his gear with him. Well, he'd leave it all and maybe he and Holly could get back there, after Connor somehow—alone and single-handed—overcame a strange alien with miraculous technology, who was probably halfway to a base where a million more like him were waiting.

Sure, he thought. *That will happen.*

But as he walked on through the frozen darkness, the other explanation began to haunt him, until he couldn't ignore it any longer. Maybe, just maybe, he was following a magical creature who lived here—someplace that had to be *close,* anyway, to the North Pole—and had a cap that gave you whatever you wished for, only everything came out *themed,* like some ad campaign for the holidays...what did that sound like?

No, it couldn't be, he told himself. A hidden UFO base made a lot more sense, didn't it?

Well, actually, no. Connor could imagine an alien kidnapping his sister, and having some kind of matter converter...that was in all the sci-fi stories. But for the alien to disguise his technology as some kind of elf hat—*that* was a stretch.

But that kind of thinking opened up a whole world of things he didn't want to remember, had thought he'd safely outgrown and left behind. Being good. Getting that special treat in his stocking. Waiting up on Yule Eve, breathless with anticipation, until somehow he must have fallen asleep, because the next thing he knew it was morning and Holly was bouncing on his bed, telling him to get up and see what Father Winter had brought them.

So if this Father Winter business was, somehow, well, *real*...what did it all mean? And why was he only finding out now? Where were the elves and the reindeer *then*, back when Connor had believed in all that? Now it was like he was being taunted with it once he was too old—and couldn't make the grade anyway, if he believed the nagging book he carried in his jacket pocket.

Suddenly, he felt cold and very alone. Back at home, he'd always had his anger ready to call up, like a fire he could use to warm himself and drive back the night. Now that fire had gone out, and the shadows were looming over him, beginning to close in.

He climbed a swell of ground and froze. A long, drawn-out howl split the air from somewhere behind him. He turned and saw several four-legged creatures racing toward him over the tundra. A pack of dogs, he thought. That could be good. A sign of civilization, right?

But the dogs kept getting closer, and larger. Another howl rose, and then another.

Wolves! Connor's knees felt weak with fear. He remembered his ray gun. *Try to scare them off, first.* He pointed it at the ground in front of the wolves and pulled the trigger.

The gun made a weird kind of wailing noise. Red and green sparks flashed from the muzzle. They didn't even melt the snow.

Connor wasn't too impressed. Neither were the wolves. They stopped for a second, then gave a derisive-sounding howl and came on.

Okay, time for plan B. Connor let the gun fall to the ground. What were you supposed to do when a wolf pack came after you? His father had gone over this that time he'd tried to teach Connor survival tactics, hadn't he? Turn and face them? Roll down a handy hill? He felt hysterical laughter rising inside him. Climb a tree?

Probably, whatever you did, you weren't supposed to run. So, of course, Connor ran, pumping his arms, kicking up snow in his frantic wake.

The wolves continued to overtake him, seemingly without effort. There were three of them. Two spread out to flank him on either side, while one kept following on his heels. He slid down the other side of the rise, and found unexpectedly deep snow at the bottom. Trying to get up, he slipped and fell.

When he looked up, he saw all the wolves crouching in a ring around him, looking at him with their tongues out. They varied in size, and the color of their fur ranged from pure silver-white to salt-and-pepper. The largest wolf was crouching not three feet from Connor. He could almost feel its hot breath as it panted.

He got shakily to his feet. Three pairs of eyes followed his every move. If I had some food, he thought. A piece of meat. Anything.

"Nice…nice wolves…good boys…" he said weakly.

When one of them *answered*, his nightmare was complete.

"Hey," said the biggest wolf in a deep voice, "you don't know who you're dealing with, here. You're just a cub, dude, and *we're* a bunch of savage beasts. Don't mess with us."

Four

Thirty Below Zero

Holly woke up with a start. She'd dreamed of falling, and for a moment her heart pounded with terror at finding herself still flying through the darkness. She didn't feel cold, exactly, but the warmth that had surrounded her was fading. She looked down, and she could see the ground again, white with snow, glittering in the moonlight.

"Good, you're awake," Snowthorn said. She turned her head and saw the elf, flying just above and behind her. He nodded toward the ground below. "She's going to let us down in just a minute."

"We're there?" Holly looked around eagerly but couldn't see much except a plain that stretched out beneath them in all directions, interrupted by a line of craggy hills. A silver line that might have been a river wound off into the distance.

"It's as much *there* as we can get, for now," Snowthorn said. "Couple hundred miles still to go, of course. But the air smells like home."

Holly sniffed. She couldn't smell anything. The air seemed pure and empty, sparkling with cold. She could see the hills below her, quite close now. They were bare rock, just streaked with snow here and there. At the foot of the hill they were passing over, she saw a big tent surrounded by bright lights. Nearby was a big radar dish. "What's that?" she asked, pointing.

"Not sure." Snowthorn craned his neck. "Maybe some kind of secret military installation. Or just a bunch of seriously high-tech hunters. Luckily, we'll be landing on the other side of that hill."

"Can they see us?" Holly asked.

"Well, I did turn off your invisibility a while back, to save a few points. But I don't see anybody watching down there, so we should be okay. Still, I miss the days when the Arctic was off the beaten path. If the Old Man hadn't moved his palace…"

"Moved it?" Holly twisted around to stare at the elf. "Where to?"

"Well, you can't expect him to keep it in one place, right at the Pole," the elf protested. "Do you know how many people visit every year? Heck, they even have a web cam there now. No, the Old Man's palace is hidden. For good reason."

As they just barely cleared the hill, Holly scooped up a bit of snow from the rocky crest, quickly patted it into a snowball, and flung it in the direction of the tent below.

Then they drifted gently down to the plain, turning a half somersault in the air, so that they landed on their feet, lightly enough that only a small puff of snow came up.

Snowthorn waved and said, "Goodbye, South Wind!"

"Goodbye," Holly whispered. She felt a warm breeze pass quickly over her face, like a kiss, and then it was gone. She looked back once, thinking of all the frozen miles that lay between her and home, and then turned to Snowthorn.

"Okay, where do we find the reindeer?" she asked brightly.

Snowthorn held up his hand. "Hang on a second. I want to make sure we understand each other first. Look, I have to take you to the Old Man's place, because of what I swore to do. But once we're there—you're on your own, okay? I mean, I'm not going to be responsible for helping you forge an entry on the List, or sending you back home, or anything like that. I owe you nothing else. Zero. Nada."

"Well, Father—I mean the Old Man will take care of me, once I'm there. So okay."

"Keep on telling yourself that," the elf said, a trifle grimly. "And one more thing. While we're trying to *get* to the Old Man's house, I'm in charge. This can be a dangerous country, outside of the Palace."

At that point, as if on cue, they heard a howl in the distance. Snowthorn nodded with satisfaction. "See? That's a pack of wolves on the track of their prey—luckily, not us. And even without the wolves—and the bears, which are worse, by the way—it's just plain *cold*."

"I still feel fine," Holly objected.

"That's because my spell is still protecting you," Snowthorn reminded her. "Without that, you'd be flash-frozen. Feels like a spring day back home to you, doesn't it? Well, right now it's actually thirty below zero, counting wind chill."

"But there's no wind now," Holly objected.

"Exactly," said Snowthorn, triumphantly. "You see my point."

"All right," she agreed. "You're the boss. So what are we going to do?"

"Well, we saw a river over there. Animals in the Arctic need water, just like they do everywhere, so I thought we'd follow it. And then..."

"Then what?"

"Then...we'll just see what happens."

Chase Me

He led the way, and Holly trudged after him. The going wasn't hard at first. The snow by the river wasn't deep, and had a crunchy crust on top.

But Holly thought it looked easier, and more fun, to walk on the river itself. It was mostly frozen over, except for an open stretch near the middle, several yards out, where she guessed the water must be running faster.

Just as she thought that, she saw a boy walking on the river, a little ahead of her and Snowthorn. He was dressed like an Eskimo in a hooded fur parka. He looked back at Holly for a moment, and smiled at her. Then he began to run over the ice.

He couldn't have said 'Chase me!' more clearly. Before Snowthorn could say anything, Holly slid down the steep bank and onto the glassy surface of the river. She started to run, getting up some speed, then slid quite a distance.

In a few moments she had almost come up even with the boy. He was standing still now, and looked back at her again with an encouraging grin.

Then he simply disappeared.

Holly skidded to a stop. She heard Snowthorn calling faintly to her. She looked all around, but the landscape was as empty of boys as any landscape could possibly be.

A scattering of snow lay across the frozen river where she'd stopped, and the ice was thick, but she thought she could glimpse something lying underneath. It looked like...people. Several people, lying down as if they were resting. Holly edged closer, until she was right over them, and carefully knelt down.

"You need to get *off* that ice," Snowthorn yelled. He was closer now.

"Just a second," she called back, without looking up. She brushed the snow away with her hand. Snowthorn's spell made it seem as warm as powdered sugar. She could see the people clearly now, like they were just on the other side of a window.

A man and a woman lay there. They were holding hands, and beside the woman was a boy that looked just like the boy Holly had followed. Holly guessed that the man and woman were about as old as her own parents. It was harder to tell about the boy. He might have been a little younger than her. They all had dark skin, and wore fur parkas. It looked like they were asleep. At least, their eyes were closed.

The woman had round, chubby cheeks, and long eyelashes. It looked like she probably smiled a lot. The boy had his mouth open a little, as if he was just in the middle of a snore. Holly stared at the man's face. He had black hair, like her own father, and a large, hooked nose. He looked proud.

Then his eyes suddenly opened. Holly jerked back.

At the same time, the ice creaked ominously under her, and a spiderweb of cracks suddenly appeared on the surface. Water welled up like blood from a wound.

Then the ice broke, with a crack like thunder. The people all disappeared. Holly began to sink into the empty, icy water. "*Snowthorn...*" she wailed.

Something rose up from underneath her. One moment she was floundering in the water, and the next, whatever-it-was had lifted her up, dripping, into the air, and deposited her gently on the unbroken ice closer to the river bank.

Holly pulled herself a little further onto the ice, then turned around to see what had rescued her. She was surprised to see a walrus resting in the water. It
seemed to be holding on to the ice with its great, curving tusks. Holly waited for it to go away, but it just hung there, breathing rather loudly and watching Holly with its small eyes as if it were very interested in her.

She heard Snowthorn puffing behind her as he finally caught up. "Snowthorn," she said without taking her eyes off the walrus, "what do walruses eat?"

"There is no cause for alarm," said the walrus, "I do not habitually include diminutive human females in my bill of fare." It had a deep, slow voice, and its whiskers quivered as it spoke. If Holly hadn't been able to see it, and had to judge only from its voice, she would have imagined it as an elderly, fat gentleman in a bowler hat.

"Oh," she said. "Sorry, you have such big teeth. So you're not fierce, then?"

"I'm a Pacific walrus," the walrus said. "Pacific means 'peaceful', so no. My diet consists mostly of bivalves."

"Bye-whales?" Holly shook her head, confused.

"Bivalves. Clams and mussels, for instance. And the occasional oyster. One of your human authors wrote a poem to that effect, featuring one of my cousins and, harumph, an itinerant woodworker of his acquaintance. Good afternoon, Snowthorn."

"Hello, Ivar," said Snowthorn. "This is Holly. Thanks for saving her from her own...um, we'll just call it impetuosity."

The habit of using big words seemed to be catching, Holly thought. She said 'thank you' to Ivar then too, very meekly since she wasn't sure what 'impetuosity' meant, but it sounded serious. She shivered, feeling her wet boots and leggings beginning to freeze. The ice water had apparently managed to get through Snowthorn's spell.

Ivar coughed modestly. "Pray don't mention it. I just happened to be in the neighborhood. Any other pinniped would have done the same."

While Holly was wondering what a pinniped was, Snowthorn did something with his hands that made a hot breeze, like a hair dryer, blow around her briefly. When it stopped, she was warm and dry again. She murmured her thanks.

"So what brings you to the river today?" Snowthorn asked Ivar.

"Oh, I have a streak of wanderlust in my nature," the walrus said cheerfully. "Besides, there's a bed of freshwater mussels in this locality that I haven't sampled since high summer. And now, indulge my own curiousity. How is it that you're conducting a human child through the wilderness, so close to the Eve?—while looking even more desperate than usual, I might add. Though you're invariably tearing your hair out over toy quotas, whenever we meet."

"Umm...I usually run into Ivar when I'm taking a break—a really quick break, of course—from the last-minute toymaking rush," Snowthorn explained to Holly. "I'm trying to make it back to the Palace," he said to the walrus. "It's a long story," he added darkly.

"Well," the walrus said, "I'll ask you to relate it another time. This is a strange Eve. The land seems more than normally restless. Not only are the, harumph, dumb creatures stirring in unwonted numbers, but an extraordinary number of spirits are manifesting themselves. For example, that interesting child who was attempting to engage you in a game of follow-the-leader," he said to Holly.

"That's right! And then I saw him...and his mom and dad...in the river!" Holly struggled to get to her feet. "We need to look for them! Help them!"

Snowthorn shook his head. "There's nothing we can do to help them, Holly. They're spirits, like Ivar said. Ghosts."

"Ghosts!" Her eyes widened. "But it looked like that boy wanted to play with me. Was he really just trying..."

"...to lure you out onto the ice?" Ivar finished for her. "I doubt that was really his intention. But ghosts may pose a danger to the living, even when there's no question of malice aforethought."

"I've never seen a ghost before," said Holly thoughtfully. "Do you think there might be more of them? Let me look! I'll be really careful to stay close to the bank this time."

"Okay, time for a little negative psychology," Snowthorn said, rolling his eyes. "Sure, Holly, go back on the ice and do a little ghost-watching on a river that will turn you into a popsicle just like them, in ten seconds or less. You can join their nice little ghost family and have fun doing nothing forever. *Or* you can listen to me and maybe have a chance of seeing your own mom and dad again."

"Your friend's advice is most perspicacious, young Holly. I would recommend that you follow it," the walrus added solemnly.

Holly could guess what 'perspicacious' meant, but she didn't get it—as far as she could see, Snowthorn wasn't sweating at all. Still, with both the elf and the walrus giving her what her mom called "The Look", she felt she had to give in.

"Okay," she said. But at least I saw them once, she told herself. *Three* ghosts. That was way more than Connor had ever seen, she was sure of it. She could tell him about it, and about how she hadn't been frightened at *all*.

"Well, I fancy it's time for me to return to decimating the local bivalve population," Ivar said cheerfully. "The pleasure has been all mine, I assure you."

If he had really been an old gentleman, Holly thought, he would have tipped his hat at this point. As it was, he waved one flipper and rolled back into the water. "Wait!" she called, as he started to submerge. "Can't you stay with us for a while?"

Ivar popped back up out of the water and blinked. "Why, since you inquire so courteously," he said, "I would be glad to accompany you a little farther. One doesn't always get a chance for good conversation. The vocabulary of mussels is severely limited."

"Hey, great," Snowthorn said. He smacked his forehead. "By the way, I should have asked—have you seen any reindeer around here?"

"Not in the immediate vicinity," Ivar said. "But some distance ahead, we will encounter a region of white water. On the further side, the river widens considerably, and its speed undergoes a corresponding decrease. Reindeer frequent that area for purposes of hydration."

Holly gave Snowthorn a blank look. "They come down to the river to drink," he translated. "Okay, this is still the way to go."

Holly and Snowthorn walked on, and Ivar swam alongside, talking to Holly as they went. The river was completely frozen over in some places. When he came to those parts, Ivar would haul himself out on the ice and move forward by wriggling and humping along, something like a giant caterpillar. Holly thought he looked very funny, but she knew it wouldn't be polite to laugh.

"You're visiting the Arctic at an auspicious time, young Holly," Ivar told her. "But it's unfortunate that your itinerary won't include the open sea. We hold great revels there, as the Eve approaches. The most prestigious event is, of course, the Marine Mammal's Ball."

"I've seen seals playing with balls," said Holly hopefully.

"Not that kind of ball. He means the dancing kind," Snowthorn told her.

"Oh, right. Like Cinderella."

"Indeed," said Ivar. "Although, unlike your renowned, but somewhat temporally challenged princess, when midnight strikes our revels are only beginning. The sparkling sea itself is our dance floor, and the Aurora Borealis serve as a chandelier of ever-changing lights. Even the whales join in sometimes—though only for the slow dances; they can scarcely manage to hold their own in a lively quadrille, I'm afraid. I refer, of course, to the Bowhead family, and the occasional Beluga. The Narwhals never dance at all."

"What do they do?" Holly asked.

"Why, they play their horns, of course," Ivar informed her. "Someone has to provide the music."

"Walked right into that one," muttered Snowthorn.

When there was a pause in the conversation, Holly could hear Ivar breathing loudly as he swam or hauled himself along the ice. There was no other sound, except for the crunch of the snow beneath her feet.

She looked up at the sky. Living in cloudy Seattle, she had formed an impression that stars were misty and fleeting things. The stars here were very different—twinkling brilliant and eternal in a sky that was like polished metal.

"Stop a moment, please," Ivar said suddenly. It was the shortest speech he had made so far.

A Shapechanger

Obediently, Holly and Snowthorn halted. The walrus stopped swimming, too, and rested with his tusks on the edge of the ice again.

"Do either of you find yourselves sensing a certain...that is, in a word, can you smell anything?" Ivar asked.

Holly sniffed. The Arctic air still smelled, to her, like nothing at all. "No," she said. "But I hear something. The river is getting a lot louder."

"The white water is directly ahead. Well!" said Ivar heartily. "This has been a most interesting adventure. But now we must part company, because I've just remembered an especially extensive bed of mussels, which, as fortune would have it, happens to be in the exact opposite direction..."

"Spare me," Snowthorn said. "What is it you smelled, Ivar? Come clean. I know you can scent a human from a hundred yards away. Is it a hunter?"

"Not human," Ivar said slowly. "At least...I don't believe so. It's been many Eves since I've scented something of this nature. I think...that a shapechanger is somewhere nearby."

"Uh *huh*," Snowthorn said. "Does your nose tell you if it's friendly?"

"Unfortunately not. So, lacking the benefit of experience," Ivar said, "I have to assess the situation based on the bedtime stories my mother told me, back when I was just a calf."

"How did the stories end?" Holly asked in a small voice.

"Oh, quite happily," Ivar assured her. "Er—that is, in the end. Farewell, Snowthorn and young Holly."

Holly knew she would miss him, and her voice caught in her throat, though she managed to wave. Ivar took a deep breath, sank into the water, and was gone.

Holly sighed and looked at Snowthorn. "Do we really have to keep going?" she asked.

He nodded.

"Should we hold hands?"

"Sure. Don't worry too much. So there's a shapechanger. I've still got my magic—a little of it, anyway. And maybe he, or she, or it will know something about the reindeer. The faster we find one, the sooner you'll get to the Old Man's place."

They went on, and the voice of the river grew louder beside them. When it was at its height, Snowthorn stopped again, squeezing Holly's hand so tightly that she almost cried out.

"I don't see anything. Where is it?" she asked.

"That must be him," Snowthorn said softly. "Look. There, in the river."

Running With The Pack

When the wolf spoke to him, Connor's head swam, and he blinked rapidly as little points of light winked in the air around him. Hey, he thought, seeing stars. Again. And before I got to the Arctic, I thought that was just some dumb expression.

Just like he'd thought that wolves only talk in fairy tales. "You...can talk," he said.

"Better than *you*," put in one of the other wolves, who was darker and smaller than the leader. A younger one, Connor guessed.

"Hey, give him a break," said the third wolf. He was nearly as big as the leader, but one of his ears looked torn, and there was a patch of fur missing from his neck. "I don't think he's from *around* here. Don't look much like he rolls with the dogs, know what I mean?"

"What about that?" the leader challenged. "Where are you from, cub-dude? And what are you doing on our turf?"

"I'm...a boy. A man, I mean. A human. Young, male human. I'm from Seattle," Connor said. This was getting surreal. *Don't* give them your address, he told himself. "And I'm looking for my sister."

"Seattle?" The younger wolf looked dubiously at him. "That's, like, south?"

"'Course," the leader growled. "Not many places *ain't* south of here, Dis. This sister of yours—she got a name?"

"Holly," he said. "See, I lost her because the wind blew her away, but I had a wishing cap, so I got ahead of her and I was waiting, but then..." It got easier as it went on, this talking to wolves thing. Connor was tempted to tell them a lot more, but the leader interrupted him again.

"Too much information, cub-dude. Once you *start* talking, you don't stop, do you? Now us, most of the year we don't say nothing, we're...what's the word?"

"Dumb beasts," suggested the one called Dis.

"Yeah, that's it. But if you hang here long, you'll figure out almost anything with a pulse talks, when the Eve comes around."

"The Eve?"

"Solstice Eve," the wolf said, squinting at him. "You must *really* not be from around here."

"No." Connor shook his head, and kept on shaking it. After a minute he was able to stop himself, but he felt a little dizzy. "So. All the animals around here...can talk?"

"Totally," Dis agreed. "Most of the year, we're just guessing what Def wants us to do. But for a half-moon around the Eve, he gets to spell it out for us. How cool is that?" He grinned, his tongue lolling out.

"So the bears talk too," Connor said. "And the..." He struggled to think of what other animals they had up here. "The reindeer?" he added, desperately.

"Bears, sure," said the third wolf, with a yawn. "Reindeer...well, they mostly give us the cold shoulder, man. But we shoot the breeze with the owls, sometimes."

"Yeah, not like they let on where the game is, though," Dis observed. "Then there's the hares and lemmings, but they only say stuff like 'Don't eat me, please—I have a wife and thirty-seven children!'" The other wolves laughed silently with open jaws at his high-pitched imitation.

"Foxes," Def added thoughtfully. "*They* talk."

"Boy, do they ever," the third wolf said. "But they *lie*..."

The other wolves nodded. "Yeah," Def agreed. "Skin you alive before you even know what's up. We hate foxes."

Connor cleared his throat. "Yes, well," he said. "It's a good thing you talk, because I can ask you...have you seen my sister?"

"Tell us what to call you first, cub-dude," Def ordered.

"Connor. My name is Connor."

The lead wolf nodded in a friendly fashion. "Con Nor, I'm Defier Of Ice Bears—Def, for short. This here is Disemboweler LemmingsBane—call him Dis. Then there's Yo." He nodded toward the remaining wolf.

"And...what's that short for?" Connor asked.

"Yo-yo," Yo said, grinning widely. "I'm a little on the *unstable* side." He seemed proud of it.

"Not his fault, really," Def said. "Some of your kind caught him once, and put a tracking collar on him. Drove him crazy. But he got it off finally, along with a chunk of his own neck. Blood all over the place. It was *wicked*."

Time to move along, Connor decided. "Okay. Well, it's, um, good to meet you all," he finished lamely.

"Now about your sister," Def went on. "She'd be human, like you, only shorter?"

Connor nodded. "Yeah. She's got red hair—you know, the fur on top of our heads..."

"Think we're stupid?" Dis growled. "We know what *hair* is."

"But we don't know where *she* is," Def added. "Haven't seen any humans all day, until you came along."

"I know where she is," Connor said.

"A minute ago, your story was you'd lost her," Yo said, cocking his head quizzically. "Make up your mind."

"Well, yes...I mean, no...anyway, I'm trying to catch up with her. She's somewhere on the other side of that hill. Someone—or something else is with her, too. I think..." Connor hesitated, then took all his courage in both hands and plunged on. "I think it's an elf."

"An elf?" Def looked dubious.

Dis and Yo looked uneasy. "Elves...hey, we don't usually mess with *elves*..." they murmured.

The wolves were actually beginning to edge away from Connor. He decided a challenge was necessary. "You're not...*afraid*, are you?" he asked softly.

That turned out to be the right thing to say. "Afraid?" Dis yipped. "We're the Pack! We're not afraid of anything!"

"There's only three of you, though," Connor said, trying to sound innocent. "That's not really—like, a *pack*, is it? I mean, seriously?"

"You bet your sweet flank steak we are," Def growled, his eyes glinting dangerously. "You're just lucky we weren't hungry when we found *you*, cub-dude, or you might have wound up on the short end of the food chain, know what I'm saying?"

"Well, if you *really* aren't afraid," Connor prodded, not too comfortable with the turn the conversation had taken, "then help me track them. My sister and the—um—other short creature. They can't be more than a few miles off."

"What's a few miles?" Yo asked rhetorically. "Nothing! Not to the Pack!"

Def's mood changed suddenly. "We can catch anything," he said. "You don't need to worry, if you're with us. Come on, Connor. We'll help you. Let's go!"

The wolves were on their feet now, running back and forth in excitement. In a few minutes Def had them formed up in a sort of ragged formation. Then they set out toward the north, Connor in their midst, breaking into a jog to keep up with the pack.

Out of Their Element

Holly saw a man in the river. He seemed ordinary enough. He stood in midstream, looming big and bulky in a hooded parka. The river rushed and foamed around the big man, but he just stood there, motionless as a stone.

Then, so suddenly she could hardly follow his movement, he stooped and dipped his hand into the wild water, and flipped something out onto the ice. It was a fish—she saw it writhing and flopping there for a second or two, and then, just as quickly, the man flicked it back into the water.

A funny way to fish, she thought. *Maybe it was too small, so he decided to throw it back?*

But as they walked up the bank, drawing even with the man, he repeated this performance two or three times. Holly wondered if *all* the fish in the river could be too small.

Then he stopped fishing and turned toward them. The fur-trimmed hood hid most of his face, but Holly could see a big, bushy beard, and the gleam of sharp eyes.

"You must be strangers here," he said in a deep voice that held the hint of a growl.

"We are," Holly agreed cheerfully, but Snowthorn put in, "Um, well, not exactly. But we're a little lost at the moment. Tell me, have you seen any reindeer around here? Lately, I mean?"

The big man stood for a moment as if lost in thought. "The caribou," he said, dreamily. "I can remember when the herds of caribou were a mile wide, and went by for days. But that was a long time ago. I haven't seen any while I've been prospecting here."

"Well, thanks anyway," Snowthorn said hastily, tugging on Holly's hand. "We'll just be on our way, then—"

But at the same moment Holly asked, "Prospecting?" She wasn't moving.

The man didn't answer, but suddenly he dipped his hand into the foaming water again, as quick as thought, and caught another fish. This one, when he flipped it onto the ice, didn't move. It stiffened and froze in place, its scales gleaming brightly in the light from snow and moon.

Holly moved as near to the bank's edge as she dared, and peered down at it. The fish was all shiny and yellow.

It had turned to gold.

"Prospecting," the big man said again. "You can never tell. When they're in the water, one looks no different than another. But if you take them out of their element, a few of them change. Then you can see what they always were, underneath, all along."

All Holly could think of to say was, "You must be really patient."

"I must be," the man agreed. His voice sounded a little weary, but he went on briskly. "So, you wanted to know about the caribou. I have no idea where they've gone, but there are some people you could ask."

"Can you tell us where they are?" Snowthorn asked.

The big man considered for a moment. "If you go upstream a few miles," he said, pointing back the way they came, "there's an Eskimo settlement there. They live in government houses, and they get supplies delivered up from the south three times a year."

"And would they know where the reindeer are?" Holly asked.

"Well, no," the man admitted. "Not likely. But if you follow the river downstream, there's another village near the shore of the sea. Those people live according to the old ways. They still hunt the caribou, so there's a good chance they can tell you where to find them."

"They wouldn't be hunting *these* reindeer," Snowthorn said.

The big man turned his hood toward the elf, and his eyes gleamed out again. "Oh, it's the other kind you're after, is it? Well, they might know something about that too. There's a shaman named Shadow-of-Birds who lives at that settlement. Have her ask her spirit helpers, and you may find what you're looking for."

"Okay," Snowthorn said brightly. He tugged at Holly's hand again. "Thanks. We'll be going on, then. Good luck in your fish…I mean, prospecting."

The big man nodded, and raised his hand in farewell. Holly waved back. Then she was trying to keep up with Snowthorn as he set off down the river at a trot.

A Strange Time

"I wanted to thank him, and find out his name and stuff," she said reproachfully.

"It's not always the best idea to get too interested in somebody's *name*," Snowthorn said, darkly. "Especially if you meet him by chance in the wild lands, near the Eve, and you have it on good authority that he's a shapechanger. Take a look back—can you still see him?"

Holly turned her head. She could still see the bulky figure in the middle of the stream, but there was something different about it. She rubbed her eyes. It looked to her now as if a huge white bear was standing there, reaching its big paw into the water, flicking out more fish that turned to gold, scattered like bright stars on the ice. The bear lifted its head and looked back at her with great, dark eyes. A moment later, it returned to its task.

After that, she had no trouble keeping up with Snowthorn. "A shapechanger!" she panted. "So that's what Ivar meant. Is he...dangerous?"

"Looks like he's not...coming after us," Snowthorn puffed, out of breath. "So probably not."

They slowed to something approaching a walk. "You see, things get a little...muddled, here, as the Eve gets closer," Snowthorn told her. "Animals can talk, for instance. You didn't seem to have too much trouble with *that*, by the way."

"Well...there are so many stories where they can. It always seemed weird to me that they *don't* talk in real life."

"Well, around the Eve, there are also animals who can turn into humans. Or maybe it's humans who turn into animals, I've never figured it out. It's a strange time."

"But how? Why?"

Snowthorn sighed. "Yeah, I've heard that you children ask questions like *that* all the time, too. How? I think it's that all the magic gathered up at this time of the year, at the top of the world, just spills over, somehow, and everything within hundreds of miles is touched by it. Why? You'll grow old before you get an answer to that one. I just know that it happens."

"It must be strange for the people who live around here," Holly said thoughtfully. "They've got to notice that there are shape-changers and talking animals around. Once in a while, they might even see an *elf*," she added slyly.

"Well, we don't get out that much, really, and we try to stay invisible whenever they're nearby. But they've seen us sometimes," Snowthorn admitted. "Lone hunters, or lost children. They have all kinds of crazy yarns about us—not much to do with what we're really like."

By this time the river they were following had taken another bend, and as Ivar had predicted, the water was flowing more slowly now. They had finally left the hills behind, and a wide plain stretched out before them.

This time it was Holly's turn to clutch at Snowthorn and whisper, "Look!"

Five

Something was moving on the plain ahead of them. Holly thought it looked, more than anything, like a snow globe. But a snow globe that floated high
in the air, lit from the inside, so you could see it far across the snow and ice. A snow globe big enough to have a house inside of it, like a doll house but bigger than any Holly had ever seen. It had a quaint, old-fashioned tower with a pointed roof, and dormers, and shuttered windows like closed eyes, as if the house itself was dreaming.

And down out of the snow globe's sky, Holly saw something flying toward the house. More than one something, but flying together with perfect coordination, wheeling and turning at exactly the same time, like flocks of birds she'd seen in the fall.

As she and Snowthorn drew closer, she saw that it was reindeer—eight of them, drawing a tiny, overburdened sleigh. The team had a driver—an old man dressed all in red, with a big, snowy beard.

The sleigh circled around the house once, and then landed softly on the rooftop.

"Like the down of a thistle," Holly heard herself saying, out loud.

And suddenly, the whole scene disappeared like a soap bubble popping. Holly looked around at Snowthorn, and the black sky dusted with stars, and the winding river. Nothing else was visible but the snow and the ice stretching out endlessly all around.

She put her hand to her head, a little dazed. "What...what was that?"

"You just called it," Snowthorn said. "Somebody's been reading that old poem again, all right."

"Poem? Oh, right. The Night Before Solstice. That's where all that came from, isn't it? But why was it floating through the air? And where did it go?"

"That was some kid's dream," Snowthorn told her. "Dreams often drift up this way, especially this time of year. Most of them don't survive, of course. But the strong ones can make it a lot further before they fade away. Some of them even reach the Old Man's palace."

"It was like a mirage," Holly said wonderingly. She pronounced it to rhyme with 'cage', but went on before Snowthorn had a chance to correct her. "You knew all along, though, didn't you?"

The elf nodded. "I've seen this kind of thing before. When I was out working on the List, of course. Even in the workshop, sometimes. Though the guys in R&D usually grab the best ones," he added ruefully.

"But it's not fair...when the kid who dreamed that wakes up, their dream will be gone!" Holly protested.

"That's not the way it works," Snowthorn explained. "Dreams are one of those special things—like love, or a cold. You can share them or give them away, and still keep as much of them as you ever had."

"Well, maybe their dream will come true, anyway," Holly said.

Snowthorn shrugged. "Not our department. Only the Old Man can make dreams come true. And he doesn't do it all the time. Not even for all the people he visits on a given Eve."

"But...he comes to every house, doesn't he? Every Yule."

Snowthorn shook his head. "Only the ones that need him. It's still more than *I* can count, and it keeps us crazy busy right up until the Eve."

Holly felt Snowthorn's words tearing at the fabric of her own dreams, ripping them so they fluttered in the cold wind. "But that means that Yule magic isn't real. Not all the time, anyway."

"That depends. Do you remember a Yule when even the grownups looked surprised, just for a second, at something you found in the stockings? Do you remember a time when oh, you got some fairy dust that made it so you could really float in the air for a second, or a music box that played whatever song you really needed to hear? If so, that was an Eve when the Old Man visited you."

"But then why doesn't everyone know about it?" Holly protested. "Why doesn't everyone *know* that he's real?"

"People forget," Snowthorn said, gently. "They say that magical things never happened, or they must have been dreaming, or they just had a little too much of Grandpa's eggnog. Grownups are good at fitting anything that happens into what they already believe. That's why I'm invisible to older people."

Holly mulled this over. "But how does the Old Man know which houses he needs to visit and which ones can wait?"

"That's above my pay grade. No one else knows as much as the Old Man. 'He sees you when you're sleeping, he knows when you're awake'—remember?"

"But if he knows everything," Holly said slowly, "and sees everything...then why does he need you elves? I mean, to help with the List? Doesn't he just know who's naughty and who's nice, without having to send you out?"

Snowthorn frowned. Holly got the feeling that he hadn't really thought of that before, and he was having to make up an answer. "Well, he could if he *wanted* to—he's got his High Seat, up in the Palace, and when he sits in it he can see everything, like you say. But it's usually easier to have us do it, I guess."

A wind had come up. Holly could hear it moaning across the plain, and the sound made her shiver. Or was it only the sound? She felt a breath of cold air across her face, and thought of the words of one of the Yule songs her mother liked. *Jack Frost nipping at your nose...*

Snowthorn noticed her shudder, and he looked a little less cheerful than usual. "It's getting harder to hold back the cold. Let's walk a little faster. The village can't be too far away, if that shapechanger was telling the truth."

What Good Is It Being Good?

As they crunched along, casting faint shadows that turned the snow blue, Holly had an uncomfortable thought. If what Snowthorn said was true, then you could be good, as good as gold, for a whole year—and *still* Father Winter might not visit you and make your dreams come true. *Then what good is it, being good?* she asked herself.

It sounded funny, but it wasn't. She didn't really want to hear what Snowthorn would say about it, not now. Probably he'd just remind her that *he* didn't make the rules.

Who *does?* she thought. That's what I really want to know. If it's the Old Man, then I'd like to have a talk with him, that's all.

They kept walking, always keeping the river on their left hand. The land began to slope gently downward, and after a while, Holly could see a great gray expanse on the horizon. Snowthorn told her it was the sea. The sky was clouding over, and it began to snow lightly.

"There they are," Snowthorn said. "We're on the wrong side of the river."

Peering, Holly made out a small cluster of round houses on the far side of the water. Igloos, she thought with a faint stirring of excitement. She had always wanted to see what real igloos were like.

There were several dark figures standing outside. They must have been able to see Holly and Snowthorn approaching, but they just watched quietly, not moving, as Snowthorn and Holly crossed the ice. A few dogs lay outside the igloos, too, watching as silently as their masters.

Holly forgot about them for a moment, as Snowthorn showed her the right places to step as they crossed the river. Safely on the other side, they struggled up the slope to where the igloos stood. There were only five or six of them.

"Is that a village? I thought they were bigger," Holly said to Snowthorn.

Apparently the Eskimos heard her. One of them, the shortest, came forward. At close quarters she could see it was a girl, not much older than she was, with a grave round face. She wore a fur-trimmed parka, some kind of lined pants, and boots that looked homemade.

"Seal skin," she said, halting a few paces away.

Holly glanced at Snowthorn, but the elf shrugged helplessly. "Seal skin?" she repeated.

The girl nodded. "My boots. Trousers, too. They work well in this climate. Can't say the same about what *you're* wearing."

Holly realized for the first time how strange she must look, in her sweater and skirt and leggings and nothing else. She supposed she was lucky the Eskimos hadn't screamed and run away.

One of the adults standing back by the igloos said something Holly couldn't understand. The girl laughed and answered in the same language. "Neither of you speak Inuit?" she asked.

They shook their heads.

"Oh, well, *kaplunas* don't, usually," the girl said indulgently. "I'm surprised at you though, dwarf."

Snowthorn drew himself up to his full height. "I am *not*," he said haughtily, "a dwarf."

The girl smiled. "Okay, dwarf, if you say so. Anyway, that means that you'll be talking mostly to me, because the others don't know much of your language. What are your names? Mine's—" she said something quickly that Holly couldn't follow. "Oh," she said, when he saw her dismayed expression. "In English, it's Duck Egg."

"Hi, Duck Egg," Holly said, feeling a little foolish. "I'm Holly, and this—" she glanced at Snowthorn and smiled mischievously. "The dwarf, that is, is Snowthorn."

Duck Egg nodded. "Well, come up to the village. That's my uncle's *iglu* up there, and he's invited you. Come on in and get warm. Or not so cold, anyway."

They followed after Duck Egg, while Snowthorn muttered to himself, "I am *not* a *dwarf*."

Connor found that the wolf pack got distracted easily. They boasted about how easy it would be to follow Holly's trail, but they were always dashing off to one side or the other, claiming they'd just seen a hare. They actually did catch one, which was shared out between Def and Dis. But the other hunts all ended the same way, with the disappointed wolf loping back into sight, tongue lolling out, while the others laughed their silent laughter.

The unsuccessful hunter would say something like, "That hare must feel lucky today. If I'd caught him I'd have torn him limb from limb" or "Did you *see* how big that one was?

Would've set a new record, I swear." Then, after a few nips and some rough-and-tumble play, the pack would finally move on.

They also had to stop when Yo noticed the moon, which had just risen high enough to be visible over the mountains. The wolves settled back on their haunches, and when Def gave the signal—"One, two, three!"—they all threw back their heads and howled. They made Connor howl too—twice, because Dis said the first time wasn't loud enough.

After that, Def spent a minute trying to convince Connor to run on all fours. "Four legs are better than two," he said. "And listen, if you're going to be in the Pack, you need to grow some real fur and get some decent teeth and claws."

"But...I'm human," Connor said.

"No excuse," Def grinned. "You just have to try. Let's see you hang your tongue out, now..."

It was beyond embarrassing. *At least,* Connor thought, *there's nobody else around to see this.*

Once they saw a snowy owl soaring overhead. It plummeted to strike something on the ground, rising up again holding a small body in its talons. The wolves snapped and jeered at it. "That's *our* lemming, beak-face.

Just drop it over here, nice and easy, and nobody will get hurt." "You call those feathers?" "Oh, yeah? Come on down *here* and say that, why don't you?"

But the owl flew on without answering.

Connor had, by this time, figured out that Holly and the creature with her were pretty much just following the river—which, according to his compass, meant more or less northward. So he didn't really need the pack. But he wasn't sure how to get rid of them. It was like having a bunch of kids follow him around—although when that thought crossed his mind, he got an uneasy image of Dis and Def tearing the hare's body between them, the blood steaming as it dripped on the snow.

At little farther on, Connor's own blood froze when they found a huge polar bear fishing in the middle of the river. It glanced at them briefly and then returned to hooking fish out of the water, adding to the few it had already piled up. Connor gave it a wide berth, but the wolves seemed to take this as a challenge to their territory. True to his name, Def trotted over until he was only a few yards away, growling menacingly at the bear.

"Back off, you big, stupid rug!" he said. "I'm gonna jack your fish. Just watch me!"

For a moment or two, the bear continued to ignore him. Def took advantage of this to dart in and seize one of the fish. The bear reacted immediately, rearing suddenly to its full height, with an earth-shaking roar.

Def yelped, dropping the fish, and turned tail, running back over the ice and up the bank. Back with the others, he shook himself, then looked back at the bear, which stayed on its hind legs.

"Well, scat!" Def said. "Hey, those fish made out of gold, or what?" He called to the bear. "Don't *need* your fish—keep 'em. They stink, anyway. I'll catch my own."

The bear growled softly and lowered itself to all fours again. "Let's get out of here," Def said to the others.

Connor followed them, now lagging behind just a bit. Maybe, if he let them get further ahead, they'd just go off in a different direction and forget about him. After a minute or two, he looked back over his shoulder at the bear, and did a double-take. There was no bear there any more—it was a man fishing in the river, a big man wearing a hooded parka.

Connor rubbed his eyes and looked again. The man was still there. I give up, he thought. I don't know *what* is going on here.

Which makes it even more important that I don't lose Holly and that...well, okay, elf.

"Hey, keep up with us, cub-dude!" Def called from ahead.

Connor sighed and quickened his pace. The snow was a little deeper now, and he could see the tracks of Holly's boots and beside them, the marks of the elf's smooth-soled shoes. Following the river, going north.

For the first time, he thought about what might be waiting at the end of that journey. He remembered his childish dreams of a secret workshop in the eternal snows. But now he knew that the quaint cottage of his vision was full of elves who were, for some reason, bent on kidnapping his little sister.

Well, how tough could they be, anyway? And if there really was a Father Winter...well, he was supposed to be jolly, wasn't he? He brought kids presents and stocking stuffers. But then if you were bad, you were supposed to get a lump of coal, right? Connor guessed he might have earned a lump or two by now himself.

Even the wolves were silent for a while as they went on. After a while, though, Connor noticed that they were acting nervous. They sniffed the air and slackened their pace. Finally, Yo just stopped in his tracks.

"Don't like it," he announced. "We've been following tracks too long, and we're close to the sea."

"Don't like the sea," Dis agreed.

"Tired of following tracks," Def added, giving Connor a significant look.

"Hungry," Yo remarked.

All three of the wolves closed in around Connor now. He tried to act unconcerned.

"Hey, what's up now? You guys going to let a little thing like being tired stop you?"

"*Hungry,*" Yo repeated, licking his chops.

Def growled, and so did Dis. They moved in closer. Connor looked around wildly. There was no escape. The only thing he could think of was to make for the river. The wolves might not like swimming. He could try to head back toward where the bear, or were-bear, had been fishing. Not that that would keep him alive much longer, probably.

He was just tensing his muscles, ready to leap for the bank and dive onto the ice, when Dis tossed his head up. "Fox!" he yelped sharply, and then, in a long drawn-out howl, "Foooooooxxxxx!"

Def turned, forgetting all about Connor. "I'm getting it too," he growled. "He's close. After him!"

"Yeah! I hate foxes!" Yo chimed in, with imbecile enthusiasm.

First one wolf, then another, streaked away through the snowy darkness. Connor found that he could breathe again. *Well,* he thought, *I wouldn't want to be that fox right now.* But from what he'd heard about foxes, it might lead the pack on a long chase—so Connor should cover as much ground as he could in the meantime.

A Frozen Sea

If he could speed up a bit, he had a good chance of catching Holly and the elf. The sea was close by, and they couldn't walk on the sea.

Then Connor remembered where he was. Okay, so they *can* walk on the sea, he told himself. But why would they? Wherever Father Winter's unimaginable place might be, it wouldn't be floating out on some random iceberg...or would it?

The river was widening out now. He must be near where it emptied into the sea, or where it would empty, if everything wasn't frozen. It had started to snow, and he couldn't see as far as before, but he thought he could make out some buildings on the other side of the river. Igloos? Well, it would make sense. He couldn't tell if anyone lived there—everything looked quiet. Connor decided that if he got to the actual shore and didn't find anything, he'd turn back and check. If Holly wasn't there, at least there'd be somebody human. Probably.

He remembered wishing for Gil and Jason to be here, but he didn't feel at all like seeing them now. The Wolf Pack, he thought. Yeah, right. They're about as lame as Dis, Def and Yo. Not much smarter, either.

Soon the sea stretched out before him, looking very different than he had imagined it. He'd visualized an endless, smooth, mirror-like surface like a huge frozen pond. Instead, because of the snow, it was hard to tell where the land left off and the sea began. Also, it seemed that some of the water had frozen in waves that were in the middle of breaking, so a lot of the surface was jagged and bumpy.

In fact, he didn't realize that he was already out on the water until he heard a crash that sounded uncannily like breaking glass, and a shower of spray and ice fragments erupted only a few feet in front of him. Connor tried to stop short, but slid a little further on, stopping only when he was eye to eye with a huge, black-and-white whale surfacing in the middle of the hole it had just punched through the thick ice.

Connor tried to backpedal, and fell sprawling. The orca rolled one of its eyes at him and opened its mouth, showing rows of razor-sharp teeth.

Maybe it talks, Connor thought. Everything talks here, right? "Uh..hi. How are you doing? You're not gonna...eat me, are you?" Good one, Connor, he told himself. If the bloodthirsty killer whale didn't happen to be thinking about food *already,* you just reminded it.

The orca made no reply except a sort of sighing sound. Then it sank back under the water with a splash, which soaked Connor's legs up to the knees.

"Turns out they don't talk much," said a voice behind him.

Connor scrambled to his feet and turned around. He was afraid the wolves had caught up with him, even though one part of his mind realized that this was a lighter, quicker voice, which didn't belong to any of the Pack.

He found himself blinking at a small white fox, not much bigger than Grimalkin, his mother's cat. It was sitting back on its haunches with its bushy tail curled neatly around its paws.

"Dolphins, now," the fox went on, "they're total chatterboxes—can't hardly get them to shut up. But orcas tend to be the strong, silent type."

"Okay," Connor said, relaxing a little bit. The fox didn't look threatening. "So now foxes talk, too. Just like the wolves said."

"Hey, I don't make the rules. I just get along the best I can. Wolves? You weren't *with* those guys, were you?" The fox yawned. "That pack of morons is somewhere inland by now, probably running over a cliff or something. I laid them a false trail. Two or three false trails, actually."

"You're a pretty sharp guy," Connor said. "So, what do I call you?"

"I'm an Arctic fox," the fox said, with a touch of pride. "Alopex Lagopus, to the scientists. But I can't say I care for that name—it translates as 'hare-footed fox', and how insulting is that? You can just call me the Snow Fox."

"I'm Connor. Listen, if you're really so smart," Connor said, slowly, "maybe you know why I'm here."

The fox inclined its head. "And I know where she is right now, too. Just come along with me, and I'll steer you in the right direction."

Feeling lost and a bit numb, Connor followed the fox as it turned inland, away from the frozen sea.

Six

Shadow-of-Birds

Holly was delighted to find that the igloo had a wooden door, fitted snugly into the walls of frozen snow. It was a half-door, like the ones you saw in old movies sometimes, with people leaning over them to talk with somebody on the outside. Duck Egg's uncle, a short man with leathery brown skin and dark, twinkling eyes, swung the door open and let Holly and Snowthorn go into the small entrance tunnel first.

Inside, it was just a single round room, not very big. At one end there was a sort of raised platform, with furs and animal hides thrown over it. An old woman sat there, cross-legged, her face webbed with wrinkles, but her eyes still bright.

There was no other furniture, except a storage chest, and something that looked like a packing crate. Each of these held an oil lamp. Holly felt grateful for Snowthorn's spell that was keeping her warm, because she noticed that even though they were inside, you could still see the old woman's breath, and though her hood was thrown back, she'd kept on her parka and the same thick leggings the others wore.

There was a pile of frozen fish, over near the packing crate. Holly wrinkled her nose at the strong smell. Even though it wasn't very warm inside, they'd started to thaw, and the fishy odor hung in the air like a cloud.

Duck Egg's uncle spoke then, and Duck Egg translated, "Make yourselves at home. Have a seat."

"Where?" Holly asked.

"Well, you could try the fish heap. We could spread a sack over it, make it a little less slippery." Duck Egg chuckled at Holly's expression. "Hey, my uncle wouldn't do that to guests. You can sit over on the bed. Don't worry, that's just my grandmother, Shadow-of-Birds. She doesn't bite. Not anymore, at least. She gave that up years ago."

"Shadow-of-Birds," Holly whispered, clutching Snowthorn's sleeve. "She's the one the shape-changer told us about."

"I know," Snowthorn hissed back. "But don't whisper. We need to be polite, remember that we're guests here. Not to mention Rule One." Aloud he said, "Thank you for your welcome, Duck Egg, Shadow-of-Birds…and sorry, what did you say your uncle's name was?"

"I didn't," Duck Egg answered. Her uncle grinned and said something in their language. "He says you can call him Uncle George."

"And...Uncle George. Of course. We're grateful for your hospitality." Snowthorn sat on the bed, on the side furthest from Shadow-of-Birds, and motioned Holly to take a seat as well.

Holly was a bit uneasy being that near to the old woman, but she didn't want to offend anyone, so she sat down gingerly on one of the hides. Shadow-of-Birds studied Holly's face, reached out a wrinkled hand to stroke her cheek, and then took one of her hands, chafing it gently. She said something to the others in a low voice.

"What...what does she want to do?" Holly asked. She had vague memories of fairy-tale witches who would pinch children, to see how fat they were, usually right before they decided whether to roast or fricassee them.

"She says you must be frozen," Duck Egg answered. Meanwhile, her uncle had taken the oil lamp off the storage chest. He opened it and took out a small parka, a pair of boots, and some pants that looked a lot like the ones that Duck Egg wore.

Uncle George brought the clothes over to Holly, smiling as he offered them to her. "Umm..thank you," she said, taking them. "Do I really need these?" she asked Snowthorn, out of the side of her mouth.

The elf nodded. "If I don't have to keep that spell going, it will help a lot. I only have a few points left. Go ahead and dress, and when you're done I'll let go and they'll keep you warm. Put them on right over your sweater and leggings, they look big enough."

"Were these yours, Duck Egg?" Even while Holly was asking, she knew it couldn't be. Duck Egg was about her size right now, so she couldn't have outgrown these clothes.

"They were my brother's," Duck Egg told her. "Bear Track."

"Sorry?"

"Bear Track. That's his name."

"Oh," Holly said. "Where is he? Does he live somewhere else?"

"Well...yes. Sort of. He joined our ancestors last winter," said Duck Egg.

"Oh. Where do your ancestors live?" Holly asked.

Duck Egg looked confused. "Umm, she means her ancestors that are—that aren't alive any more," Snowthorn whispered.

"Oh. I'm sorry." Holly didn't know what else she should say, and she was distracted by having to figure out the parka and leggings at the same time.

"He went with my father to hunt the caribou," Duck Egg explained. "Then a storm came, and they were lost in the night. Probably they fell through the ice somewhere. We never found them. Not too long after that, my mother fell ill, and she went to our ancestors last summer. My uncle took me in, because he had no children of his own, just my grandmother to take care of."

"It was good of him to do that," said Snowthorn. Holly noticed that he was wiping away a tear.

She felt like crying herself. Now she knew who were the ghosts that she'd seen before, frozen under the ice. She almost said something, but Snowthorn shook his head at her.

Well, she thought, at least the ghosts were all together now. But what about Duck Egg? What would it be like to lose your whole family? Holly's own father was away a lot. But he always came back. And he would be home for Yule, she told herself. He *had* to be.

But a small voice in her mind said, *Sometimes there's a crack in the ice. Sometimes, fathers don't come back.* She pushed that voice away, and instead concentrated on the time she'd seen him last. He'd promised to be there in time to see her open her presents. And her dad kept his promises. "Your word should be your bond," he'd often told Holly. "Only people with no honor break their word."

But then probably Duck Egg's father had promised that he'd come back from the hunt with food for his family. He didn't know he wouldn't be able to keep his promise. And Duck Egg seemed like a nice person. Her Uncle George, too. But if she and her family were honorable and good, why would something like this have happened to them?

Maybe, she thought, they did something naughty a long time ago, and that was why. That wasn't much comfort, though, because it made her think of times she had done things other people told her were naughty.

But I was always sorry, she told herself. *Really* sorry.

Holly didn't dare look at Snowthorn or Duck Egg again, just then, so she looked at Shadow-of-Birds instead. The old woman looked back at her, her eyes dark and deep as the river.

The Moon Is Cooler in the Summer

"Hungry?" Duck Egg asked cheerfully. Her uncle was holding out a chunk of some kind of meat to Holly.

Gratefully, she seized on that distraction. "You bet. I could eat a *horse*!" She felt a sudden misgiving. "It's not *really* horse, is it?"

Duck Egg made a mock grimace. "No way. We never touch any stuff like that. This is seal meat. Almost as good as caribou marrow. Go on, give it a try."

Holly gingerly accepted the piece of meat and nodded her thanks. Uncle George gave Snowthorn a piece, too. Holly took a tentative bite. The meat was cold, nearly frozen, but it had been sliced thin, and she hardly needed to chew it. It seemed to melt in her mouth.

"It *is* good," she said, amazed.

Duck Egg, her own mouth full, nodded. When she could speak she said, "My grandmother is a shaman, you know."

"So we've heard," Snowthorn admitted.

"Well, when she was younger she used to fly up to the moon a lot," Duck Egg said.

"Why?" Holly asked.

"Cooler in the summer," she said. "And it's easier to sleep, too. You just have a few stars shining in the sky, just like night lights, instead of the sun hanging on the horizon twenty-four seven."

"That sounds fun," Holly said. "Why did she come back?"

Duck Egg said something to her grandmother, who replied with a short speech. "Missed the frozen walrus meat," she said, straight-faced. "It's her favorite."

Holly saw the twinkle in the old woman's eyes. "Uh *huh*," she said. Then she remembered Ivar, and turned to Snowthorn with a horrified look. "But how can anybody eat…" she started to say, then stopped short when Snowthorn gave her a sharp glance and put his finger to his lips.

A moment later, she gasped as she felt a trickle of cold water run down her back. Uncle George looked up at the roof and said something. "Oh, just a little melt," Duck Egg told Holly. "You get more than three or four people in here, it gets really hot inside, and the walls and ceiling might melt a bit. No big deal."

"What happens in the spring?" Holly asked.

"*All* the igloos melt, along about June," Duck Egg said, matter-of-factly. "Then we put up our hide tents for the summer. "

"How long does that last?"

"Three months or so. Then everything freezes over and we build the igloos again."

Holly shook her head in wonder. "My mom and dad don't like how much it rains sometimes. But living here sounds harder. How did your people decide to come up here?"

"How did the Inuit come up here? Now *there's* a story," Duck Egg said. "Just keep in mind, this is the unofficial version, okay?

"Once a hunter was looking for seal. He went out far on the ice, and found a breathing hole where he knew a seal would come up, sooner or later. Maybe a walrus, and then his family would eat for weeks. But he had to wait a long time, and it was dark, and all the seals had gone far out to sea, so he fell asleep. When he woke up, he was going to head back to camp, but there was a mile of open water in the way."

"Because the ice floe broke off, and floated up north here, and he could never find his way back," Holly broke in, excitedly. "Then he made a wife out of snow, and they had a family, and that's how all of you came to be."

Duck Egg shook her head. "Hey, nice story. You've got some imagination, don't you? But no. It turned out that the whole *mainland* had broken off, and kept on floating south, until it ran into some other continent. There was a big smash-up, that's where the mountains come from, and the fjords and all that other stuff.

"So the hunter just stayed where he was, and after a while, his family came up to be with him. They said it was way too crowded down south. Not to mention the earthquakes, and the bugs. If there's one thing we can't stand, it's bugs." Holly nodded thoughtfully. "And that," Duck Egg finished, "is why my people have never felt like moving anywhere else."

"That is one...great story," Snowthorn said, with a note of grudging admiration in his voice. He cleared his throat. "But, umm, we have something to ask. You've been very hospitable, but I need to be getting home to the...well, the dwarf country."

The Old Man's Herd

Uncle George said something then, and Duck Egg translated. "My uncle says you dwarves have strong magic of your own. How can *we* help you?"

"*Had*, is the key word here. *Had* strong magic, which I, well, lost...through no fault of my own." Snowthorn gave Holly a significant look, then went on, "Anyway, we need to find the reindeer to help us home."

"The caribou?" Duck Egg sounded bewildered. "How will the caribou help you get home?"

"Not the normal caribou," Snowthorn said, lowering his voice. "There's a special herd...the one that belongs to the Old Man."

Duck Egg glanced back at her uncle and grandmother. They traded rapid-fire phrases in their language. Uncle George seemed a little nervous, but the old woman's face stayed serene, as far as Holly could make out in the dim light.

At last Duck Egg turned back to Holly and Snowthorn. "My grandmother knows all the spirits around here," she said, carefully. "She knows Nuliajak, the Old Woman Under the Sea. Nuliajak owns all the creatures in the water, and we need to ask her permission when we fish or take a seal. And there's Nanuk, who rules over the polar bears. But the Old Man that you're talking about—he must be Tekkeitsertok, it can't be anybody else. The caribou belong to him, and birds, bats—anything that travels in the sky."

"Yes," said Snowthorn softly. "Exactly. And what we're looking for is just that. The reindeer who travel in the sky."

Shadow-of-Birds spoke again, and Duck Egg's uncle said something brief and nodded.

Duck Egg smiled. "My grandmother says those aren't caribou that a man would ever think of hunting, and my uncle agrees. But my grandmother says, if you stay with us tonight, tomorrow she'll ask her spirit helpers to guide us. They fly around and see everything, so they probably know where the Old Man's herd is. If they do, we'll take you there."

A Cozy Den

The Snow Fox trotted along easily, and Connor didn't have much trouble keeping pace with it. *I'm following a fox now,* he thought. *I used to have a magic wishing cap...and a plan...but now I'm following a fox.*

Still, he couldn't think of what else to do. The elf had his sister. She didn't know Connor was anywhere near, and anyway, maybe she hadn't been taken hostage. Maybe she was here by choice. A faint echo of her words back in their house came back to him. "I'm asking *for* you..."

Somehow, he thought, she'd known. She knew all this crazy stuff about elves, about Father Winter, was real. And so she'd decided...what? She was going to walk right up to his front door? *With* an elf, forgetting for a second where she even *found* an elf? And then what? This old guy with a white beard, would just come out and say *Hey Holly, welcome. So tell me, what do you and your brother want for Yule this year?*

Why couldn't she just write him a letter, like any other little kid in the entire freaking world?

"A little slippery here," the Snow Fox warned Connor, bringing him back to the present. He scrambled with the fox down a short, steep slope. There was a cliff face there, not very high, and in it was an opening like the mouth of a cave, ringed with stones.

"My den," the Snow Fox said, tail swishing proudly. "You'll be my guest tonight. Your sister's not going anywhere until the morning. Go on in."

Connor hesitated, eying the opening. It looked like he'd have to go through on hands and knees.

"Don't worry. The further in you go, the bigger it gets," the Snow Fox assured him.

Connor sighed. *So I'm going to spend the night in a fox's den,* he thought. *This would have sounded pretty cool...back when I was eight years old or so.*

He crawled inside, ducking his head to avoid the rocks above. Once inside, the passage sloped down through smooth rock, narrowing a bit. Connor had a moment of panic—*what if I get stuck and can't get out?* The narrow part only lasted a few feet, though, and then the space opened out—more of a cavern than just a den. Connor found he could actually stand upright, and he did, as quickly as he could. His hands and knees hurt from crawling over cold stone.

It was warmer in here, though, and when his eyes adjusted to the dim light Connor saw why. The fox had, of all things, a fireplace. There was a fire burning there right now, purring contentedly as a cat. The chimney was a natural fissure in the rock.

Feeling almost beyond amazement, Connor looked around at the coziest den that anyone could imagine. There was a low table with a couple of chairs pulled up to it, not far from the fireside. A bed stood in one corner, with a pillow and real sheets, one edge turned down invitingly. There was a little wooden door set in the rock wall opposite the fireplace, which looked like it led to a pantry or something equally comfortable.

First Course

While he was gazing in wonder, the Snow Fox emerged from the passage. "Stand back," he advised. "The snow's melting, and I need a good shake. You can take your things off, too."

While Connor complied, the fox shook himself, sending a shower of water around the room. Then he jumped up in the chair closest to the fire, curled his tail around his legs, and gave a contented sigh. "So, what do you think?" he asked cheerfully.

Connor sank down into the opposite chair and spread out his hands. "What are you doing with a table and chairs? I mean, you're just, like, an animal."

"But not a *dumb* animal. You never know when somebody's going to drop in, so you need to be prepared. All the comforts of home," the Snow Fox said complacently.

"So...what's in the other room, over there?" Connor indicated the door he'd thought led to the pantry.

"Oh," the Snow Fox said, brightly, "that's where I hang all the kids who come to visit me, once I'm finished with them."

The fox seemed to be waiting for some reaction from Connor. He looked around coolly, stifling a yawn.

"Tough audience." The fox winked. "Actually, it's my pantry. That reminds me, you must be famished. And thirsty too. How about if we have a little something?"

Connor nodded. His stomach seconded the motion with a loud grumble.

The Snow Fox jumped down from his chair and trotted over to the door, which Connor saw now stood a little ajar. He nosed the door open and disappeared inside. Visions of fat sausages and thick slices of cake began dancing in Connor's head.

When the Snow Fox returned, however, he was carrying something in his mouth, and stood up on his hind legs to drop it on the table. Connor stared, his mouth suddenly dry. It was some kind of fat rodent, looking very dead with its short tail hanging over the table edge.

"What—" His voice came out as a harsh croak. "What is this?"

"The appetizer, of course," the Fox told him. "It's a lemming. Great eating. Quench your thirst, too. Drink the blood, eat the flesh— nothing better. I always start with the liver, myself, but that's a matter of taste. Dig in, while I go grab another one."

"This is one of those things that jumps off cliffs? No thanks. It's like...some kind of rat, or something."

Connor poked the lemming with one finger, distastefully. His heart skipped a beat when the seemingly dead rodent opened its eyes, squeaked, and jumped off the table, skittering away over the floor to vanish into a hole in the rock wall.

He thought the fox was choking on something, but then realized that it was laughing. At him. Sure, he thought. Cheap shot, but whatever.

"Okay," the Snow Fox said when he'd recovered. "I'll stop trying to yank your chain now. I just caught that lemming in the pantry, it was after the real stuff. Come in with me and we'll have the table spread in no time."

Pure as the Driven Snow

Connor's hunger was strong enough to conquer his misgivings. On the other side of the door was a small room, its walls lined with wooden shelves. The sausage of his vision was there, along with a toasting-fork, which the Snow Fox carried in his mouth.

And there was a small cake to follow, along with bottles of some kind of drink. Connor carried the other things over to the table. He had to go back a couple of times to get everything.

Connor toasted a sausage for each of them. They were good, full of spices, juicy meat, and sizzling fat. There were no plates, but Connor ate his sausage quickly enough that he didn't even need to put it down. He cut himself a piece of cake afterwards. It was poppyseed, or something a lot like that. The Snow Fox wouldn't eat the cake, but he accepted some of the drink, poured into a shallow bowl he'd had Connor fetch on his second trip.

"The best drink in the world," he said, lapping some more up and smacking his lips.

"What is it, anyway?" Connor asked, taking another sip. It was cold, and had almost no taste at all. When he swallowed, he felt chilled to the bone, just for a few seconds, but then that was replaced by a spreading sense of clarity, a sort of crystalline energy that made his fingers and toes tingle.

"Just water," the Snow Fox said. "But it's pure as the driven snow—in fact, that's what it was, twenty thousand years ago: driven snow. It's from a glacier up in the mountains, in the broken country. I'm the only one who knows about it. Ice water. Water from the Ice Age that has never thawed since, winter or summer. Water with the ancient sun and air locked up inside of it."

"I heard the glaciers are all melting now," Connor said. "Where did you say this one was?"

The Snow Fox looked at him reproachfully. "You can't expect me to reveal my trade secrets. Nobody does, up here. Do the elves tell you how they make their toys? Does the Old Man tell you how his reindeer fly?"

There it was again. Connor shook his head. "So...cut me some slack. I just found out that all this stuff is real—Father Winter, or Santa, or the Old Man, whatever you call him, and the elves sitting around running a toy assembly line, and whatnot. Why doesn't anyone else know? I mean, when you're a kid, everybody tells you Santa is real, sure. But as far as *they* know, they're lying about it."

The Snow Fox somehow managed to shrug. "Just because people think that what they're saying isn't true, doesn't mean it isn't. When you're a little older, you'll find out that lots of truths are only told by accident."

"And *then*," Connor went on, "they say they're going to come clean, give you the low-down on how things really are—and what they tell you is completely *wrong*."

"Well, not *completely*. You know that your mother fills your stockings, yours and Holly's. You hid and watched her doing it, the year you turned nine."

Connor froze. "How do you know that?"

"I know lots of things. Trade secrets, remember?" The Snow Fox winked at him. "Anyway, so here's the deal—Father Winter, Santa Claus, or whatever you want to call the Old Man...he doesn't bring presents. His big goal is to make sure that people who aren't being 'good'—according to *him*, and who made him the judge and jury?—*don't* get what they want. That's his real job, the rest is all PR."

"But I remember some good times at Yule," Connor protested. "At least...you know, when I was six. Or five." Before Holly came, he added to himself silently.

"Yeah, well. The Old Man doesn't visit every house in a given year. But do you remember any Yules that were especially dull, when you didn't get anything you wanted but everybody expected you to act all excited anyway, and dinner was burned and your sister was being a pain in the neck, but everybody blamed you instead of her?"

"Yup." Connor was sure he remembered more than one year like that.

"There you are," said the Snow Fox. "*Those* were the times that the Old Man visited your house."

Connor turned this over in his mind, staring at the fire, while taking another swallow of the ice water. Looking at it in the cold light of rationality, the pure, rarified air that surrounded him now, it made sense. He felt a growing admiration for the Snow Fox. Everyone else believed what they were told. But nobody could put one over on *this* guy.

Connor didn't stop to think that the Snow Fox might not be telling the truth either. Although he'd used a magic wishing cap, and followed an elf to the North Pole, it wasn't too long ago that he hadn't really believed in anything.

At this point, there was no way he could keep *that* up. But he still found it easier to think that supernatural things, if they existed, must be bad. He was like many people who don't quite dare to believe in angels, but know for sure that demons are real.

The ice water might have had something to do with it, too. Connor took another sip, and the cold spread to his heart, feeling like a soothing piece of ice laid on a sore place. He thought of Holly then, and though she seemed far away, he knew that he ought to ask about her.

"My sister, though. Why is she here? What does she have to do with all this?"

"Because she buys into those stories they put out about the Old Man," the Snow Fox answered at once. "She got the elf to bring her to the North Pole because she thinks that he'll give her something. Give *you* something, actually. You know that she really came here because of you, don't you?"

Connor remembered Holly saying "I'll ask *for* you", so he had to admit that he did. "But I never asked her to," he protested.

"Of course not. You're too smart for that. You know the score. She has no idea it's all a game, so she's acting like she can really make things come out differently. She thinks she can make the Old Man change his List."

"His list?"

"Naughty and nice...does that ring any bells?"

"Oh. *That* list." Connor thought suddenly of the book he'd found, back home, and that still lay in his jacket like a stray lump of coal. Was that somehow part of the List?

"*You're* probably down as naughty," the Snow Fox said. Connor felt a faint pride at recognizing this as a compliment, even before the Snow Fox continued, "I know *I* am, along with anybody else who's more interesting than a sea cucumber."

"Sure," Connor agreed. "Who wants to be *nice,* anyway?" It was a milk-and-sugar word, he thought. Cloying. Sickly sweet. Almost exactly the opposite of the clear, cold, pure atmosphere that filled his spirit now.

"And anyway, the Old Man doesn't let anybody *see* his List, much less change it. So she's going to fail, that's all," the Snow Fox said, matter-of-factly. "Nothing that anybody can do."

"But what will happen, then? What will they do with her?" Connor asked, feeling a faint stir of concern.

"Steal her dreams—that's what the elves do to children. Keep her there until she hasn't got any left."

Connor found this hard to believe. "But what about the toy making, and all that? If the elves hate children, why do they do that stuff? The toys are for children to play with, aren't they?"

The Snow Fox sighed. "The elves make the toys, but they don't give them away," he explained patiently. "They *collect* them. Haven't you ever heard 'he who dies with the most toys wins'? That's actually an elvish saying. Humans borrowed it and it wound up on bumper stickers. I'm not sure how things like that happen, by the way, but they do."

"So...they steal dreams..." Connor took another sip of the ice water, and found it easier to see the truth of that. In fact, he could see it all now. Everything was falling into place, all the pieces of the puzzle, forming a perfect, crystalline pattern. A thing of beauty, really.

But one thing was still nagging at him, the smallest of missing pieces. Oh, right, he thought. Holly.

"But what would happen to Holly then? When she doesn't have any dreams left?"

"Where do you think all the elves came from, in the first place?" the Snow Fox asked with a pitying look. "They're all children. Children who were stolen away from their parents. Children who will never grow up, no matter how long they live—and some of them have been there for hundreds of years."

Connor pondered this. He began to feel as if there were cracks in the ice that was encasing him, heart and mind. Somehow, it wasn't okay that Holly was part of this picture, this pattern that he was seeing more and more clearly, with every sip of ice water he took.

"It's a good thing you stole his cap, though," the Fox was saying.

"His cap? Oh, yeah, the wishing cap." Connor had almost forgotten about it, running with the wolves. "Sure, that was fun. But I didn't really need it," he added, with a nonchalant air.

"Maybe *you* didn't. If the *elf* had it, he'd have wished himself right up to the Old Man's palace. They'd already be measuring your sister for one of those tacky fur suits, right about now. Good work. Of course, the elf probably has a backup plan, but you bought some time, at least."

"Bought some time," Connor repeated. He had an uncomfortable feeling, growing stronger by the moment, that since he had this time, it was up to him to do something with it. Holly might be dumb, but she was his sister. He'd protected her before—not lately, it was true, but once when they'd been at the same playground, he'd made a bully back down and leave her alone.

Another memory floated up, cracking the ice that was spreading over his mind and heart—his father saying, *Take care of your little sister, Connor. Whenever I'm not around. I'm counting on you.* But almost right away, another voice spoke inside his head. *Sure,* it said. *Easy for him to talk. But it's his job to take care of her, not mine, and he's always going away. Rescuing other people.*

Connor found himself nodding in agreement with the second voice. And even if I did promise, he thought, I can't disappoint my dad anymore by what I do or don't do. He's gone, and with every minute that passes, his own chance of getting rescued is going down. So it doesn't matter now.

He was hoping the first voice would agree with that, and tell him how grownup and realistic he was being. But there was no answer—he was just left listening to the hollow echo of his own words: *it doesn't matter now.* Something stirred deep inside him, and he realized that he didn't really believe that. No matter what anybody said, no matter what he said himself, it really *did* matter.

The Snow Fox yawned. "Well, time to sleep. You can have the bed—I'm going to curl up right here by the fire."

Connor finished his ice water, and stood up, stretching. He felt sleep falling over him like a blanket. He should have been on edge, especially after the tricks the Snow Fox had played on him earlier, but he found that he trusted the Fox now. And anyway, he was so tired. More tired than he had ever been in his life...

"But we'll find Holly in the morning," he mumbled, as he pulled back the covers and lay down on the bed. "I'll get her back, somehow. You'll help me, right?"

"We'll talk after you sleep on it," the Snow Fox said soothingly. "You just need to think about what you want. What you *really* want."

Connor looked up at him. *Up?* part of his brain repeated, in disbelief.

For just a moment, though his half-closed eyes, Connor saw a man standing over him—or maybe a teenager, because his smiling face looked young, despite his white hair. Then Connor's eyes closed all the way, and darkness swirled around him, warm and comforting.

He thought he heard one last whisper. "Sweet dreams."

At the same time, Holly and Snowthorn were lying with Duck Egg's family on the wide bed platform, tucked up under layers and layers of furs and hides.

They'd blown out the oil lamps, and most of the room lay in deep blue shadow. But a bit of soft moonlight still glowed through a window of ice, set high in one of the igloo's walls.

Tomorrow they would find the magic reindeer, somehow, and then...

Holly couldn't imagine any further. She could see the Old Man himself, but not where he lived. Where could it be, that you had to ride a flying reindeer to get there? Up on some high mountaintop? Up in the air itself, built on clouds?

Snowthorn would say only that it moved around. But then how would they get there at all? The reindeer would know, she told herself. The reindeer must know.

Suddenly she felt a sharp yearning for home and for her mother. It made her want to cry and curl up as small as she could. But there was no way back now, she knew. She had to go onward, with Snowthorn, to the Old Man's palace.

Just after she dropped off to sleep, but before she knew for sure that she was dreaming, she found herself at the foot of a spiral staircase that wound up and up, until it was lost in shadows far above her. She heard her mother's voice, telling her that she needed to look for her father. So she started to climb.

As she went up the stairs, there were small windows in the wall at the turnings so she could look out. Through the first, she could only see snow and ice, jagged mountains and a frozen sea. Through the second she saw something that looked like a map spread out beneath her, like she was looking down at the world from high in the sky.

When she stopped the third time and looked out a window smaller than the first two, she finally saw her father.

He was walking somewhere—where was his plane, she wondered?—and dressed for the outdoors. But it felt somehow like he was inside. Everything was dark at first, until her father turned on his flashlight and moved it around. Then a huge hall made out of crystal loomed up around him. It must be ice, Holly realized. This was one of the ice caves, up on the mountain, that her father had told her about once.

The ice reflected back his light like thousands of glittering stars. There were big boulders of ice strewn around the floor, and her father moved around them slowly, as if he was tired. Icicles hung from the ceiling, too, like bright, shining swords suspended over his head.

It was a winter wonderland, just like in the Yule song, but her father kept looking around and shaking his head. Once Holly thought he looked right at her, but he didn't seem to see her. There was no hope in his face, nothing but weariness.

It came to her that he was looking for a way out, trying to get back to her.

"I'm here," she murmured, "Daddy... Papa...come find me..."

But he couldn't hear her, either, and something seemed wrong anyway. Wasn't *she* supposed to find *him*? But how could she, when she was still lost herself? Her thoughts tangled in confusion, she drifted down into sleep.

And Holly's nightmare drifted off into the black sky, moving like a shadow across the face of the moon. Finally it floated out over the sea, where the North Wind tore it into little pieces of darkness that were lost in the night.

Some Things Even You Can't Do

Connor dreamed of his mother that night. What he saw seemed real. But of course, it couldn't have been. How can you dream about things that are really happening somewhere else?

He saw his mom sitting at the kitchen table, her face buried in her hands. He knew somehow that she had already called 911, and told them all about what had happened, what Connor had said and how he'd looked, what Holly was wearing. She'd called Charlie and told him too. She'd walked up and down the neighborhood asking people. There wasn't a voice talking to him in the dream, or anything like that—he just knew.

After a while she got up. Her face was set. She went into the dark living room and looked at the tree, with its branches spreading empty. Grimalkin came out with her, and rubbed against her leg now, purring softly.

Connor watched his mother as she took strands of lights out of their boxes, wound them around the tree, and plugged them in. Suddenly a thousand little stars came to life, red and yellow and blue and green, steadfast, holding the darkness at bay.

In that light, and the light of the electric fire, with its false logs that burned endlessly but never changed shape, Connor's mother hung the stockings on the mantel.

When she was done, the stockings dangled empty, slack-mouthed, on their hooks. *Nobody's coming to fill them, Mom,* Connor thought. *And you won't even do it yourself, not if you're all alone. Why do all this? Why pretend that there's some special day in the year that's magic, that can somehow bring you happiness? Might as well pretend you can fly...*

But of course, Connor wasn't really there. Anyway, his mom couldn't hear what he was thinking. She went on with her ritual, carefully hanging all the ornaments on the tree, one by one, stacking the empty boxes neatly in the closet as she finished each of them. She found a high branch for the glass pickle that Connor usually got to hang. Holly's favorite, a little gnome with a red hat, went a little lower.

After she'd hung all the ornaments, Connor's mom went to one of the side tables. He saw that she'd set up a little altar there. Along with the incense and candles, and a statue of some goddess whose name he couldn't remember, a picture of his dad lay on the tabletop.

She opened a drawer and rummaged around for a while, then took out pictures of Connor and Holly, and lay them down beside the one of his dad. Connor didn't like the picture of him she was using—she'd caught him by surprise, and he looked clueless and nerdy.

Connor watched his mom as she lit the altar candles and said a few words under her breath. Nobody hears, Mom, Connor thought at her. Or okay, given the weird stuff he'd found out, maybe they *do*. But they don't care, because they made the world on purpose to be the way that it is.

Then his mom went over to the picture that hung on the living room wall, the one that showed two children crossing a ramshackle bridge, with an angel watching them from above. The picture had been a present from Connor's grandmother, who was Catholic, and their mom had kept it though she didn't usually have Christian things around. Looking at it always made Connor a little nervous, even though the bridge wasn't very high.

His mom kissed her hand and touched, first the girl who was guiding her brother, and then the barefoot boy.

Then she sat back down with a sigh. Grimalkin came over, waving his tail in the air.

He looked at the tree, then at her, seeming to approve. He jumped up into her lap and curled himself up, purring.

"Maybe I should start talking to you, Grimalkin," his mom said to the cat, who blinked up at her sleepily. "Hey, too late. I am already."

She stroked the cat absent-mindedly, gazing at the tree. She stayed like that for a little while, and then Connor could see her make up her mind to do something else. Grimalkin mewed reproachfully as she stood up, dumping him unceremoniously into the chair.

She walked back to the brightly lighted kitchen, pushed the map of the mountain as far to one end of the table as she could, and got a pen and a pad of note paper decorated at the borders with snowflakes and holly leaves. She sat for a moment chewing the end of the pen, and then began.

Dear Father Winter, she wrote.

Not him! Connor shouted at her without making any sound. *He's the worst of them, Mom! What has he ever done for us? For you? He took your daughter away, that's what!*

But she went on writing. And the dream wouldn't let Connor look away, so he couldn't help but read his mother's letter.

Dear Father Winter, it's been a long time since I've asked you for anything...

His mom sighed, nibbled the end of her pen for a minute, and then went on.

But now there's a big thing I have to ask. I don't know if it's even possible. And I know there are some things even you can't do.

But I have to try. I've lost my family. I don't know where they are, any of them, and I need them.

It's hard to think of Don being lost. Sure, Connor thought, she would think of my dad first. But he still felt a twinge of jealousy.

He always acts so sure of himself, his mother wrote. *But then I remember when we first met.* She smiled, and for a moment, her face seemed younger and less careworn.

He was in the Air Force then, on wilderness maneuvers. He got lost and wound up walking into my parents' backyard. A little later, we started dating.

It wasn't a story Connor had ever heard before. It was strange to think of his father actually getting lost. But in a weird way, it was also reassuring. My dad isn't perfect, he thought. He makes mistakes too. Of course Connor had always known that, but it still felt, just now, like a revelation.

He always says, "I wasn't really lost that day, Megan. I was looking for you...and I found you."

His mom stopped writing for a moment, and Connor saw tears on her cheeks. He wished he could comfort her somehow. But of course, he wasn't there. And anyway, the ice water the Snow Fox had given him didn't make it easy to think of comforting things.

If you can, please make it be like that now. That he's not really lost. That he's looking for me, and at the end of the journey we'll be together. That he will be home for Yule, like I told Holly.

Please, if you can, make it so.

His mom had filled up a whole sheet of paper, so she put it aside and started a new one. *I graduated from nursing school, and Don and I got married. Connor came along a year later. We were so happy. Connor was so like his father, and they were always close.*

That's what mothers always say, Connor thought.

But then Holly was born, and Connor was jealous of her, I think.

Sure, Connor thought. Jealous of my kid sister. But deep down, he felt that his mom might be right. A little.

Connor seemed to be drifting away. We couldn't tell at first, because it was so gradual, but we were losing him. We tried a few different things, and then last year, Don tried taking him up in the plane. Connor couldn't handle it, and since then, things have gotten worse. He's gotten more and more moody and withdrawn. He hangs out with friends who aren't good for him, and now, I can't even talk to him anymore. Holly still can, a little.

I haven't said anything about Holly yet. She believes in you. That's the most important thing about her. Her faith. Other than that, she looks a lot like me, her hair is red like mine, but curly. She's got a missing tooth right now in front, it looks really cute when she smiles...

His mom sighed. Connor could see her thinking that it didn't make any sense to give a description to a guy who was magic, and was supposed to know everything. She started a new paragraph.

They might be together. I hope they are, so they can help each other. But no matter where, I just want you to find them. To guide them back home.

Just then it started to rain again. It sounded like thousands of tiny fists pounding the roof. His mom looked up for a minute, then started to write again.

I'll leave a candle in the window.

She skipped a few spaces and added, *Thank you, Megan.*

Connor watched his mom slowly seal the envelope, and write the impossible address on the outside, like a prayer. She got up from the table and put on her jacket. He knew she was going to splash down the street, through the rain, to the mailbox to post the letter. The same mailbox he'd hidden behind, what seemed like a hundred years ago.

But when he tried to follow his mother out of the house, he found himself lost on a dark, frozen plain where stars glittered like windows into a world of ice. Somewhere ahead of him a bridge arched up far into the sky, and he was going to have to cross it, alone.

Connor whimpered in his sleep, trying to push the dream out of his head and far away. After a dark, feverish struggle, he succeeded.

The dream left him, drifting over to the Snow Fox's chimney, and floated upward. It rose out of the chimney with the woodsmoke and kept on going up in a lazy spiral. Bands of red and green light flamed across the sky, and the dream moved along with them as if following a road. Inside the dream, the image of Connor stepped hesitantly onto the bridge, and began to walk across it. The dream-bubble itself drifted toward an especially bright star that shone, cold and fixed, at the end of the road formed by the Northern Lights.

But Connor slept the rest of the night in a warmer darkness that was free of stars and dreams alike.

Seven

Luckily Holly, being used to the gray skies in Seattle, didn't rely on the morning light to wake her up. She opened her eyes just a little when their hosts began to stir.  Uncle George had produced a small camp stove from somewhere and was brewing something—some kind of grown-up tea? Holly wrinkled her nose. Her mother drank coffee, and she liked the rich smell of it, but it had tasted bitter and awful the one time she'd asked for a sip.

She shook Snowthorn, who'd been sleeping next to her. He just grunted, and burrowed deeper under the covers. She shook him again, harder. This time, he threw off the covers and sat up, blinking as if his eyes were dazzled by the faint light.

"Good morning," she said brightly.

"I'm not a morning person," Snowthorn muttered, though it came out sounding more like 'nodda munning perse'. "And this time of year, I'm about ready to climb into bed for a few *months*. This is unnatural, is what it is. Hey, is that tea?" he asked, perking up a bit.

Duck Egg brought the elf a cup, and handed him and Holly each a slice of some different meat: "Caribou," she explained briefly. Then she went back to the other side of the bed platform, where she, Shadow-of-Birds, and her uncle sipped tea and talked with low voices in their language.

Holly looked at Snowthorn, who seemed to be lost in his own thoughts. She cleared her throat. "Sorry to erupt," she said politely.

Snowthorn choked on his mouthful of tea. When he could speak again he said, "*In*terrupt. You're sorry to interrupt. What are you interrupting, anyway?"

"Well, you looked like you were thinking."

"I do, sometimes. Terrible habit, I know, but you might try it sometime. It grows on you."

"I'll think about it. Anyway, I can't eat this." She gestured with her slice of caribou meat.

"Why not? Mmmm, good." Snowthorn made a show of chewing his slice, his eyes closed in ecstasy.

Holly couldn't help it. She knew it should be funny, but tears filled her eyes. She'd flown hundreds of miles on the South Wind, chased ghosts, talked with a walrus and slept in an igloo, but having cold reindeer meat for breakfast was the last straw. She wanted to be home. She wanted the warmth and the cheerful sounds of her mother's kitchen. She wanted...

"A sausage sandwich," Snowthorn said, in a resigned sort of voice.

Holly smelled the toasted muffin, the melted cheese, and the spicy meat before she realized what she was holding.

"Thank you," she said to Snowthorn. "How did you know that's my favorite breakfast?"

"We elves just know these things," Snowthorn said. He didn't look especially happy about it. He took his Elf Help card out of his pocket and looked at it with a sigh.

"How much do you have left?" Holly asked.

He turned the card around and showed her the strip on the back, which was now completely gray and empty. "Absolutely nothing," he said. "That was it. I've hit bottom." Then he brightened. "But hey, don't worry about it. I was just kidding myself. I was never going to get into R&D anyway. A bad boy like me? Enjoy it, that's all I ask."

Holly felt guilty about Snowthorn giving up his last bit of magic just to get her breakfast. What was he going to do for the next five hundred years? But as she took bites, the familiar food did seem to comfort her heart and make her stronger. She understood for the first time what her mom meant by 'comfort food'.

She would have to be nicer to Snowthorn, she decided. She'd been so focused on her quest that she hadn't really thought of all he'd done to help her. For some reason, she thought of her mom, too. Of course, she had always done things for Holly, but Holly had taken it for granted.

She looked thoughtfully over at Uncle George. He was just giving his last piece of meat to Duck Egg. He laughed and said he wasn't hungry that morning, but Holly knew somehow that he wasn't quite telling the truth.

But I'm doing things for other people, too, she reminded herself. *I'm making this journey just because of Connor. Just to make him happy. So then my mom and dad can be happy again too.*

In a few minutes their hosts had finished their breakfast, and Uncle George stood up, said something, and went outside. "He's going to harness up the dogs to the *qamutik*," Duck Egg informed them. "The sled, that is."

Still Night

Holly clapped her hands, her brief sense of guilt forgotten. "We're going to go on a *dog sled*?"

"We will, if you want to get there today," Duck Egg said matter-of-factly.

In a little while Uncle George called from outside, and they went out to join him. Holly was surprised when they ducked through the low tunnel and emerged from the igloo. There was only a faint glow of light on the horizon, and the sky, as well as the air, it seemed, were a deep blue, almost black.

"But it's still night!" she exclaimed, forgetting where they were.

"This is as light as it gets, this time of year," Duck Egg said.

"And where we're going, it will be even darker. This is polar twilight. Around the Palace, it's polar night all the time, until the spring. *Astronomical* polar night," said Snowthorn, with an air of satisfaction.

Holly nodded, trying to make it seem like it wasn't a big deal. She turned to look at the sled. Uncle George had harnessed eight of the wolf-like dogs to it. It had a light framework with long runners turned up at the ends, and looked ready to start skimming over the snow any moment.

"It will be fun to ride," she said.

Duck Egg nodded. "When you're on a trip like this, or heading out for supplies, it is. When you're on your way back, or when we move in the fall and the ground's not quite frozen, it's different. The sleds are heavy and piled high with stuff, and the dogs get pretty tired, so it's slow going. Hey, that reminds me, uncle. I'll get some fish for us to bring."

Holly made a face; she'd hoped to get away from the fish. "The dogs won't run without food," Duck Egg said, with a smile. "Don't worry about the smell, we give them the fish that are really frozen stiff. They don't care, they just snap them right up."

After Duck Egg brought a bucket of fish, her uncle stood in the front of the sled and took up the reins. Duck Egg sat in back with Holly and Snowthorn.

Shadow-of-Birds walked over slowly, carrying a small drum made of some kind of skin stretched over a frame of bone, and took her place in the front, next to Duck Egg's uncle.

Uncle George called to the dogs, and they began to run. The sled caught on some rough ice, and they bounced jarringly, then settled down to a smooth glide, quickly leaving the small cluster of igloos behind in the distance.

You Have To Decide

For a moment, when Connor woke up, he thought he was back in his own room. He yawned and stretched. *So it's all right after all,* he thought. *We didn't get caught yesterday. I'm not even suspended from school, I'm still at home, and I can do whatever I want. It's Yule Eve, and it's warm, and the fire smells like hot spiced cider...*

Fire? His eyes snapped open and he sat up in bed. He felt dizzy for a moment as it sunk in that he was still in the fox's den, lying on a pallet on the floor. He looked around, half expecting to see the young guy he'd glimpsed the night before, but only the Snow Fox himself was curled up in front of the fire, tail over his nose. As Connor sank back down, the Fox stirred and yawned.

Connor let his head fall back, and closed his eyes. *It's Yule Eve,* his thoughts ran on, taking a different course, *and my sister's been kidnapped by an elf, and my mother probably thinks we're dead, and my father might actually be dead. And last night, I crashed with a fox.*

"Rise and shine," the Snow Fox said cheerfully. "Wake up and smell the coffee."

A *crazy* fox. "There isn't any coffee here," he said. "Unless you have some in your pantry?"

"Hey, anything's possible. All you need to do is believe," the fox said. He trotted over and nosed Connor's face.

Connor yelped. "That's cold!"

"So I'm healthy. Come on, you really do need to get up. Your sister's awake already, and the Eskimos are making tea and thinking of getting the sled out. Today's the day, Ray. It's the *Eve.*"

That got him moving. He went over to the fire, where the fox had thoughtfully moved his parka and his other gear. He pulled the warmed clothes on and stood up. "So where do I go?"

"Now you're getting ahead of yourself. We've still got a few minutes. How about some breakfast first?"

"Breakfast, sure." The fox jumped up in one of the chairs, as he had the night before, and Connor sat in the other. He noticed that there was nothing on the table, other than two empty bowls.

"Umm...should I go get something from the pantry?" he asked.

"First," the Snow Fox said, "you have to decide."

"Decide what?"

The Fox looked at him thoughtfully, resting its chin on its paws. "I like you, Connor. You're the smartest creature I've met in quite a while—other than myself, of course." He coughed modestly and went on. "So I'll give you a gift. And because I know you can handle it, I'll let you choose your own gift."

"Okay..." Connor wondered why the Fox was taking so long to get to the point. "So what are the choices?"

"For one thing, I could help you catch up with your sister."

His dad had taught Connor to play poker a while ago, and he called on that training now to keep his face expressionless. "How can you do that? She's with an elf, you know."

"Elves!" the Snow Fox said contemptuously. "They're nothing but children, I told you that. I don't care how old they get. Their magic is as childish as they are. I can run rings around them. You can, too, with my gifts."

"Which are...?"

"First, the power of invisibility."

"Invisibility?" Connor remembered the wish he'd made back home, before he'd even tried the wishing cap, and wondered if the fox had read his mind somehow.

"It means," the Snow Fox explained patiently, "that nobody will be able to see you."

"I *know* what it means," Connor snapped. "What I meant to say is, how does it work?"

"Telling you *how* it works isn't part of the offer," said the Snow Fox primly. "Second, the gift of swiftness. You'll be able to run as fast as the fastest sled dog, without tiring, for days if need be."

"Okay, I get that. So I'd be able to run them down, and rescue my sister without the elf knowing I'm there. But then how do we get home?"

"Oh, I thought you understood about that. You don't. Unless you figure out a way to get to the Old Man's palace. He has the power to send you home, if he feels like it."

"And if he doesn't?"

"Look, Connor," the Snow Fox said, with a touch of annoyance. "I can only do so much for you. After that, you need to rely on your native powers. Your quick wit, your blarney, your gift of gab."

"Right," Connor muttered. "It's like, a quest. We don't want things to be *too* easy."

"Exactly. Oh, and by the way, the powers I give you won't last forever. And I can't tell you exactly when they'll go away. It might be sudden."

Connor nodded. "Sure. Makes it more interesting. So what about the other choice I have?"

"Oh, that. Well, I could just send you back home."

"What?" Connor sat bolt upright. "But you just said..."

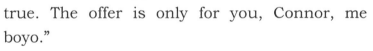

"I didn't. I said that I couldn't send *both* of you home. Which happens to be true. The offer is only for you, Connor, me boyo."

"But...how can you do that?"

"Never mind *how*," the Snow Fox said. "I told you not to ask how, didn't I? Let's just say that foxes are masters of twists and turnings. We always have plans B, C, and D, and we always have a back door handy. What I would do is let you use my back door, just for this once."

"Your back door?"

The Snow Fox pointed with his nose toward the back of the cave. Connor saw that there was indeed another door in the rock wall. He felt as if cold water was trickling down the back of his neck, because he was suddenly certain that it hadn't been there the night before.

"It can't be," he whispered.

"Believe, Steve. Go on. Open it, I've got nothing to hide. Go ahead."

Connor got up and walked over, feeling as if he were wading through invisible mud. This door had a knob just like his bedroom door, at home. Then he noticed some chips in the paint, and the holes where he'd tacked up a horror-movie mask, last Halloween, before his mom made him take it down.

It *was* his bedroom door.

He turned the knob, and the door gave a short creak, just at the right time. He looked through into his own room. Everything seemed to be just as he'd left it. Of course, he thought, it was only yesterday. What would have changed?

Wait. He frowned. Something was wrong with this picture. His bed had been neatly made, with both the pillows fluffed up. And there wasn't a pile of dirty clothes in the corner where it always was, right next to the electric guitar he'd gotten two Yules back—which his father had picked up 'just to show Connor a few things', and wound up playing riffs that practically melted the fretboard. Connor had barely touched it since.

He swung around to confront the fox. "That isn't my room. It never looks like that."

"Your mom came in and straightened the place up," the Snow Fox said. "Looks like *that* move was long overdue, by the way."

"She never comes into my room," Connor said defiantly. "I don't let her."

The Snow Fox sighed. "She knows you're not home right now," he pointed out. "She has no idea where you are. She has to do something, and this is one thing she can do. Make your room look nice. I'm no therapist, but I think it makes it easier for her to believe that you'll really come back. What do you think? Is she right?"

Connor opened his mouth to argue some more, but he thought of his dream, and his mom wandering around the empty house, and somehow he knew that the Fox was telling the truth. Slowly, he raised his hand and reached forward. He didn't meet any resistance. This was no picture, it was the real thing.

"You could walk right through," the Snow Fox said. "No strings attached. One small step for Connor-kind."

Realizing that he was holding his breath, Connor let it out slowly. His stomach felt as if it had been tied in knots. He turned away from both the Snow Fox and the room on the other side of the open door, trying desperately to think.

"If it helps," said the Fox from behind him, "think of this. Your sister believes. She's really into all this North Pole shtick. She'll be happy, being an elf. She won't see anything but the illusions that the Old Man creates for them. And your mom might think losing one kid is better than losing both."

"You said we could get back, that there was a way from the Old Man's palace," Connor said, swinging back to face him.

"Oh, that was just to make you feel better. I have no idea, really," the Fox said brightly. "Never been inside the place, myself."

Connor squeezed his eyes shut. He imagined going home, just lying there in his own room, breathing in the smells that were all full of comfort, even the bad ones. And anyway, he wouldn't leave dirty clothes lying around his room, ever again. That was nothing, if he could go home. He'd have that quiet dinner with his mom. He would make things up to her. There was still time to turn things around.

And then, of course, she would ask Connor about Holly. No problem. He'd just tell her...

What? That he'd been kidnapped, along with her, but he'd gotten away. And left her there. In a place he couldn't describe, with things that weren't even human. And time would go on, and his mom would keep up that little shrine he'd seen in his dream, and she would always be acting like Holly, or maybe even his dad, might show up at the door some night. And her hope would die slowly, inch by inch, year by empty year, until nothing was left.

And he would be stuck being the man of the house—forever. I never signed up for that, he thought. I'll leave home as soon as I can, go to school if there's money, get a job, anything. And I'll forget all about this, leave it all far behind me...

Sure, he thought. That'll happen. He might grumble and complain, and he was pretty sure he would, but in the end he knew that he wasn't going to walk through that door. He drew a deep breath. Without looking behind him, he swung the door closed. The short, sharp creak sounded like the cry of something in pain.

"I'll take the powers," he said. "I'm going after her."

I Don't Feel Any Different

"Your choice," the Snow Fox said, in an *it's-your-funeral* kind of tone. "All right, *now* we can have breakfast. See what you can find in the pantry, I never know what's going to be in there myself."

Connor took a few steps and then looked back. The rock wall was sheer, with no sign that a door had ever been there. He went inside the pantry. The same shelves lined the walls of the tiny room, but the contents were entirely different this morning. Where the sausages had been were stacks of oatcakes. He brought a few of them and a couple of bottles, which he found were full of milk.

Connor munched his oatcakes quickly. It wasn't that different from his usual breakfast, which was oatmeal, but it was dry enough that he was glad of the milk, and drained the entire bottle in a few gulps.

The Snow Fox licked his chops, having polished off his cake, and lapped up his bowl of milk, in the meantime. "Nothing like an oat cake when you're going on a quest. It's in all the stories. All right, time to go. The Eskimos are whipping up the dogs, and your sister's getting onto the sled."

"So do I have those powers now? I don't feel any different," Connor said, holding up his hand and looking at it suspiciously.

"Not yet. You need to put on that ring." The Snow Fox nodded toward the table. Connor saw something lying in the middle. It looked like a bit of white fur.

"That's a ring?" Connor peered at it.

"Well, okay, it's made from my fur," said the Snow Fox, a little defensively. "How else is it going to work? I'm magic, okay? Just twist it around your finger, and away you go."

Connor held up his hand. "Wait a second. So it's a ring and it makes me invisible? I think I've heard this story, and I don't like the way it ends."

"*Your* story is different. I mean, it's not a story at all, of course," the Snow Fox added hastily. "You're in control of your own destiny. Captain of your own soul. A free agent. You the man, Stan."

"What if it falls off?"

The Snow Fox grinned. "Believe me, that's the last thing you need to worry about. It will only fall off when you forget all about yourself."

"Huh. Well, that's just what I want to do," Connor said. He thought of looking into the mirror in his room, seeing that face he had to carry around whether he liked it or not. Then he pushed that thought away, because it made him think of being in his room, of being home, and for a second he knew he was about to change his mind, to beg the Fox to open that door again...

But there was the swatch of fur lying on the table. He reached out and stroked it, and somehow, it seemed to come alive at his touch, twisting itself around his finger. It felt uncomfortably tight. He tried to slide it off, but it wouldn't budge.

"See? What did I tell you?"

"But I don't feel any different," Connor protested.

"Just close your eyes for a minute, and you will," the Snow Fox assured him.

"*Okay.*" Connor closed his eyes.

He heard the Snow Fox say softly, "Catch you later, frater."

Then there was silence. Connor opened his eyes. Once again the world reeled around him. He was outside now, standing up, at the side of the frozen sea, with cold stars shining overhead, bringing out a few answering glints from the jagged ice.

Well, what was a bit more magic? "Later, dude," he whispered.

Eight

Impossibly Green

Holly enjoyed the sled ride. The air was clear and crisp, and everything was quiet except for the faint swishing of the runners over the snow, and the panting of the dogs. And while they were moving quickly, it was easier not to think of other things, like what the Old Man might think of her trying to trick him, and what would Connor wind up getting for Yule anyway, and would her father really get home in time—she wouldn't let herself think about her nightmare.

She tried to look around and figure out where she would go, if she were giving directions, but it wasn't easy. Holly was used to finding her way around in parks and city streets—places where there were trees, and houses, and signs. Here there was nothing, just a big, open country where the air cracked with cold, and every now and then there was a range of jagged, broken hills, that looked just like every other range of hills they'd passed. The only landmark she knew was the river, and they'd left that behind long ago.

But Shadow-of-Birds seemed to be in no doubt about where they were going. After a while she began to beat on her drum, keeping it up until it merged with the panting of the dogs and the swish of the snow, and seemed like some kind of strange heartbeat belonging to the land itself. Every now and then, she talked in her own language to people who weren't there, seeming to pause politely so that they could speak, too. But there was no answering voice that Holly could hear. She was a little scared at first, but Duck Egg and Snowthorn assured her that all this was normal, for shamans.

After a while she could feel that they were going uphill. The dogs began to pant and strain. Holly, peering ahead, could make out a strange, conical hill rising over them, made of dark rock just streaked with snow in some places. It looked far too steep to climb, and Holly wondered what they would do next.

They paused at the base, where the sheer rock began, and Shadow-of-Birds and Duck Egg's uncle exchanged a few words in low voices. Then George turned the sled, called encouragement to the dogs, and they began to go around the hill's base.

"What are we doing?" Holly asked under her breath.

"Just wait," Duck Egg told her.

What they were doing, it turned out, was driving around and around the hill in circles. Shadow-of-Birds was chanting now, her voice a high, thin wail, like the song of some lost ghost. She kept up the drumbeat, too, until the whole thing seemed to Holly like some kind of strange dance, a dance that would go on forever.

They circled the hill several times. Holly lost count, then thought she caught up again. On what, as far as she could tell, was the ninth time, the sled crunched suddenly to a halt. Uncle George and Shadow-of-Birds stared up at the hill. Snowthorn and Duck Egg had risen to their feet so they could see. Holly scrambled up to stand beside them.

She was gazing right at the hill when it suddenly dissolved, like a dark cloud before a strong wind, leaving only empty sky. She blinked and rubbed her eyes, but the hill was gone for good. Instead, there was a little valley opening before them. And the valley was vividly, impossibly, green.

Duck Egg drew her breath in sharply, and her uncle muttered something Holly was glad she didn't understand, and moved his hand like he was pushing something away. Only Shadow-of-Birds stayed calm.

"How can it be?" Holly stared down at the land below. Somehow, in the middle of the Arctic twilight, a glow like sunlight filled the valley. She glimpsed a bright, unfrozen stream down there, winding its way through green fields. And by the river, a few scattered, slow-moving shapes, looking like a herd of....

"Reindeer," said Snowthorn softly. "There they are."

Uncle George said something in a low voice to the dogs, and tossed them each a fish or two. They lay down in the snow and chewed their food, giving a thoughtful growl now and then, just as if they were making conversation while eating their lunch.

A thought struck Holly. "Do they talk this time of year, too?" she whispered to Snowthorn.

"I think it's just the wild animals," he said. "Or if the tame ones do, then they sure don't let *us* know about it."

Duck Egg cleared her throat. "Okay, this is as far as we can go," she said. "My uncle says he and one of his friends saw this valley once, years ago, but as soon as they did, they broke their spears, turned their clothes inside out, and walked away. *Backwards.* He says a hunter's life isn't worth a frozen seal's flipper if he gets within bowshot of one of those caribou."

Holly and Snowthorn climbed down off the sled. She turned to Duck Egg and hugged her impulsively. "Thank you," she said. "And tell your uncle and grandmother thanks for us."

Duck Egg looked a bit taken aback, but in a moment her smile returned. "You're welcome. You're the nicest *kapluna* girl I've ever met."

"How many others have you met?" Holly asked.

"Well, just one. But you're *way* nicer than she was. I hope you find what you're looking for. That Old Man..." She shook her head. "I've heard he can be very tricky."

"You can say that again," Snowthorn muttered.

Holly turned to Shadow-of-Birds, and for the first time, the old woman smiled. It made Holly think that she knew what it would be like in the spring up here, when the sun finally made the skies bright again. "Goodbye," she whispered.

"*Tavvauvutit*," said Shadow-of-Birds, stroking Holly's cheek. Her hand felt as light as a feather.

Uncle George insisted on solemnly shaking hands with both Holly and Snowthorn. Then they watched as he roused the dogs, and they started off downhill again, back towards the river and the village. Duck Egg raised her hand and they waved back. Shadow-of-Birds looked over her shoulder and said something more, but her words were lost in the wind.

"What did she say?" Holly called to Duck Egg.

"She said, may the spirits protect you," she called back. "You're definitely going to need it."

After they could no longer see the sled in the deepening twilight, Snowthorn took Holly's hand. "Let's find us a reindeer," he said. "We're almost home."

Almost Home

"*You're* almost home," Holly said. "Is it...well, is it safe? Duck Egg's uncle seemed to think..."

Snowthorn laughed. "Safe? Nothing up here is *safe*. Is this the same little girl who made me promise to take her to the Palace, so she could break in and forge an entry on the List? Safety didn't seem high on your list of concerns, back then."

Holly looked back at him, and her lip trembled again.

"Okay, okay. It's as safe as…well, getting on an airplane. Safer. I'm an elf. The reindeer know us. And these are the *retired* reindeer, so…"

"Retired?"

"Well, yes. The magical reindeer don't age much more slowly than the other kind, so the Old Man has to break in new ones for his team, every few years. So, as I was saying, these guys are…"

"Old?"

"*Experienced.* One of them will be glad to help, and once we're up and away, all we need to do is find the bridge."

"The bridge?"

"The bridge of light. The Northern Lights, humans call them."

"Oh." Holly grew interested again, in spite of herself. "That's the same thing as the Roaring Bore-it-all-us that Ivar talked about, isn't it?"

Snowthorn just smiled, not bothering to correct her this time. "That's right. And on the other side is the Old Man's palace. Come on, let's go down to meet them."

They picked their way down the slope into the green valley. It was strange for Holly to be walking on grass again. There wasn't a path down, exactly, but it wasn't hard going.

The air grew warmer as they went down, also. At the bottom it was almost like a spring day. Holly threw back her hood and let the mild air caress her face. She could hear the babble of the stream not far away. How could nothing more than the sound of running water make her so happy?

The air was so fresh and fragrant, so full of promise. She took a deep breath. It was like the air on the first day of vacation, when you came out of the school and left behind all the walls and the closed doors, and saw a golden summer stretching endlessly before you.

The next thing she knew, she was sitting cross-legged on the grass, though she didn't really remember deciding to rest. There were dandelions growing all around her, and some had gone to seed. She plucked one and blew on the globe, turning it until she had blown all the seeds off, watching them as they floated away on the mild breeze. Then she did the same with another flower, and another, until all the air was full of the tiny feathery seeds, like warm snowflakes drifting lazily down...

Then she saw him again—the ghost of Duck Egg's brother, Bear Track. He was standing between her and the stream, and the dandelion seeds were floating all around him and through him. This time, he wasn't smiling, or trying to get her to play any kind of game. He frowned at her and seemed to be saying something, but though his lips moved, she couldn't hear any sound.

"What is it?" Holly asked, scrambling to her feet.

But Bear Track had vanished again, and all the seeds went spiraling down to light on the water, or bury themselves in the long grass. Holly shook her head, too, to clear it, and then she remembered where she was. A chill went down her spine as she thought how she had, for a moment, forgotten all about the Old Man and her quest, and even Connor and her dad.

Suddenly she realized that she'd also lost track of Snowthorn.

When she looked for him again, she saw him walking away from her, keeping close to the brook. She ran to catch up with him and took him by the hand.

Dreaming

"Snowthorn! Where are you going?"

He turned to her, and for the first time since she'd met him, he looked peaceful. "Going?" he said, blinking in the warm sunlight. "Where would I be going? I'm going to stay right here."

"But we've got to go talk to the reindeer. They're back the other way," she said, tugging at his hand.

She might as well have been trying to pull up one of the small trees that leaned over the brook. "Plenty of time," Snowthorn said dreamily. "Lots of time to talk to reindeer. First, I'm going up the brook. There's a waterfall up there, you know. You can sit on the bank, with flowers all around, and listen to all the stories the water's voice is telling. Can't you hear it?"

Holly almost could, and that made her afraid. She shook Snowthorn's shoulder. "We've got to *go*," she said urgently. "You need to get back to the Palace, remember? You want to get into...what was it, the R and R department?"

Snowthorn didn't make any attempt to move or resist her, and it was strange to see him answering calmly as his head flopped back and forth from her shaking. "Well, just lately, I've been thinking of retiring…it's so nice here…not a troll in sight…"

She stopped shaking him. "You have to help me find the List. You *swore* to do it!" she said, close to tears.

At those words, Snowthorn drew a deep, shuddering breath, and looked at her. Suddenly his eyes were focusing again. "Oh. Right." he said, and his voice sounded more like the elf she'd come to know.

She stepped back from him. "Just don't…fall into a dream again. I was starting to feel it, too. It's this place. It must be magic."

Snowthorn nodded. "You think? The Old Man wanted to make sure the retired reindeer would be happy here. So yeah, a bit of magic went into this. Some good work, too," he added, thoughtfully. "I can think of worse places to retire. Maybe if we just go take a look at that waterfall…just for a minute, mind you…"

"Your promise," Holly reminded him. "My brother, Connor. Reindeer. The List."

"Okay, okay." Snowthorn held up his hands in defeat. "I'm awake. And speaking of reindeer…" Snowthorn looked over his shoulder. "Look, they're coming over here to meet us," he said in a low voice. "Four, no, five of them. Now don't be afraid."

Holly nodded. The reindeer advanced with dainty steeps, their hooves hardly seeming to make a mark in the soft ground. They stopped a few yards away and stood looking at the elf and the girl, their antlered heads lowered, as if in doubt.

She let Snowthorn take her hand again, and lead her toward them.

Connor watched as Holly and the elf got off the sled. For whatever reason—maybe it was a result of using the wishing cap so much, or just hanging in a place where there was so much magic floating around—Connor could see the elf clearly now. He wondered why Holly wasn't screaming and trying to get away. The elf had yellow eyes in a withered face, and hands that looked like crooked claws. Once, when he smiled, Connor could swear he saw pointed teeth.

He must look different to Holly, he realized. The Snow Fox had talked about the Old Man's illusions. More magic.

The valley's sudden appearance had surprised Connor, but not much. It stood to reason that he wouldn't be the only invisible thing around here. He did wonder why the Eskimos had brought Holly and the elf to this place, though. It looked more like Shangri-La than a place that Father Winter might live. Green grass, here? But who knew.

As the sled dogs lay and crunched their doggie treats, the elf looked around, but his eyes swept right over the place where Connor stood. Connor felt exultant. Hey, now you know how it feels when somebody else has more mojo than you, he thought. He felt like making faces, jumping up and down and waving his arms, and generally acting like a triumphant idiot. But he didn't. He watched from a few yards away as the Eskimos shook hands with Holly and the elf, then started off downhill on their sled.

Holly and the elf talked for a minute. Connor could only catch a word here and there, since he didn't want to push his luck by getting too close. He heard something about "safe" and "bridge", and then a phrase, "...on the other side is the Old Man's palace".

Then they started to go downhill, into the valley.

He frowned. So there was some kind of bridge to cross. Okay. He felt uncomfortable, remembering the ending of his dream last night. But he couldn't see a sign of any bridge, down below. There was a glint of reflected light from a little stream winding through the valley, but it looked as if you could jump across it with no trouble. What could they be talking about?

He stayed a discreet distance behind them as they went down the slope, so Holly had reached the bottom while he was still only about halfway. The elf was a bit behind her too, and Connor saw it look bemused, then begin to wander off down the brook. He stood still for a moment, tensing every muscle, and his heart raced. Now was his chance, he could grab her and carry her back up out of the valley, before the elf could catch him, and then—

Yeah, right. And then? They'd be stuck in the middle of the Arctic with no way to get home. Maybe they could find their way back to the Eskimo village, before they froze or starved, or maybe the Snow Fox would offer more help. Maybe. But the Fox himself had told Connor that the only way out—for both of them—was through Father Winter's palace.

While he was thinking, Holly had gone over to the elf and taken his hand again. Now Connor, too, noticed the reindeer gathered down by the river. A wild suspicion dawned on him. But no, he thought. None of those guys looks anything like Rudolph. They seemed too small, for one thing. These couldn't be *those* reindeer, the Donner-and-Blitzen type reindeer, that flew through the air. No way.

But if they were...what did that mean, about where they were going? For the first time since the Snow Fox had twisted the magic ring on his finger, Connor felt afraid.

We Have Time

"Greetings," Snowthorn was saying to the reindeer. "I trust you are all well."

The reindeer in the middle, who had the largest set of antlers, tossed up its head. "The snow and ice never come here, and we have the best grass and leaves to eat," it said, in a deep voice. "How would we not be well?"

"Just making conversation," Snowthorn muttered.

"And how did an elf, and a human child, find their way to our hidden valley?" asked another reindeer, looking from Snowthorn to Holly.

"Well, it's a long story," the elf admitted.

"Tell us," said the first reindeer. "We have time."

They all sat down, tucking their legs underneath them. As they settled themselves, making various grunting and snorting sounds, Holly realized that they all looked *old*. Their racks of antlers had many branches, their pale brown fur was grizzled, and they moved slowly, with a hint of stiffness.

"Can't rush this," Snowthorn whispered to her. "They're retired, you know. No sense of time any more."

"We haven't lost our hearing, though," one of the reindeer said, pointedly. "But we don't get a lot of news around here. The sooner you tell us the story, the sooner we can get on to whatever you came here for."

Holly sat on the grass beside Snowthorn as he regaled the reindeer with their adventures. He told it fairly well, she thought, though he exaggerated sometimes, especially when he talked about Grimalkin, who wound up sounding like a man-eating lion. The reindeer were a good audience, grunting politely to indicate interest at the right places, and sometimes making a sort of honking noise that seemed to be their way of laughing.

Snowthorn drew near to his dramatic conclusion. "And so," he intoned, lifting his hands, "through untold perils we have made our way to this remote valley, to ask a boon of you. I have to be back at the Old Man's palace before the Eve, and this human child has a mission there as well…"

"What kind of a mission?" interrupted the first reindeer who'd spoken to them.

"A *secret* mission," Snowthorn said. "As I was saying, we need to get to the palace, and since we can't fly by ourselves…"

"You're not asking us to *fly* with you, are you?" asked another of the reindeer. He shook his head. "Why should we leave our valley? Life is good here."

The others nodded and snorted in agreement.

Snowthorn flung up his hands. "I'm talking about going on an *adventure*," he said. "It's not like you're doing anything special today. So what, you're just going to stay here and munch your lotus leaves?"

"I don't know what you're talking about, but it sounds like nasty stuff," said one of the reindeer primly. "*We* eat grass, willow leaves, and every now and then, a bit of lichen. And there's plenty of all that here. The Old Man has been good to us."

"Yes," said another of the reindeer. "We gave him faithful service for years, and we're tired."

"He gave us this place so we could *rest*," murmured still another.

Holly felt the spell of the valley rising around her again, with its dreamlike feeling of peace, but she shook it off. "But we need your help," she pleaded, her voice sounding harsh and discordant in her own ears. "Please," she added, as an afterthought.

But even that most powerful of magic words failed, this time, to have the effect her mother had always told her it would. The reindeer were shaking their heads, and one or two began to yawn.

"Can't help you," the first reindeer said. "Go ask the younger ones. The ones who are flying on the Old Man's team now. They're game for anything."

"But they're already *up* there," Snowthorn pointed out. "We need you to get us there in the first place!" A note of desperation had crept into his voice.

"Not our problem," the first reindeer said.

"And what about me? I came here for my brother," Holly pleaded. Her eyes blurred with tears as the reindeer pushed themselves up from the ground and turned away.

"Sorry," said one of them. "But it was a long time ago. I'm not sure I even remember how to fly."

On, Dancer!

All of the reindeer were moving away now. Holly hung her head and sobbed. Then she felt Snowthorn's hand on her arm.

"Holly," he said.

She looked up. One of the reindeer had turned back and now stood close to them. He—or she, Holly felt somehow that this one was female—was slighter than the others, and her fur was a bit darker. She might have been a year or two younger. As she faced them, she kept lifting her hooves up and taking tiny steps in place, almost prancing, like an excited child who's been told to keep still, but keeps shifting from foot to foot.

"I'm sorry the others are acting that way," she said softly. "I think most of them really have forgotten. But not me. I'll go with you."

"Thank you," Holly said, hugging the reindeer and putting her face into its soft fur. "What's your name?"

"Once, before I retired, I was Dancer," she said shyly. "I'd like it if you could call me that. Though my niece joined the Old Man's team last winter, so the name really belongs to her now."

"Thank you, Dancer," Holly said in a muffled voice, before releasing her.

"You don't have to thank me," she said, looking up to the sky, where dark clouds had begun to gather. "I do remember flying. And I miss it. To be up in the air, among the stars, and on the Eve, too...there's no feeling like it."

"Well, it's getting late," said Snowthorn gruffly. "We should get started. You won't have a problem taking both of us?"

Dancer made the honking sound again. "Neither one of you is very big. Do you know how heavy the Old Man's sleigh is, on this night of all nights? Yet just eight of us pull it around the world."

"All right. Holly, you get up first. That way I can help make sure you won't fall."

"You won't fall," said Dancer reassuringly, standing still as Holly wriggled up onto his back. Snowthorn followed.

"All aboard?" the reindeer asked. "All ready?"

"Ready," Holly said in a small voice. "But...how high up will we have to go?"

"It depends. We need to find the bridge of light—that's the only way to the Old Man's palace. Sometimes it will appear as low as the clouds, sometimes higher than the tallest mountain. But don't look down, at least until we find the bridge, and you won't feel the cold and the wind. I have a bit of my own magic left," Dancer said gently.

Snowthorn gave a sigh of relief. "Well," he said, "let's get this show on the road. So to speak."

Dancer tossed her head, took a short run along the river, and in a few moments they were rising into the air, clearing the rim of the valley.

The other reindeer lifted their heads to watch. "Young people," one of them remarked, half grumbling, half with envy.

On, Blitzen!

Connor's worst fears were confirmed when the reindeer flew off with Holly and the elf on his back. His stomach lurched. The Snow Fox wasn't such a great buddy after all, he thought. No matter how fast I can run, I'll never catch *that* reindeer. And being invisible doesn't get me any points, either. Why didn't he give me the power to fly, too? Now *that* would have been useful.

As it was, he'd have to hitch a ride with one of the reindeer himself. He didn't know how the elf had persuaded that one to fly. Some kind of magic, probably. He'd talked to them for a long time, but again, Connor hadn't heard most of what he'd said. He felt nervous about coming too close because when he did, the reindeers' nostrils had flared and one or two began to look around suspiciously.

Or it could be, he thought, that the reindeer were in on it—the whole Yule conspiracy thing. In that case, they would just be helping the elf because they were on his side. And the elf was stuck otherwise, without his wishing cap. So *this* was his backup plan.

Two could play at that game, Connor thought, with a wolfish grin. With his powers, catching one of the reindeer should be a snap. They couldn't see him coming, and he was probably faster than they were, on the ground at least. How hard could it be?

A few minutes later, he changed his opinion. Catching up to the reindeer—sure, that wasn't a problem. But somehow, when he tried to grab one or leap onto its back, it would dodge to the side so that he fell sprawling, or put on just a little extra burst of speed, leaving him empty-handed. One had even stopped stock still when he'd been running alongside, timing his jump to lead it, so that he overshot and crashed to the ground a few feet ahead.

Okay, he thought, now they *have* to be getting suspicious.

His fears were confirmed when the latest reindeer asked, while facing in his general direction, "So what kind of creature are you, anyway?"

What the heck, Connor thought. I haven't tried *talking* yet. "I'm not a creature. I'm a boy," he said.

The reindeer sniffed suspiciously. "Boys aren't invisible," he observed.

"Well, this one is," said Connor, a little belligerently.

"You do smell something like a boy," the reindeer allowed. "But I won't really believe it until you become visible. Show yourself!" he challenged, with a stamp of his hoof.

Connor didn't want to admit that in fact, since he couldn't get the ring off his finger, he couldn't become visible if he tried. *Another* little detail, he thought, that the Snow Fox had somehow forgotten to tell him. "Um, I can't. I'm..." he thought desperately. "I'm under a curse."

"Hey, that's too bad," the reindeer said sympathetically. "Why don't you tell me all about it?" He sat down, tucking his legs under him, and assumed an expression of polite interest.

"But I need help. There's no time to waste. I need to...let's see, I need to get to, um, the Old Man's place before he flies out tonight. To break the curse."

The reindeer was visibly impressed. "Wow, I've never heard of anything like that before. *What* a day we're having in the old retirement home. I guess it makes sense, you can't really enjoy the holiday if you're under a curse."

"So if you could please fly with me...if it's not too late, the other reindeer left a while ago..." Connor begged. I could fall on my knees, he thought, but the reindeer wouldn't see it.

"Sure, no problem," the reindeer said, getting up. "You should have told me your story first. Would've saved you a lot of trouble. You must have gotten all out of breath trying to catch me."

He turned around, looking back over his shoulder toward Connor, obviously waiting for him to mount.

"So...you'll take me?" Connor asked, hardly able to believe it.

"That's the general idea," the reindeer said, patiently. "I just realized, seeing Dancer soaring up there, how much I've been missing flying myself. Besides, she's been pretending not to notice me lately."

Connor wasted no time, scrambling up onto the reindeer's back, grabbing a handful of its neck fur to hold on.

"Relax," the reindeer said, beginning to break into a canter. "I won't let you fall off. Although you do seem pretty heavy, as invisible boys go."

"So they're lighter, and they have a head start," Connor said nervously. "Do we still have a chance of catching them?"

The reindeer snorted. "You call that a head start?" he asked. "Listen, I may be retired now, but they didn't call me Blitzen for nothing."

Connor's stomach was left somewhere far below, and the scream he was starting to let loose was sucked right out of his lungs, as they shot up into the sky like a deranged rocket.

Nine

Holly found that riding Dancer wasn't at all what she'd expected. It was very different from being carried by South Wind, and although she had often
dreamed of riding flying things—dragons or griffins, usually—those creatures had wings. Dancer didn't, and so her movements—up, down, or sideways—always seemed unexpected. It was like riding a carousel horse that had somehow broken loose from the merry-go-round and gone soaring off into the sky.

Also, unlike traveling with South Wind, Holly was very conscious that there was nothing keeping her on the reindeer's back as they soared through empty space. If I were alone, she told herself, I'd be scared.

After a few seconds, she quit pretending. She *was* scared. She tried to burrow into Dancer's fur, while simultaneously clutching her neck in a death grip.

"Need...some...air," the reindeer said, in strangled tones.

"Oh. Sorry." She relaxed her grip by a miniscule amount.

"I've got you, Holly," Snowthorn said. His arms encircled her, and she felt less frightened, and warmer. The elf was stronger than he looked. For a moment, she could almost imagine that it was her father holding her, and if she closed her eyes she could hear his voice, singing her an old lullaby.

Go to bed first, a golden purse...go to bed second, a golden pheasant...

But she couldn't keep her eyes closed. They snapped open again when Dancer swooped up sharply and came, impossibly, to a stop, hovering in midair.

"Just taking my bearings," the reindeer said reassuringly. "Good thing it's a clear night. We won't be needing Rudolph."

"Is there really a Rudolph?" Holly asked, interested enough, for the moment, to forget where she was.

"No, he's just a—what do you call it, urban legend. But there have been some foggy nights when we could have *used* somebody with a headlight for a nose, I can tell you. By the way, whatever you do, don't look down."

Of course, Holly looked down right away. The ground was further away than she could have imagined. They were above most of the clouds, which streamed across the white landscape below, a ragged, tattered veil that did nothing to soften or conceal the broken rocks and jagged, icy hills that jutted up toward them.

She moaned faintly. "Not long now," Snowthorn told her, holding her even more tightly than before. "You know, this is actually kind of fun. Like a roller coaster."

"I don't *like* roller coasters!" Holly wailed. "I don't even like *Ferris wheels.*"

"Your father flies over mountains," Snowthorn reminded her. "He must go almost as high as this, all the time."

"My father," said Holly decidedly, "is a *very* brave man."

"Hang on," Dancer said, coming to a decision. "We'll head up and toward the North Star. I think I saw some lights in that direction, but they were shifting and flickering. Let's go and take a closer look."

She soared up again, and Holly was actually glad when they had risen far enough that she could no longer see any details of the land below, just a formless mass of white, with gray clouds passing over it like shadows.

Once again she tried closing her eyes, though she wasn't able to relax as much as she had at first. After a time of silence, except for the rushing winds, she felt Dancer come to a standstill again.

"Here we are," she said softly.

Holly opened her eyes and gasped. They were poised right in front of a shimmering curtain of light, deep red at its top, shading down to greens and blues below. It was like a bridge of starlight—for Holly knew that all the stars were really suns of different colors, and even though she was used to seeing them from far away, so that they looked like plain pieces of glass scattered across the night sky, you would be able to see all the colors if you got close enough.

The other thing it reminded her of was days when the sun would find a hole in the clouds, and its rays would beam down from that one spot as if it was a door that opened into some marvelous world of light. But those moments were usually fleeting, and this one went on and on.

She realized that they were slowly rising up, with a gentle motion now, more like the thistledown in the poem. At the same time they drifted closer, so she could see how, if you looked steadily at a single part of the bridge, it flickered in and out of sight, while the whole structure went on looking just as solid as before.

Holly found her voice at last. "It's beautiful. Like a rainbow."

"But there's something better than a pot of gold, at the end of it," said Snowthorn. "Look."

She saw it, finally, the palace that they had talked about for so long. The bridge of light led right up to its gate. It shone with such a strong, pure white light, that for the first moment it was hard to look at. She could hardly take in the soaring towers, the spires, the windows full of light, that outshone the stars and the aurora itself. But as complicated as it was, it seemed to be all of a piece, as if it had never been built, but had simply crystallized there, the essence of the northern skies.

Stronger Than You Can Imagine

Holly also saw tiny white birds circling around the spires, and perching on the roofs in rows. "What are those?" she asked Snowthorn.

"Snowy owls," he told her. "They're bigger than you think. Those birds could carry off a reindeer if they wanted."

Dancer snorted.

"Well, *two* of them could," Snowthorn conceded.

"It's a wonderful place," Holly said. "No wonder you wanted to get back."

"Not that they'll roll out the red carpet for me," Snowthorn said, a bit grumpily. "But yes. I'm glad to be here again."

"And I'm glad to have seen it, even once."

Dancer cleared her throat. "Yes, well, me too. I wouldn't have missed this for the world. But this is as far as I go."

"You won't come into the palace with us?" Holly asked. "Not even the um, courtyard?" She was fairly sure that palaces had such things.

"I'm getting tired. Not as young as I used to be," the reindeer answered. "Besides... I don't really want to watch the Old Man getting the sleigh ready, if I'm not going along," she said shyly. "And they'll miss me down in the valley."

"We'll miss you too," Holly said, patting her neck. "So we just...walk over there, then? Will it hold us?"

"It's stronger than it looks," said Dancer. "Stronger than you can imagine."

"But," Snowthorn added, "it doesn't last forever. So let's keep the goodbyes on the short side."

Snowthorn dismounted first, then helped Holly to climb off Dancer's back. "Well, what do you know," he said, as he eased her down to the bridge, which felt unexpectedly firm underfoot. "We have some company."

Dancer looked behind them. Another reindeer was hovering near the bridge, this one riderless. "It looks like Blitzen," she said. "Our latest ex-Blitzen, I mean. He must have just come along for the ride. He always was a bit of a showoff." She yawned ostentatiously, but Holly noticed she kept watching the other reindeer out of the corner of her eye. "Well, I guess I can keep him company on the way back. For old time's sake."

She moved restlessly, impatient to be off. Holly barely managed to give Dancer a brief hug and a kiss before she cried "Goodbye!" and launched back into the sky, with a toss of her antlers.

Holly looked down at her feet. She was standing on light itself. The colors were changing now, getting brighter, shifting through orange to a brilliant yellow. It was like Oz, she thought, when Dorothy had to follow the yellow brick road. Except that then the road shifted back to a deep red, then began changing with every few steps she took, to green, and blue, and other colors in between, for which she couldn't find any names.

"It's not far now," Snowthorn said, taking her hand.

Snowflakes

They walked together over the bridge of light. Holly felt so full of wonder that there was no room for fear any more. Besides, the air was suddenly still now, as if they had gone to a place above and beyond where any wind could reach. It was cold, though, so cold that each breath was like drinking ice water. She could feel it all the way down her throat to her lungs, as if she were breathing in the huge, empty spaces of the sky, and the cold fire of the stars.

As they walked, and the great, glittering palace drew closer, it began to snow. Holly didn't look closely at the snowflakes at first, but then one fell right in front of her eyes, and she gasped again.

For the snowflake was alive.

It was larger than the ones she remembered seeing at home—that one time, years ago, when it had snowed. Those had come down blurred and half melting on the wind, and had dissolved in a moment when she caught them on her tongue, or brushed her cheek with a brief, cold kiss. And this snowflake wasn't just an abstract pattern of diamonds and stars and branching feathers. It looked like a perfect little maiden made of snow, with an dress of intricate lace, and a crown that glittered with all the colors of the rainbow. She had a face with finely etched features, with crystal eyes that reflected the starlight and, for a fleeting instant, Holly's face too.

She seemed to see Holly, too, in the instant she fell past, and for that moment Holly felt that they knew and recognized each other, somehow. Then the little snow maiden sank into the light, falling *through* the bridge, and Holly couldn't see her any more. She felt a brief, sharp sense of loss, as if she were missing a friend.

Another snowflake floated down, close enough to touch. This one was a small warrior, in fantastic crystal armor and an ornate helmet. Somehow he was holding six swords at once, their bright blades all pointing in different directions—the glimpse was too fleeting for Holly to see whether he had six arms and hands, too. His gaze was calm and challenging as he too spun down and disappeared through the bridge of light.

She stopped and caught Snowthorn's arm. "What *are* these?"

"Snowflakes," Snowthorn answered matter-of-factly.

"They don't look like any snowflakes I've seen before," she said with conviction. "And how can they fall through the bridge? It seems so solid."

"For you and me, it is. The bridge isn't meant for them. They're born in the clouds, and their whole lifetime passes as they're falling. Before this, you've only seen the ones that made it all the way down to the earth. By that time, they're dead, or dying. Up here they're still alive."

"So they're only alive for the time it takes them to fall? That can't be," Holly said, indignantly. "That's too sad."

Snowthorn squeezed her hand. "*They* don't feel sad. Look, up here we're on eternity's doorstep. Here, something that lasts for a few seconds can be as important as something that lives for...well, a thousand years. That's the way that the Old Man sees it, anyway."

"Well, *I* don't," said Holly rebelliously. She wondered, for a moment, how the Father Winter she had always loved could have no problem with a world where snowflakes lived and died in the space of a few minutes. What could she say to him, if they did meet? No, the other plan was better—just change the List. Change the rules of the game, because it wasn't fair in the first place.

A Broken Dream

"Anyway, trillions of snowflakes have been born and died, before you ever got here," Snowthorn said, in what he might have thought was a comforting tone. He tugged at her hand and she began to walk with him again. "There are more of the dreams, too," he said, nodding toward the gates of the castle ahead.

The bridge of light sloped upward, the last part of the way, and they were forced to slow down. Rather than looking at the snowflakes that continued to drift down past her, Holly studied the dreams, which were clustered around the gate like drifting soap bubbles.

She could make out finer details now. The nearest dream to her showed a small boy playing with a model train set. He had laid the tracks all around a Yule tree, complete with tunnels, mountain bridges, and stations in the middle of busy towns with trees and houses and pedestrians. He looked perfectly happy as he watched the train chug around the track.

In another dream, a blonde girl sat under a tree—it was a smaller tree than Holly was used to seeing, with fewer ornaments—and opened a book, touching the pages gently, as if she was afraid she might tear them. Now and then she moved her lips as she ran her finger along the words.

Next to that dream floated a scene with another boy opening a present. This one looked pale and thin and unhealthy. He took something out of the package that looked like a bottle. He opened it, sipped from the contents, and suddenly his eyes were bright and his cheeks rosy. Whatever was in the bottle had healed him.

"Only the strongest dreams make it this far," Snowthorn said.

Holly's brow wrinkled. "So there's a girl who really wants to learn how to read, and that boy is sick, and he's asking to be cured. But who needs a *train* that much?"

Snowthorn shook his head. "It's not so easy to judge a dream from outside. You have no idea what that boy's life is like, or what that train means to him."

"Okay, okay. Wait...look at this one—there's a girl who looks a lot like me!"

The little girl was peeking out from behind a snowman, and smiling. The snowman had two fine branches for arms, one a good bit shorter than the other. A trail of pebbles gave it a lopsided smile and two mismatched eyes. Its carrot nose wasn't quite straight, and its hat leaned at a rakish angle.

Holly watched, fascinated, as the girl with the curly red hair turned away to start rolling another ball of snow.

"We look like sisters," Holly said. "Twins, almost. She's even wearing those boots with the ladybugs on them, like I used to have."

The girl looked over her shoulder and called something to someone who wasn't visible. The next moment, a tall boy with dark hair came into view, carrying a shovel. He grinned and said something back to the girl, who made a snowball quickly and threw it at him. He pretended to cower back as it missed him a foot.

Holly's eyes widened. "It's Connor! That means...it *is* me. It must be. It's my dream. How can that be?" she demanded, as if it was somehow Snowthorn's fault.

"Take it easy. You just have a very persistent dream. That's something that you want very much."

"The *snowman*?"

"Well, that too, but I'm betting it's mostly that you want your brother to be with you again. To have fun with him, like you used to."

"But I came here for *him*." Holly gestured helplessly. "Not to ask for something for me. Connor needs my help. He needs the Old Man's help."

"People need to ask for themselves. I told you that."

"But he doesn't *believe*! How can he even ask?"

"Come on, we're not going to go over all of this again, are we? We might as well have stayed back in Seattle. Which reminds me," Snowthorn went on, with an expression of dawning hope. "Maybe, now that you've seen what your dream *really* is, we can rethink this business of sneaking in and trying to change the List…"

Holly stamped her foot, and the dream-bubble burst. The bright images broke into a thousand pieces and scattered, falling through the bridge like tiny shooting stars. One of the fragments fell on her boot and rested there a moment. It was part of the dream girl's smile, her own smile. She shook it off and it fell through the bridge with all the rest.

"…or not," Snowthorn finished, forlornly.

"We're going to go through with it," she said, quivering with anger and blinking tears from her eyes. "I'm going to change the List if it's the last thing I do."

"The last thing *I* do, more likely," Snowthorn said, under his breath. "Okay. You're pretty sure of what you want, I guess. Let's see if the gate will open for us."

In a few steps, they were standing before the gates, which were covered with elaborate carvings, forming an intricate design of wreaths and candy canes and sprigs of holly. There was no hint of a latch, or any kind of way to open them from the outside. Holly ran her hand over the surface, trying to find if there was any crack, and immediately forgot her anger.

"It's made of ice," she said. "It's all made of ice. But it's so thick you can't see through it. It's all white and milky."

She brushed away her tears, which had frozen, and they made a quiet tinkling sound as they fell to the bridge.

"What else would you build it out of? This is the Arctic," Snowthorn reminded her patiently. "We don't have a lot of trees up here, but we're not about to run out of ice."

"But how can you keep it warm inside?" Holly asked practically, remembering Duck Egg's igloo. "Wouldn't the walls start to melt?"

"So you're standing in front of a palace floating in the air a mile over the North Pole, and what really bothers you is, how does the *heating system* work?" Snowthorn spread his hands. "It's *magic*. This is where all the magic comes from."

"Okay. So how do we get in?"

"I was working on that, before you started wondering about the...*mechanics* involved, here."

Snowthorn reached out and gave a series of sharp, but polite, raps on the gate with his knuckles. Holly expected there would be footsteps, or an answering voice. But instead, the gates just started to swing inward, moving ponderously on unseen hinges, with a sound like a glacier pushing boulders along to grind down mountaintops.

"Get ready," Snowthorn said to Holly, in a low voice. "Since it's the Eve, they should all be out in the courtyard, taking care of the last-minute details. They'll be loading a few last things on the sleigh, the reindeer will be champing at their bits...even the Old Man might be there already, or he'll be up getting the List right now to take with him…"

The gates finished swinging open. Holly took a few unsteady steps into the courtyard, Snowthorn at her side.

The elf's jaw dropped, and he stopped in his tracks.

"We're too late," he said.

For the rest of his life, Connor remembered the ride up to the Bridge of Light with Blitzen. He was afraid of heights, of course, but this was different somehow.  When he recovered from the first burst of acceleration as they rushed up into the sky, he found himself whooping with delight.

It wasn't too long before they had Dancer in sight. "I could fly rings around her," Blitzen said, with some satisfaction. "It would be kind of fun, actually. Maybe she'd finally be impressed. How about it?"

"Uh, no, thanks," said Connor, hunching down on the reindeer's back by instinct, even though he knew that he was invisible. "Let's keep a low profile, okay? I don't want to get too close."

"Something to do with the curse, eh?" Blitzen nodded understandingly. "Well, don't worry about it. I'm sure the Old Man can help you out."

"Yeah?" Connor wondered how much this 'retired' reindeer really knew about what went on in the Old Man's palace. "Do you think he'd do that?"

"I couldn't say for sure." Blitzen hovered thoughtfully for a moment. "But look, he didn't just turn us out on the tundra, did he, after we weren't up to pulling sleighs anymore? He gave us that valley to live in. So why wouldn't he do something for you?"

Well, it's pretty obvious, Connor thought. *He bought them off, probably to make sure they wouldn't talk. Or maybe the reindeer are like Holly. He's pulled the wool over their eyes, and they really believe the story about flying around delivering toys to all the good little boys and girls. Maybe that's even what they see happening.*

"Glad to hear it," he said noncommittally. "Hey, watch it, we're drifting a little close to them for comfort."

Blitzen nodded. "Okay, we'll just hang back here and do loop-the-loops for a while."

Hanging back, Blitzen-style, was exciting enough that Connor didn't notice much else for a while. But then, when Blitzen pulled out of one of his loops and shot forward, since Dancer had pulled ahead in the meantime, the bridge was suddenly—*there.* Like frozen lightning, it appeared in an instant and filled half the sky, swirling with all the colors of the rainbow.

Connor watched as Dancer rose to the top of the bridge and hovered there. Blitzen followed discreetly, keeping back a hundred yards or so.

"Okay," Connor said. "I don't think they've seen us yet. Now, when you get onto the bridge, try to walk really softly…"

"Onto the bridge?" Blitzen twisted his head around to stare at the place where Connor was. "I never agreed to that. Time for you to do your part, invisible boy. You can't break a curse by having someone else do all the work. How fair would *that* be? Besides," he added, in a kinder tone, "you'll kick yourself later, if you don't feel like you've earned it."

"But…how am I going to get to the palace?" Connor asked helplessly.

"You have feet, don't you, even if I can't see them?" Blitzen nodded toward the bridge. "The palace is right there. You walk."

For a moment, Connor couldn't see anything at the other end of the bridge. Then, slowly, like when your eyes get used to a dark room and you can start to see details, a castle sketched itself into existence. It was all black, hard to see against the dark surrounding spaces. Then he saw that the smooth walls and soaring spires gave back dim reflections of the stars and the rainbow colors of the aurora. It must be made of something like glass, he realized.

The hairs prickled on the back of his neck. There were glass castles in some of the fairy tales his mother had read to him, and they usually had giants or ogres living in them. Maybe with a captive princess or two hanging around to offer you good advice. If you were lucky.

"Look, Dancer is letting her people off there," Blitzen continued. "*They* don't seem to have any problem with it."

Connor watched in frozen horror as Holly and the elf swung down to stand on—nothing. Just beams of light, colors streaming through empty space. But somehow, they didn't fall. Holly even looked like she was smiling.

"It's holding them up," Connor said wonderingly.

"Something to do with quantum physics," Blitzen remarked. "I'm not quite sure how it works. I always thought I'd have more time to study once I retired, but you know how it is. All right, this is where you get off. I have a feeling Dancer will head this way, after they say their goodbyes. You don't want her to know you're here, and I don't need you hanging around cramping my style." The reindeer looked back at Connor and winked.

"But..." Connor said, feeling as if he were frozen in place. "I can't...I mean, I have a hard time believing in all this."

"You don't have to believe," Blitzen said. "It will hold you up whether you believe in it or not. You just need to trust me."

Right, Connor thought. *Trust me.* But wasn't that just another kind of believing? And where did it get you? Somebody says "trust me", and if you do, they leave, flying around mountains and rescuing every single person in the world who might be in trouble, except *you*, then getting themselves buried in avalanches, smashed at the bottom of crevices, "destroyed entirely" as his mother would say, without even a few last broken words for their family...

Hey, he thought, *where did all that come from? I tell you what, Connor, my boyo, after this you'll never in your life need to pay for therapy.*

"I almost forgot," Blitzen said. "One other thing you need. Courage."

Connor nodded stiffly. Courage. That, he could understand. It was the only possible reason he was still here, other than complete insanity, which at the moment seemed more likely.

Moving as if in a dream, he swung one leg over Blitzen's back and lowered himself to the bridge. He half expected to drop right through. Sure, it will hold elves and little girls up, he thought, but they're so *light*.

Somewhat to his surprise, the bridge felt at least as firm underfoot as the frozen sea had, when he'd barely escaped being eaten by the orca. Though when he thought about it, that wasn't a comparison that made him feel exactly comfortable.

"Goodbye," he said to Blitzen, who was already rising up further into the night sky.

"Good luck," the reindeer called down to him. "Hope everything works out for you, with the curse and all. Merry Yule!"

Then Dancer rushed by overhead, not seeming to see Blitzen—and for sure, not seeing Connor—and Blitzen turned and tore after her. In a few moments, they were lost to view in the distance.

"Merry Yule," Connor answered, to the empty air. It occurred to him that it was the first time he'd said that in a couple of years, at least.

He turned and saw that Holly and the elf were already moving toward the palace. He walked quickly after them. There's probably some sort of gate, he thought, and it might only open for a moment. I'll have to be close enough behind them to slip through...

At that moment, something like a bubble floated by to one side. A bubble with a small, perfectly formed scene inside. Connor saw a living room with a big tree, and presents piled high under it. But as he watched, a greenish creature in a red fur suit slithered down the chimney, came out of the fireplace, and quickly grabbed all the presents, stuffing them into a big sack. Then it seized the tree, and started shoving it up the chimney.

Connor turned to look after the nightmare, and his eyes were drawn downward, to the toy-size mountains and frozen sea spreading out beneath him like a relief map. Suddenly the reality of his situation came home to him.

He'd thought the hard thing would be getting off Blitzen's back and stepping onto the aurora bridge. One small step for Connor-kind, then take a bow, collect your medal, and wave to the crowd. But it turned out that was only the beginning. Now he had to walk over this bridge—this fairly *narrow* bridge, with just enough room for Holly and the elf to walk side by side, made of nothing more substantial than moonbeams—with no railing, nothing but empty space on either side.

His heart drummed wildly in his chest, and suddenly the air seemed too thin. He was gasping for breath. He broke out in a cold sweat.

But all the time, Holly and the elf were getting further away. So he forced himself to move, stiffly at first, lurching to one side and then catching himself just in time. He finally steadied himself by keeping his eyes straight ahead, focused on his sister, looking neither to the left nor to the right.

One foot in front of the other, he told himself. *Don't think about what you heard in school that day, how walking is really the same as falling, except you catch yourself just in time. Just think about Holly. I need to catch up to her. I need to save her. Bring her home. But how can I? I have some powers now, sure, but how long will they last, in that place? No, don't think of that either. Never mind, just don't lose her. Stay with her. First things first.*

Don't think of how cold it's getting, either. He looked up at the dark palace, looming closer now, and realized that it couldn't be glass. That would shatter into a million pieces up here, wouldn't it, in this frozen sky? No, it had to be made of ice.

Black ice.

Now and then a living snowflake fell close enough to him that he couldn't ignore it. He saw diamond-winged dragons, and bull-headed men with spiraling crystal horns, and flying skeletons with glittering eyes and lacey wings.

The air was filled, too, with more nightmares floating up from the world below, like sinister balloons that some demon child had let go by accident. They kept pace with him as he walked, as if stalking him. He saw visions of children stolen from their bedrooms, while strange lights shone in at the windows. He saw endless rows of boys and girls working at small tables in a dark, windowless room, dwindling and withering before his eyes as they toiled, until they looked like the elf-thing that had taken Holly.

And he saw another floating bubble that held a mountain, with snow swirling around it. A plane flew close by, then started to spin, out of control, and slammed into a rock face. An avalanche came roaring down, and the plane was swept away into the depths.

But that can't be, he thought. *I fixed things with my wish, didn't I? Don't think about how the other wishes didn't work... Or about how it's almost two days now, if my dad hasn't made it back home yet. Think about the bridge. Think about Holly.*

"Is that the best you can do?" he cried aloud. The dark castle walls absorbed the sound of his voice, giving back no echo. He might as well have been talking to himself. Probably he was.

Connor brushed the frozen tears from his cheek, and went on.

Back in Seattle, Connor's mother started awake. She'd fallen asleep while still sitting at the table with her map and phone. But almost as soon as she closed her eyes, a nightmare hit her like dark lightning.

She saw Holly and Connor walking on a bridge together. It was like the picture that hung in the living room, except that Connor was stumbling along, far behind Holly, and the bridge was beginning to crumble and fall to pieces behind him.

Holly was walking ahead, sure-footed. She had already almost reached the other side. But unlike the girl in the picture, who was guiding her brother along with her arm around him, Holly seemed to have no idea that Connor was in danger.

But what made her wake up with a cry of despair, breaking the spiderwebs of dream that bound her, was that there was no angel watching over them. Nothing but cold stars and an empty sky.

Ten

Where My Tears Won't Freeze

"This can't be," said Snowthorn dazedly, for what seemed like the hundredth time. "It's the *Eve*. Where *is* everybody?"

"Maybe they finished packing the sleigh, then went off to get warm by the fire and toast some marshmallows," Holly said, hugging herself against the cold. "Sounds like a good idea to me."

"But they should have been waiting for me," Snowthorn said. "I hadn't brought back my part of the List. Not that I actually *have* it any more, of course," he said with a grimace, "but they should have waited. I'm not *that* late. Am I?"

Only half listening to Snowthorn, Holly looked around at the nearly empty courtyard, which was framed by the palace's outer wall, with towers on the other three sides. Directly before them, a large tree stood, with stars in its branches—not ornaments made to look like stars, but real stars. Holly could tell, somehow.

Instead of grass, the ground was covered with snow, which had been carefully groomed at some time not long ago. But there was also a trampled path leading around the tree, on both sides, out to the center of the courtyard, where the footprints mixed with hoofprints and a large, rectangular mark that must have been made by something big and heavy.

Next to where the sleigh had rested, several huge sacks stood. They looked like they'd been stuffed like sausages. Holly wasn't sure how anyone, even Father Winter, could lift them.

"Look," she said. "They left all those toys and things. He'll have to come back for those, right?"

Snowthorn seemed to wake up from his daze for a moment. "Well, sure," he said. "But not til tomorrow night. Remember that people celebrate on different days. We get all the shipments ready in advance so we can..." He yawned. "Hit the hay sooner."

"Oh," Holly said. "Can those sacks really hold enough presents for all the people that he visits?"

"Bigger on the inside," Snowthorn said absent-mindedly.

Holly noticed that the snow was littered with scraps of wrapping paper and ribbon, and tiny bells like the ones you put on presents so they jingle when you hand them to someone to open.

After so many wonders, it made her feel strange to see things that looked so normal. It reminded her of their living room at home, after all the presents had been unwrapped and exclaimed over. She remembered the bits of bright paper scattered across the floor, and how the tree looked so bare without all the boxes piled around it.

Then she looked a bit more closely, and saw that the snow beneath sparkled with all the colors of the rainbow.

"Maybe we should check inside," she said, stamping her feet to try and get the pins and needles out.

Snowthorn let her grab his hand and lead him around the tree, toward the tower ahead.

"They should have waited for me," he muttered. "Although it would have been a lot harder for you to sneak in, with the courtyard packed with elves."

"You'd have thought of something. Disguised me as a present, maybe," Holly said impatiently. "Come *on*."

Snowthorn pulled his hand back. "Wait a second. If he's left already..." He stopped short, staring at Holly. "Don't you get it? If he's already gone, what good is it changing the List *now*?"

Holly took a deep breath. Could she have come all this way, come so close, just to have things go wrong at the last minute? She felt herself beginning to cry again, and brushed impatiently at her eyes. At least, she thought, let's get inside where my *tears* won't freeze.

"Let's go in there," she repeated. "*I'm* going there, anyway, no matter what happens."

She marched away, following the path that curved around the tree. She smelled its scent as she went by, and slowed down, thinking of winter mornings with that cool, spicy fragrance filling the house. Then she shook her head impatiently, and went on toward the tower.

She felt a sudden pain in her heel. "Ow!" she said, glaring back at Snowthorn, who had just rounded the side of the tree. "Watch out! You stepped on my foot."

Snowthorn raised his eyebrows. "Ummm...I don't see how that I could have."

"Well, there's nobody else here," she pointed out, with unassailable logic.

"Oh, okay. Sorry...I guess," Snowthorn said, looking around in puzzlement.

"Well, come on," she told him.

The tower door was standing open just a bit, as if someone had been careless and forgot to close it all the way. Holly pushed and pulled, and the ice cracked and creaked, but she could only get it to open a few inches further. There was just enough room for her to squeeze past.

Snowthorn looked around again, then shook his head with a sigh and followed Holly into the tower.

Connor didn't have to worry about getting through the castle gate. It was still standing wide open when he got there, just a few seconds after Holly and the elf had gone through. At least he didn't have to touch the black ice.

As he passed, he glanced briefly at the designs carved on the gates, which were filled with menacing elves holding icicle daggers and snarling snowmen with fangs, and shuddered.

Once inside, though, he heaved a sigh of relief. He had crossed the bridge. Of course, he knew that he wasn't really any safer, since he was standing on a chunk of snow and ice just floating in the stratosphere, along with a castle that looked like it weighed about five million tons. But he still felt better.

The courtyard was daunting, though. The space was dominated by a twisted, leafless tree, its branches full of black, flickering candles. Next to it, coal was heaped up in huge piles.

Of course, Connor thought, *that's what they always say. If you're not good, Father Winter will leave a lump of coal in your stocking. Well, looking at this setup, it's a good bet he's expecting a whole lot of bad people this year.*

He saw a clear path trampled in the snow, curving around the leafless tree, toward the black, smooth tower that loomed ahead. It was tall—Connor could hardly gauge its height, looking up at it—and there were a few high windows, where a red, sullen light flickered.

Right, Connor thought, *That's where Holly and the elf are going. To that thing that looks like the Dark Tower of Mordor.* They'd been standing and looking at  the tree and the heaps of coal for a while, apparently in shock—which was, Connor thought, totally understandable—but now they were on the move.

The elf was lagging behind now, though, and Connor came up close behind Holly, so close that he stepped on her foot by mistake.

She cried out and looked around, and he immediately backed up a couple of yards. Holly glared at the elf instead, until he apologized. Serves him right, Connor thought. I'll bet he's done *something* he should apologize for.

But then he realized, with a jolt, that the elf looked different now. Instead of a withered changeling, he just looked like a normal, chubby, balding middle-aged guy, except for the ears. Some instinct made him look back at the courtyard behind them, and now a huge evergreen tree loomed there, studded with twinkling, multi-colored lights.

What about the mountains of coal? He retraced his steps around the tree. Now, huge sacks taller than he was stood there, with a few presents peeping out at the tops. He went over and touched one. They were real, all right. There was something written on the outside. **MAGIC SACK, COMMERCIAL GRADE,** he read. **MULTI-MILLION STOCKING CAPACITY.**

Maybe I'm beginning to see what she's seeing, he thought. His powers must be starting to wear off, just as the Fox warned. But he felt the ring of fur still twisted firmly around his finger. And he was obviously still invisible, or else Holly wouldn't have blamed the elf. Something must have gotten transferred to him from Holly, when he accidentally touched her because he was following too closely...

Too closely? Now they were getting away from him, while he was wasting time here trying to figure out magic that made no sense anyway, no sense at all.

He raced back around the tree and to the tower. He went up to the door, wrenching it open a little wider, though the tower still looked as if it was made of black ice and he shrank inside at the thought of touching it. It felt like frozen oil under his fingers.

He stepped inside. As soon as he stepped over the threshold the door, with perfect haunted-house timing, slammed shut behind him. But Connor hardly noticed. He stared wide-eyed at the scene that was unfolding in front of him, feeling as if his own blood had turned to ice.

Holly found herself standing in a large ante-chamber. It was mostly empty, but straight ahead a series of shallow, wide semicircular steps rose up to a curving gallery where there were two doors, both closed. And standing on the steps...

Dance of the Nutcrackers

There were ranks and ranks of them. Nutcrackers. Not like the small figures that her mother usually set up on the sideboard, a couple of weeks after Halloween's ghosts and witches were packed away, but more than life-size. There were two different kinds. One looked like an ordinary soldier, and wore red jackets crisscrossed with gaily painted shoulder straps, and shiny black boots. They had black villain-style mustachios under their sharp noses, which would have been good for twirling if they hadn't been painted on, but their hair was white, and they had a shock of white beard showing under their prominent teeth. They held silver wooden swords up at the ready.

The other type was taller, and there was only one per stair. *It must be some sort of commander*, Holly thought. These Nutcrackers had tall white fur hats and white fur boots, and their uniforms were silver. Their white hair was longer, streaming over their shoulders, and their mustache and eyebrows were white too. Their round blue eyes stared at her coldly, and their beards hung down like icicles. Instead of swords, they held some kind of staff topped with a crystal star.

There are two kinds of children—those who like Nutcrackers very much, and those who don't like them at all. Holly had never liked them. Seeing dozens of them ranged before her, all over seven feet tall, made her like them even less, if possible. But hearing Snowthorn come in behind her, she decided all at once to pretend that she wasn't afraid.

She walked up to the nearest officer, on the lowest step, and looked up at him with her hands on her hips. "Let us by, you...you block of wood!" she said rudely, and gave his beard, which she was only just able to reach, a sharp tweak.

Immediately, with a sharp *click*, like a trap springing shut, the Nutcracker's jaws opened and closed.

Thrown off balance, Holly fell back onto the floor, and the Nutcracker moved toward her stiffly.

Holly screamed. It was like a nightmare, when something that never should move at all suddenly comes alive and darts quickly toward you, and you start awake, your heart pounding. But she didn't wake up. And the Nutcracker kept on coming.

Holly scrambled to her feet and backed away. She bumped into Snowthorn and hung onto him like grim death. All the first rank of Nutcrackers were alive now. They weren't actually moving very fast, but if anything, that made it all the more horrible. They didn't bend their knees, just swung one leg stiffly forward, planting that foot, before beginning to move the next one.

And all the while they held their swords high in menace, and their jaws champed in unison, *click, click,* with every step. The officers rapped their staves smartly on the floor at the same time. The loud sound echoed in the big room, like the ticking of some huge clockwork mechanism.

Holly realized that she had backed away nearly to the door. "Do something!" she cried to Snowthorn. "How do we make them stop?"

The elf looked panicky too. "You think *I* know? When I use the Wishing Cap, it takes me right into the main toymaking hall. Or I take the pedestrian bridge from the dormitory. I haven't been this way on foot in a hundred years."

"But can't they see you? Don't they know you're a...*good guy*?" Holly waved her hands.

"They're just machines! They don't know anything!" Snowthorn wailed.

"Use your magic on them, then!"

"They're *magic* machines! We made them so other magic won't work on them! There's a password....oh, if I could remember...there's too much noise, I can't think! We have to get out of here!"

"We can't turn back," Holly heard herself saying.

Snowthorn didn't answer. One of the Nutcrackers had leaned over stiffly and seized him in one of its clumsy, mitten-like hands. It lifted the wriggling elf high, its painted jaws chomping in what suddenly looked like an evil grin.

"Let him *go!*" Holly tried to jump high enough to pull Snowthorn down. Failing at that, she aimed a kick at the Nutcracker's knee. She yelped in pain as her foot connected with its hard wooden leg.

Then another Nutcracker was bending down, one of the commanders. Its round blue eyes stared directly into Holly's. This close up, you could see that they were nothing but dots of blue paint. There was no soul there to turn them into a window. The snowflake maiden, falling past Holly on the bridge, had been real. The Nutcracker wasn't.

Then the red jaws clashed, and the Nutcracker was lifting her, too. Holly felt that she should be screaming, but instead she felt a sort of frozen horror that didn't keep her from noticing small details of what was going on. She saw, for instance, that the Nutcracker's other hand, the one that held the staff, could never open. It and the staff were fused together.

She noticed also that the Nutcrackers had no joints in their legs or feet, just at the hips, which was why they had to swing their whole legs stiffly as they walked. That was one reason, she thought in a dreamy sort of way, that it hadn't been a specially good idea to try and hit one in the knee. They didn't really *have* knees.

Meanwhile, the two Nutcrackers were carrying her and Snowthorn up the stairs. There was still some sort of commotion going on below, nearer the door to the outside, but on the stairs, the other Nutcrackers had mostly frozen again, standing there with their jaws closed tightly, as if they'd never moved at all.

"Thanks," said Snowthorn, who was jolting along right next to her.

"Whattt...forrr?" Holly managed to ask, between jolts.

"Trying to rescue me. It was nice of you. Really nice. Completely ineffective, of course, but...nice."

"Anyyy...tttime," she assured him.

They lurched on up toward the door and whatever was waiting for them on the other side.

Connor had stayed locked in place, unable to move, as the Nutcracker soldier picked up the elf. Then he saw Holly try to kick the soldier, and the other Nutcracker bending down, and its hand closing on her.

Going to Pieces

He leaped after Holly. Unfortunately, another one of the Nutcrackers lurched across his path at that moment. He wondered, in the split second before they collided, if it knew somehow that he was there. But its movement had seemed random.

An instant later, Connor bounced off the intruding Nutcracker, knocking it off balance. It teetered for a second, and then crashed to the floor, breaking apart, its legs and arms flying off in opposite directions, the head rolling over to settle upright in front of Connor. The jaws champed once more, then gaped open and still.

Right away, a few of the other Nutcrackers wheeled clumsily and began clomping toward the spot where the first one had fallen. However random their actions had been before, this was purposeful. Connor had a feeling that they wouldn't stop searching until they found him. Being invisible wouldn't matter—he wasn't sure these things could really *see* anything, anyway.

He rolled over, barely escaping being trampled by several pairs of wooden boots, and scrambled to his feet. He ran at the nearest Nutcracker and gave it a push. It crashed down and flew to pieces, just as the first one had. This time, its sword hand, with the arm still attached, landed right next to Connor. He needed to dodge out of the way as the arm flailed out convulsively, aiming several sword cuts in his general direction.

In a second, more Nutcrackers closed in on him. At the same time, he realized that while most of the others had frozen again, the two ahead had already carried Holly and the elf nearly up to the top of the stairs. A black door at the top of the stairs swung open slowly as they approached.

Good one, Connor told himself. *You come in like a knight in shining armor or something, only you don't even need a horse, because you have this super-fast invisible thing going on, see, and while you're busy smashing up a bunch of windup toys, their buddies are getting away with your sister. Again.*

Yeah, big hero.

He gave up trying to fight the Nutcrackers, and merely dodged, running between two of them as they took stiff swipes through the air with their swords, missing him by inches. He pounded up the stairs after the two Nutcrackers carrying Holly and the elf, just as they disappeared through the door.

Not Too Late

Holly forgot her fear as the Nutcrackers took them through the door and, after a few more paces, jolted to a halt. Looking around, she saw that the room they were in now was vast. The ceiling was so far away, and so lost in shadow, that she couldn't really be sure there even *was* a ceiling. It reminded her of the train station downtown, where they'd met her dad once when he came back from a trip.

She finally found her voice. "What *is* this place?"

"Toymaker's Hall," Snowthorn said. "My home away from home. Welcome...I guess. That's the fore-elf's desk there."

They were standing in front of a large wooden desk, which was littered with pieces of toys or machinery: Holly saw, among other things she couldn't identify, wheels, levers, sails, and wings. An elf in a red suit like Snowthorn's was snoring there, his head resting on the desk. He wore tiny spectacles, and had on a long nightcap, but from the white hairs peeking out around its base, Holly judged that he was even older than Snowthorn.

Then she was shaken again as the Nutcrackers went into motion. They lowered Holly and Snowthorn to the floor and then released their grip. Ponderously, they turned around and strode out of the room. The big, heavy door closed behind them.

The elf at the desk stirred at the sound, and looked up, blinking at them. "Oh," he said. "Snowthorn. I should have known. What do you think you're…"

His eyes glazed over, he nodded, and then his head thumped down on the desk as he began snoring again.

"Why did the Nutcrackers let us go?" Holly asked.

"I guess they're just designed to capture intruders, and bring them in for judgement," Snowthorn hazarded.

"Judgement? Who from? Him?"

At that moment the elf raised his head again, and went on just as if he hadn't fallen asleep in the middle of a sentence.

"...doing? The Eve is here, and for the first time in three hundred years, the Old Man had to fly off with the List unfinished..."

He paused to sigh peacefully, and his head sank back down on the desk.

Holly nudged Snowthorn. "You heard him! The List isn't finished. That must mean the Old Man will have to come back, doesn't it? We're *not* too late!"

"Well..." Snowthorn frowned. "They might just copy over the entry from last year. Sorry to say it, but most people don't really change that much, from one year to the next."

"But there's a *chance*," Holly insisted.

"Okay, there's a chance." Snowthorn threw up his hands. "Anything is possible. I've never known an Eve like this one."

Holly turned back to the old elf, who was snoring gently again. "Why is he so sleepy?"

"I told you that we sleep all winter," Snowthorn said. "Do you have any *idea* how many hours we put in, right up until the Eve? I can't blame old Silverfrost there. The rule is, we hit the sack as soon as the sleigh flies."

"But why is he still at the desk, then?" Holly asked practically.

"Good question. Actually, everybody gets to go to sleep *except* the duty elf. We take turns, each shift is about a week, and you wake up the next one when your watch is over. Come to think of it..." Snowthorn frowned. "Oh, yeah. I was supposed to take the first watch, this year. Something else for me to get in trouble over. Guess I'll find out if elf points can actually go negative. No wonder Silverfrost is so mad."

"He doesn't look mad," said Holly, as Silverfrost smiled in his sleep.

She started as the old elf's head jerked up again, and he shook an admonishing finger at Snowthorn. "...and if you think you're going to get *away* with this, you can just..." His eyes closed again, and his mouth fell open, but this time he stayed upright as he resumed his snores.

"...think again," Holly finished for him. "Let's not wait for him to finish yelling at you, okay? Then it really *will* be too late."

"Sure, let's move on," Snowthorn agreed. "When he wakes up again in another minute, he'll figure it was all just a dream."

Holly walked away from the desk, and Snowthorn followed. "So this is where you make the toys," she said in wonder.

The hall was like a cave, huge and dimly lit, so she couldn't tell all that might be in it. But judging by what she could see, the whole room was filled with row on row of desks, with all sorts of odd gadgets attached to them sticking out in all directions, stretching away endlessly into the shadows. There were narrow aisles in between, and large tubes hung in the air above them. Other, smaller tubes branched off from the main ones, leading down to each desk. At the end of the aisles nearest to Holly, the tubes opened up into large, downward-facing mouths. Large bins, shaped like stockings made for somebody with blocky feet, sat under the openings. Holly peered into one, and found a few toys on the bottom.

"Look, they forgot some toys," she said, picking up a small doll who looked something like Belinda. "That's *another* reason the Old Man will have to come back."

Snowthorn shrugged. "Not really. We almost always have some left over. Do you realize how hard it is to figure out exactly how many toys you need, when you're filling millions of stockings every year? And it's better to have too much than not enough."

The doll had a small tag attached to it. Holly held it up close to her eyes to read.

50% cotton, the tag read. *50% wool, 100% magic.*

She worked the sum over a few times, then frowned. "That doesn't add up."

Snowthorn came to look over her shoulder. "Sure it does. The cotton and wool make a hundred percent, and there was magic in *both* of them, so that makes two hundred percent. Easy as pie. What kind of math do you study in school, anyway?"

"I'm learning the times table," Holly said with dignity. "This must be higher math, like triggernomancy or something." She patted the doll's head and put her back.

Just then there was a sound like a sigh and one more toy fell from the tube, bouncing softly to rest. Holly looked at Snowthorn.

"No, I don't think anybody's still be awake and making toys," he told her. "This one must have gotten stuck in the system."

Holly picked the toy up and looked at it. It was a small, truculent-looking stuffed elephant. She turned it over and checked its label.

"*40% velveteen, 30% cotton, 15% magic,*" she read. "Okay, now this one *can't* be right. It adds up to...ummm...well, it doesn't even add up to a hundred."

Snowthorn shook his head. "No, that's right. Not one of our better efforts, I'm afraid," he added sadly.

Holly dropped the elephant back into the bin—it hit with an forlorn-sounding squeak—and went up to one of the desks. It was neat and clean, unlike Silverfrost's, but underneath it was a storage area where there were bins of parts. A computer monitor was attached to the desk on an arm that could be swung out of the way. On the side was mounted one of those woodworking machines like her dad had in the basement (a lathe, she thought, that was it), and on the other side, some brackets holding, among other things, goggles and a welding torch.

She pulled out a drawer just below the work surface, and found that it was stocked with more kinds of tools than she could imagine. There was a high swivel chair behind the desk, and she could see how the elf sitting there could finish a toy, then spin around and drop it into the small tube behind them to come out ready to be picked up in the bin at the end of the aisle.

"This isn't what I imagined at all," she said.

"Oh? You probably thought there were these big assembly lines all over the place?"

"I guess so."

"Where would the fun be in that? We elves are craftsmen!" Snowthorn said. "We take pride in our work. Not all of us can be in R&D, but everyone, even the greenest, wettest-behind-the-ears apprentice, gets to put whole toys together."

"Doesn't it make things go...well, slower?"

"No problem. If we need to speed things up, we just add more elves."

"What's this?" Holly pulled something out of a holder mounted below the torch, something that looked like a butterfly net, except that the net was so fine and shimmering you could hardly see it, as if it had been made from spiderwebs sown together without any seam.

"That's a dream catcher. Watch it, they're fragile." Snowthorn took it out of her hand and gave it a gentle shake.

"But dream catchers are...these sort of hoops with feathers hanging from them," Holly protested. "My mom put one in my room when I was having trouble sleeping. But it didn't always work," she added thoughtfully.

"Yeah?" Snowthorn gave her a sidelong glance. "Oh, okay, I know what you mean, but those are for *bad* dreams. We use these to catch the *good* ones—at least, any that make it all the way up to the workshop." Snowthorn looked up, scanning the vast space under the shadowed, vaulted ceiling. He pointed. "Look—there's one now."

Faintly, Holly could see one of the small bubbles floating past above them. It was far too high up to reach, but she caught a glimpse of the dream. A little girl was peeking out from behind a snowman, smiling. She had curly red hair...

It was her own dream again. But how could it be? She'd burst that dream-bubble while they were still on the bridge.

Snowthorn recognized it at the same time. He whistled. "Now *that* is one persistent dream you have there. Want me to catch it?"

"Can you?" she asked automatically, though she wasn't really sure if she wanted him to.

"I can try." He flexed his wrist a couple of times, warming up, and then cast the net like a fisherman casting a fly. The net stretched out, impossibly far, and snared the floating bubble. Then it contracted again, slowly, bringing the captured dream down within reach.

Holly peeked into the net. "Where did it go? There's nothing here but this." She reached in and held up a small flower with a withered-looking blossom.

"Even the strongest dreams are fragile," Snowthorn said, putting the dream-catcher carefully back into its holder. "When you catch them, they'll change. Sometimes you get lucky, and they become models or blueprints. But usually, they collapse and you're left with the seed, whatever started the dream in the first place. Sometimes it's like this, a flower petal or a bit of feather—I remember one where all that was left was a tiny seashell—and once, just once, I saw a dream that turned into a single tear when it was caught."

Holly turned the flower over in her hands. She frowned as she noticed that the dry flower head wasn't still growing on its stalk. It had been taped there.

"What's the story with that?" Snowthorn asked her.

Holly closed her eyes. The memory came back to her so strongly that for a moment it seemed as if she stood in her yard again, looking down at the flowers in her little garden patch that her mom had helped her plant.

"It was fall," she said. "The flowers were starting to die, and their heads were drooping and starting to fall off. I thought it was because I wasn't watering them enough, or maybe I hadn't kept them warm like I was supposed to. But I wanted things to still look nice, and I didn't want it to be my fault. So I gathered the flowers that fell, and taped them back onto the stems." She opened her eyes, smiling through her tears. "Then they *did* look nice again…for a day or so."

"But it wasn't your fault," Snowthorn said gently. "You know that now, right? Sometimes things just come to an end. And you can't make that not happen. You can't turn back the clock. It's how the world was set up."

Holly didn't really want to think about what Snowthorn was saying. She just knew that she didn't believe it, that she would never agree, no matter what Rules had been laid down, or even what the Old Man might say about it.

There *had* to be a way to fix things.

But just then she smelled something, something here and now and delicious, that made her forget all about dreams and memories. She put the flower down and sniffed the air. Her stomach began to rumble.

"It smells like chocolate and caramel and cherries and sweet cream and...what *is* that?" she asked.

Snowthorn pointed out another of the giant stockings, several aisles down. This one was filled with candy. Holly's stomach grumbled again, reminding her that the last thing she'd eaten had been a few fragments of bannock while they were on the sled, looking for the reindeer's hidden valley. She reached in and took a big handful.

"Hey, don't touch those," Snowthorn said sharply from behind her.

Holly looked back at him, her mouth already full. "Why?" she said indistinctly. "Because it's magic food, and if I eat it I'll fall asleep and stay here forever?"

"No...I was thinking about what your mother would say. You didn't even bother to bring a toothbrush, did you?" Snowthorn tried hard to look severe, then gave up. "Oh, go ahead. Try the green ones, and the chocolates shaped like diamonds—they have coconut and almonds and stuff in them, so you might actually get a little nutrition by accident."

Holly munched away happily for a few minutes. When she finally felt like stopping, she glanced at Snowthorn and caught him in the middle of a yawn.

"You're sleepy too?" she asked.

"Sleepy? I can hardly keep my eyes open. Look, I'll just put my head down over here on one of the confectioner's desks, while you look around. Have some more candy..." He broke off to yawn again, his jaws cracking.

> Look Out

"You need to help me to get to the List first. You *swore*," Holly reminded him.

"Oh, right. I wasn't trying to pull anything, I just...forgot about it for a second." Snowthorn nodded, then jerked his head back up. "So," he said brightly, "what were we talking about?"

"The List," Holly said, feeling a little scared. "Take me to it. Now."

"Oh," said Snowthorn. "Well, it's right around here. You just need to go back out the way we came..."

"Where the Nutcrackers are?" Holly asked over his yawn. "I'm not going back there. No way."

"....and go in the other door," Snowthorn finished. "Simple."

He leaned on one of the desks and nodded again. Holly shook him. "But *then* what do I do?"

"I...don't know. I've never been in....the Old Man's chamber...it's on a need to know....basis..." She could see Snowthorn's eyes glazing over as he spoke. Then they fluttered closed, and he began breathing softly and regularly, clearly asleep on his feet.

"Snowthorn, wake up! I can't go alone!" She shook him harder, without much result except to tip him over toward the desk, which stopped his fall. He stood propped there with one foot off the floor.

A moment later, though, his eyes opened again. "Holly," he said. "You're still here. Look, I'll miss you...I wish I could go further...it's been fun and..." He smiled slowly. "I'm just glad I could help you..."

Slowly, he slid down to the floor, and lay there, no longer moving at all. He began to snore.

Holly straightened up. She took a deep breath and tried to keep her heart from pounding. She'd told Snowthorn she couldn't go alone, and she knew it was true. But she had to. There wasn't any choice.

She had just turned away when Snowthorn roused again. "I forgot...Holly, look out..."

She ran back and knelt down beside him. He blinked up at her, bemused. "What...was I saying?" he asked.

"Look out. You were telling me to look out. What for?"

He nodded. "Look out...for the Hall...of Rejected..." The nod lengthened and his head drooped on his chest. A look of peace came over his face. He obviously thought he'd delivered his message, whatever it was.

The Hall of Rejected...what? Holly wondered. Well, unless there was a big flashing sign hanging over the entrance, she was out of luck. She stood up again, taking a few slow steps toward the door.

Then she stopped. Had somebody called her name? She looked around. Nobody was there but Snowthorn, sunk in blissful sleep.

Then she felt as if cold fingers were touching her arm, and she shivered. Suddenly, the great deserted hall was a spooky place. Snowthorn was there, but he was asleep, and she decided that having someone around who was sleeping wasn't much help. You were still alone. If anything, it made it scarier that someone else was with you, but not really *there* at all.

Immediately, she wished that she hadn't thought that. "And they're still waiting outside," a small voice in her head reminded her, irresistibly. "The Nutcrackers. They're still waiting for you…"

Just then, some of the candy in the bin seemed to leap into the air. It hovered there in a loose mass for a moment, then started to pour slowly back down, as if something invisible had scooped it up and was letting it run through its fingers.

Holly screamed and ran blindly for the door.

Eleven

Connor had just managed to slip inside the big door before it thudded shut behind the Nutcrackers. One of his sleeves caught in the door, and he'd spent a minute vainly trying to tug it out before he thought of shrugging off the coat. By then, the Nutcrackers had already set down Holly and the elf, done a clumsy about-face, and were coming toward him again. He darted out of the way as the great door groaned open again. His coat fell to the floor. The door swung to again with a noise like thunder, and he was alone in the room with Holly and the elf.

A Known Associate

Except, as he saw when he came up behind them, there was another elf there. But that one was acting like he'd been drugged or something, talking and then falling asleep in the middle of a sentence. Connor gathered, though, that Holly's elf was being scolded for being late, and the List not finished.

The List! Suddenly it all came together. The Snow Fox had mentioned the List, too. And

Connor had, all the time, been carrying the little book he'd found, back in the house.

He checked the inner pocket of his Air Force jacket, that he'd had on under the parka. The book was still there. *Just as well*, he thought. If this mysterious Old Man, who had somehow managed to convince everybody that he was a 'jolly old elf', didn't have the full story on the misdeeds of one Connor Morrison, that was all to the good.

On impulse, he pulled the book out and flipped through the pages until he came to the one with his name. He scanned down the list, looking for any change. He did find a new entry, but it wasn't very helpful.

A known associate of the notorious Snow Fox.

Typical, Connor thought. Here he was trying to rescue his sister, fighting off every temptation to abandon his quest, but he wasn't getting any points for *that*. He thrust the book back into his pocket.

The drowsy elf finally went down for the count, and Holly and her elf moved on down the hall. Connor followed them, staying close but at a loss as to what to do. Obviously, they still couldn't see him. And he was bigger than the elf. Maybe stronger, though you never knew what kind of magic the elf might have in store.

But somehow, Connor wasn't quite as ready to jump the elf now that he looked like some harmless old guy. And right at the moment, it didn't seem like Holly was in much danger. The elf was acting more like a tour guide, pointing out to Holly one of the desks, looking like a cross between an artist's easel and a machinist's work station, that filled the whole huge room as far as Connor could see.

He watched the elf bring down Holly's dream, too, and knew that it was a real dream, not a nightmare. And the elf didn't act like he wanted to steal it, either. What if Holly was seeing things more the way they really were? Connor wondered. And now he was, too, since he'd accidentally touched her?

In a little while Holly's elf started yawning, like the other one, and clearly was about to fall asleep. Connor's pulse began to race. This was his chance! He tried calling to Holly as she straightened up, leaving the elf snoring on the floor, and looked around the room. She looked around, but after a moment she shook her head. He could see her thinking that she must be hearing things.

He came close and touched her arm. She felt something, all right, but from the way she acted, she still couldn't see him. She just shivered as if there'd been a cold wind.

Then she turned away and began to walk back toward the outside door.

Desperate, Connor went over to the bin of candies that Holly had been rummaging in a minute ago. They looked good enough that it was all he could do to stop from cramming a handful right into his mouth, but he wasn't that trusting yet—who knew what would happen if you ate something here? Instead he began to juggle handfuls of the candy, throwing it up in the air and letting it fall back into the bin.

Oh, she saw *that*, all right. Holly looked back at him, obviously seeing nothing but a bunch of candy floating in the air for no good reason, screamed, and ran. Brilliant plan, Connor, he thought. Letting the rest of the candy drop, he raced after her, almost slipping as he stepped on the loose pieces skittering over the floor.

Another Door

Without any clear plan, Holly ran toward the door. Her footfalls echoed in the deserted hall. That sound, and the fact that she was moving, getting away from whatever the invisible thing by the candy bin was, made her feel a little less afraid.

She was surprised to see the door creaking open before she got to it. Then she remembered Snowthorn saying that doors opened by themselves in the palace, if they opened at all. She passed the fore-elf's desk, where Silverfrost was still snoring, and put on speed.

As she went through, she caught sight of a parka lying crumpled on the floor. That hadn't been there before, she thought. What could it mean?

Then she was outside, and the ranks of Nutcrackers stretched down toward the outer door before her.

She stopped dead, her heart in her mouth. But not a single one of the Nutcrackers moved. Not one even champed its jaws. They stayed facing away from her, swords and staves at the ready, watching for something that might come through the outside door.

Of course, she thought. *They're machines. They're not as human as the reindeer, even. They were made to guard against something getting in from outside, so that was what they did, and nothing more.* She and Snowthorn had been dealt with and forgotten. She was in no danger from them now.

Still, she slowed down and even went on tip-toe over the polished floor. The other door seemed a long way away.

Then she was standing right in front of it, feeling smaller than she had in a while. She had gotten used to being with Snowthorn, who was no taller than she was. But this door was clearly made for someone larger. There was no doorknob, but she saw a reindeer's head holding a ring in its mouth, made of some shiny metal, too high for her to reach. It must be a knocker, she realized.

Above that, something was written in fancy letters. Holly puzzled it out. *Sanctum sanctorum*, it read. She shook her head. What could that mean? Anyway, it wasn't about rejecting anything, so this wasn't the place that Snowthorn had warned her about.

She waited a few moments, but the door showed no signs of opening. All of a sudden she remembered her mother saying, *It's polite to knock.* She looked up, and saw that either the knocker had moved, or it hadn't been quite as high as she'd thought in the first place. She could reach it, if she went up on tiptoes again, and stretched her arm as far as it could go...she could just reach it...

As firmly as she could, she rapped the knocker against its metal plate, once, twice, and a third time. The sound of the knocks reverberated through the tower. She let the knocker go and glanced back over her shoulder, a little afraid that the Nutcrackers would wake up. But they were as motionless as ever.

Then, slowly and in complete silence, the door swung inward.

Holly took a deep breath, and went in. Inside it was very quiet, and the air felt different. The room didn't seem as large as the toymaking hall, yet somehow, she felt like she was in the middle of a vast, open space. In the dim, sourceless light, she could see that there were hardly any furnishings. On her left was some sort of podium, with a large book lying open on top.

Checking the List

Further into the room, to her right, rose a spiral staircase. It reminded Holly unpleasantly of her dream in Duck Egg's igloo. The stair wasn't attached to anything, and didn't seem to go anywhere but up. She followed it with her eyes, and realized that this room must stretch all the way up to the top of the tower. Far, far above, she could see that there was some kind of window or skylight.

That was where all the room's light came from, the light of stars and moon, and it was there that the spiral stairway stopped.

It was as if she'd stepped inside a lighthouse. She lowered her head, feeling a bit dizzy. Then she realized what the book on the podium must be.

The List.

She took a few steps toward it, feeling as if each one carried her a distance of miles. She thought of all the frozen lands between her and home, of her mother and father, of the bridge of light and the empty sky that held up the floating palace, and of Snowthorn.

And of course she thought of Connor. *This is it,* she thought, *the good part of the story at last.* The List hadn't been finished, and so the Old Man—Father Winter—would surely come back, before he finished his rounds this Yule Eve. And when he did, he would look for Connor's name, and see that he was Nice. So he would get what he wanted, and then, naturally, he would stop being naughty. He would be happy. And so would Holly, and her mom, and her dad. They would all live happily ever after...

The podium was too tall for Holly, too, but luckily there were some library steps right next to it. Maybe some of the elves had to come in and make their entries sometimes, or look things up there when a question came up. She climbed up the steps and stood, finally, looking down at the List lying open before her.

She paused for a moment, feeling as if someone was watching her. She looked around quickly, but there was nobody there. Her heart beat faster. It had been one thing to think about changing the List, back when she was at home, or had Snowthorn close by. It was quite different here, in this still, empty room with the terribly long stairway winding upwards toward the sky.

She focused on the book again, thinking how old it looked. The pages were yellowed and slightly brittle to her touch. She eagerly scanned what was written there, but all the entries were in characters she couldn't recognize. She turned over page after page, but it all looked like gibberish to her. Strange signs like faces frowned or scowled at her, but there was nothing at all she could understand.

Her heart sank. The List was the biggest, thickest book she had ever seen. Bigger than the phone book. Bigger than the unabridged dictionary her mom had shown her once, at the library, that needed a little table all to itself just like the List had.

What good was it, everything she'd done, everything Snowthorn had done too—if in the end she couldn't even find Connor's name? It could take days to search through the List. Father Winter would be back long before then.

She remembered that when her mother had a decision to make, she would sometimes shuffle a pack of cards with funny pictures on them, and then just turn over the one on top. Holly had never understood how that worked, but at the moment, she didn't have a better idea. So she drew a deep breath, and looking away, lifted many pages at once, turning to a place nearer the end of the List.

When she looked back at the page, she saw:

Holly Morrison.

She felt a thrill of hope. Surely Connor's entry would be close to her own! Then her gaze strayed over to the opposite column, and she saw the word:

Naughty.

She felt as if she'd just gotten an electric shock, but it only lasted a second. There must be millions of girls named Holly Morrison, she told herself. Well, thousands, anyway. Still, she had to be close.

But when she looked back at the List she found that it now read:

Holly Morrison who lives in Seattle, in the yellow house with a plum tree in the back yard. This means you.

She looked away. "But I'm nice," she said out loud, as she had said—how long ago it seemed now—to Snowthorn, back in her room. "I've *always* been nice."

Then she darted a glance back at the page. The name had changed, she thought. Maybe whatever else it said could change too. But...

Naughty, the List went on saying, severe, uncompromising.

Angry tears stung Holly's eyes. "All right, then," she told the List. "Somebody made a mistake. It's probably because I made Snowthorn drop his book and he didn't bring it here like he was supposed to. Just wait, I'll fix it."

She noticed that there was a shelf just underneath the tabletop where the List rested, and she found an old-fashioned quill pen and an ink bottle there. After a few false starts, which left an inkblot or two on the page—maybe the elves make mistakes too, she thought despairingly, maybe even the Old Man does, he *must*—she laboriously crossed out the

'Naughty' next to her name and wrote 'Nice' next to that, the letters looking a little cramped because she had to squeeze them in close to the edge of the page.

But when she ran her eye up and down the List, searching for Connor's name so that she could finally finish her work, she saw nothing but her own name, endlessly repeated.

Holly Morrison – Naughty

Holly Morrison – Naughty

Holly Morrison – Naughty...

She dropped the quill pen, nearly upsetting the ink bottle, and flipped through all the pages. As far as she could tell, the entire List now was filled with only one name, her own—repeated over and over again, for hundreds of pages, thousands, more than she could possibly count. It was as if someone, some immortal and yes, *naughty* person, had been set to writing those words endlessly, for all eternity, as some kind of punishment.

Naughty...

With a wrenching sob, she turned right to the very last page of the book, and looked at the very last words written there. Something like 'They lived happily ever after', or even 'The End', would have been some comfort. But instead she read:

You're still being naughty. Please stop!

"It's not fair," she cried out loud. "It's not *fair!*"

For some reason, Snowthorn's words came back to her again. *Rule Four: no guarantees.*

Holly gave up. She opened the List back up again, to somewhere near where it had been at first, and smoothed the torn edge of one of the pages. Shakily, she stepped down to the floor, and stood there with tears running down her cheeks. She cried for a long time, and her sobs were still the only sound in the whole vast chamber.

At last, after Holly's tears had slowed down to an occasional sniff, she dried her eyes as best she could, and thought about what to do next. The worst had  happened already. Her quest had failed. Now, there was only—what? Waiting for the Old Man, telling him she was sorry? She wouldn't argue, she decided, even if it *wasn't* fair. She would just say, *Yes, I've been naughty. I'm sorry. Can I go home now?*

Then her gaze was drawn upward again, up the staircase that spiraled toward the skylight above. For the first time she realized clearly what it was. *The Old Man's high seat,* Snowthorn had called it. *When he sits in it, he can see everything. Anything he wants.*

She walked over and set her foot on the lowest step. She felt a little shiver run through the structure, and stopped, feeling a thrill of fear. *But the Old Man climbs up and sits in the seat,* she reminded herself. *He's a grownup. A* fat *grownup. That means it should be safe for me.*

So she went on, stepping quickly and, after the first few turns, not looking down. Above her, the skylight grew closer. She could see, after a few more spirals, that it was really a dome, made of glass or—*of course,* she thought—pure, perfectly clear ice. It was like an observatory. Maybe, she thought, the Old Man had moved the Palace up here, floating in the sky, just so the tower could look out over the whole world.

At first Holly tried to count the number of steps, but she kept losing track and having to start over. It was hard to count when she felt so dizzy. Around and around she mounted in an endless spiral, always upward, clinging to the railing to help her keep moving along...

Then, unexpectedly, she rounded one last sharp turn and reached the top. She swayed for a moment, feeling dizzy, and glimpsed the stone floor far below. She closed her eyes and breathed deeply. Then she climbed up into the wide, tall chair that waited empty on the platform there.

Her hands gripping the arms, she felt calmer, and she forgot how scary the climb had been when she looked out at the moon and stars, and the blue and white Earth below.

She found that when she looked at the Earth, if she didn't shift her eyes, after a moment it seemed as if the ground or water was zooming up toward her, and she could see pictures of whatever was happening down there, tiny but perfect in every detail. She amused herself following a cruise ship for a while as it steamed toward an island with palm trees. Moving her gaze up toward the pole, she saw big cities, and then out on the open plain, a herd of non-magical reindeer grazing.

When she looked up at the stars, though, her vision didn't show her any more details. They were beautiful and unchanging. Only the Moon seemed to change a little when she looked steadily—the man in the moon seemed to be smiling at her at first, but then his expression changed to one of cold indifference, and the craters that were his eyes looked dark and empty as the eyesockets on a skull.

So she concentrated on the earth. It occurred to her that she might be able to see her family. Her mother and Connor were in Seattle, of course, and she knew where that was on the big globe in the living room. That wasn't the part of the Earth that she could see right now, but she found that if she called up her mother's face clearly in her mind, her vision zoomed in and moved closer until she saw a big city surrounded by water, and then, a house that she recognized.

She could see inside, too. She didn't understand it—it seemed to be more a matter of looking *around* the walls than through them, somehow. But her mother was there. She was sitting in the living room, and the tree was decorated now, with all the lights on. But she didn't look happy. Grimalkin was with her, rubbing against her leg and opening his mouth to meow, though Holly couldn't hear anything, but her mother paid no attention to him. Her face was haunted, and there were dark circles under her eyes.

Holly realized clearly, for the first time, that her mom must be worried about her. She hadn't really thought about how long it might take, finding the List and changing it. Magical adventures weren't supposed to take any time at all, were they?

But Holly remembered now that it had been a whole day and night since she'd been home. "Don't worry, Mom!" she called. "I'm okay. I'm with...I mean, I'm at the Old—at Father Winter's place. I'll be home soon...I think."

But her mother's worried expression didn't change at all. Even though it was a real picture Holly saw, it wasn't like being there. She couldn't hear her mother, and her mother couldn't hear her.

What about Connor? She brought her brother's face into her mind, and tried to remember him looking happy, the way he used to, not with that sneer that he wore so often lately. She was confused, though, because no picture of Connor came to her. Instead she kept getting jumbled images of the room she was in, as if she were back down on the floor, looking up at the night sky above.

Even the High Seat can't find him, she thought. What does that mean? Is he doing something bad? *Really* bad? Is he...

But she shied away from that thought. Connor had been fine when she left. There had to be some other reason she couldn't see him. Maybe it had to do with her trying to change the List. Yes, that must be it. She was being punished in some strange way, for wanting to make Connor be nice.

Other doubts rose up in her mind, but she pushed them back and at last allowed herself to bring up the picture of her father's face. *Where is he?* she asked silently. *Is he all right? Will he...will he really be home for Yule?*

In her vision, she was rushing over seas and plains, and finally the scene settled: a big mountain with slopes of snow and rock and ice. Then, all of a sudden, it was as if she was seeing *inside* the mountain. She saw some kind of cave with a glittering roof and walls. Huge boulders gleaming with a bluish light were scattered over the floor.

An ice cave. Holly recognized it from a picture her dad had shown her once. Then, all at once, she remembered her nightmare.

Inside the cave, a star was shining. It twinkled in the middle of the cold and darkness, calling up a thousand broken reflections like cold flames from the ice. As it moved closer, she saw it wasn't a star, but a flashlight someone was carrying.

It was her father. She saw his face clearly for a moment as the flashlight beam moved around and the light leaped back from the icy walls. He looked tired and scared.

"But where is he? What's he doing there?" she wondered aloud. "He's up in the blue yonder. Flying home. He shouldn't be out in some cave..."

Then Holly noticed something else. Trickles of water coming from the roof. Suddenly a huge icicle crashed down, with a sound like a hundred mirrors breaking at once.

The cave was beginning to collapse.

Holly started up out of the chair. "Daddy! *Daddy!* You'll get buried, you have to get away, now!" She stretched her arms out blindly toward the vision of her father, and took a step toward him, then another...

One too many. Her consciousness came back, with a jerk, to the chamber and the High Seat, as she clutched at emptiness and fell down toward the stone floor far below.

I Hate Rule Four

Connor found that his magical swiftness, if nothing else, had definitely worn off now. Holly had a head start on him, and she widened her lead when he slipped and nearly fell. I never knew she was this fast, he thought. Good thing I didn't rattle a chain or anything, she'd be halfway to Seattle by now.

He saw the door open for her, but it was closing again by the time he got there. Man, he thought, no breaks for guys who just happen to be invisible. That's *cold*. This time, though, he managed to get through without getting caught, and even picked up his discarded parka on the way by—once you'd spent time wandering around the Arctic, you weren't likely to pass up a chance like that.

Like Holly, he studied the Nutcrackers cautiously before going on. He was tempted to push a few of them down the stairs and see what havoc they would wreak on the way down. But no sense stirring them up, he told himself. He just had to stick close to his sister, until the magic in the Snow Fox's ring wore off, and she could see him and believe it was him there talking to her.

He was standing directly behind Holly when she lifted the knocker—which he could have sworn was higher up the door, a minute ago—and knocked at the door. *Sanctum Sanctorum*—he couldn't remember the exact translation was for that, but he was pretty sure it meant Private. Why couldn't she go back to the nice hall with all the toys and candy?

When the door opened, she went in without hesitating. Connor followed, starting to wonder now just who had kidnapped who. The elf was out like a light now, sleeping with the toys. But Holly still acted like she knew what she was doing. She hadn't just been running away from Connor's haunted house act. She'd been running *toward* this room, too.

And whatever was waiting inside.

Connor looked up at the spiral stair until his head swam, then watched as Holly climbed the podium steps and started leafing through the List. "I wouldn't do that if I were you, kid," he said. "The part *I* got to look at wasn't exactly a hot read."

No reaction. Of course. Connor remembered wishing to be invisible, way back in Seattle. Now all he wanted was for Holly to be able to see him. *Be careful what you wish for,* he thought. *Yeah, just one more of those old sayings you never believe until it's too late.*

Then he saw his sister stiffen. A moment later, she started to cry. He came up behind her and looked over her shoulder.

Connor Morrison – Naughty, the entry at the top of the page read.

"Don't worry about it," he advised Holly. "Not like we've never heard *that* before."

Holly rummaged on the shelf below and pulled out a pen and an inkwell. "No, no, don't try it," Connor said, becoming genuinely alarmed. He remembered the way the little book he'd found had changed when he just looked at it. What would this book—this much *bigger* book—do if you tried to actually *write* in it?

He tried to pull Holly's hand back, and she almost spilled the bottle of ink, but kept right on going. He looked over her shoulder again after she'd stopped writing.

"See?" he said. "No difference."

His sister gave an angry sob, then started flipping through the book's pages, faster and faster. Then she backed down the steps and stood there sobbing as if her heart would break.

"Hey," Connor said. "Look, I said don't worry about it." Awkwardly, he tried to put his arms around Holly. She shivered a little, but grew quieter. After a minute she looked up at the spiral stair and moved toward it, determination in her face.

Connor knew that look. It was the same look she'd had when they talked last, in the hall at home. He tried to keep her back, but it seemed he'd really turned into a ghost now. She broke his hold as easily as walking through a cobweb.

"Okay," he called as she set her foot on the stair. "Okay. I am *not* going up there. You're on your own now."

He saw the stairway shiver as she climbed. No way, he thought. I flew on the reindeer. I walked on the bridge over nothing. I did all that heavy-duty quest stuff. But I am *not* climbing up there. Besides, I must still weigh *something*. I'd probably just bring her down along with me.

The sounds of her footsteps echoed down to him. After a long time, they stopped. There was no other sound for a long time. Connor moved around the stairway, peering up. He could just make out some kind of platform at the top. What could she be doing up there?

Then he heard his sister's voice, crying faintly from far above, and then a long, drawn-out wail. He looked up and saw her falling toward him.

She rushed closer, silent now, her arms spread out, her eyes wide and looking as if she'd just seen something way, way worse than the stone floor rising up to meet her. Connor reacted instinctively, holding out his arms and gathering her in, knocked backward and downward by the force of her fall. Pain flared in his back and tailbone, but he had her, he was cradling her in his arms, she was safe.

At the same time, he felt the ring made of the Snow Fox's fur loosen and fall away from his finger.

Holly looked up at him, and suddenly he knew that she saw him at last, and his own eyes filled with tears.

"Oh, Connor," she said. "*Connor*. Rule Four. I *hate* Rule Four."

Then her eyes rolled up and she fainted.

> Now You Believe Too

Holly was only out for a couple of minutes, but it was long enough for Connor to get a creepy feeling about the chamber they were in. For some reason he was more spooked now that he was visible again. Before, with his special powers, he'd been like one of the zillion other supernatural creatures wandering around here. Now, he was just himself again, and he had Holly to look out for into the bargain.

He wasn't sure what to do with her, but had a vague memory, maybe from some movie, that chafing her wrists and gently smoothing her hair back might be a good idea. When she finally stirred, he felt relieved and stopped. In a moment, she sat up, blinking.

"Connor," she said wonderingly. "So it wasn't a dream. But how did you get here?"

Awkwardly at first, then warming to the story, Connor told her about picking up the wishing cap and following her and the elf. He tried to tell everything as honestly as he could, though he left out the part when he'd wished for his gang to appear, and he glossed over how tempting it had been when the Snow Fox showed him a way to go back home.

Holly listened wide-eyed. "So we've *both* been on a quest! And now, you believe too. Don't you?" she asked sharply, at Connor's dubious expression.

"I believe in *something*," Connor said slowly. "I'm just not sure what."

"But you're seeing things the way I do now," Holly pointed out. "The High Seat, and the List, and the elves…"

"Well, sure," Connor said grudgingly. "But how do we know this is how things really look here? Maybe I was seeing the truth before, and now I'm not, because I touched you and…picked up whatever kind of spell that elf—"

"Snowthorn," Holly interposed.

"—Snowthorn, put on you," Connor finished.

"I don't think spells are like colds or the flu. They're not *catching*," Holly said thoughtfully. "But anyway, now let *me* tell *you* what happened. Then we can decide."

Connor stayed quiet while Holly told her story, even when he felt that she was going off on tangents once or twice. It occurred to him that he had never listened to her talk for this long before.

When she finished neither of them said anything for a while. They'd just reminded themselves of how much had happened, in only one night and day, and the old ways they had of talking felt out of place now. The stories had carried them this far, but now that they were told, they felt shy again, as if meeting each other for the first time.

"I wish you'd gotten to meet Duck Egg," Holly said at last.

"Yeah. She and her family sound pretty cool," Connor answered absently. "But Holly, we've got to think about what to do next. Mom is missing us. For all she knows, we've been kidnapped—that's what I thought too. I know you weren't, really," he added hastily, "but it looked that way. So we've got to think about how to get home. She went in and *made my bed*, Holly. That's serious."

His sister nodded soberly. "It's even more important for us to get back, if Daddy...well, you know," she finished, rubbing her eyes.

"Yeah." Let's not dwell on *that*, Connor thought. "So what do you say we have a look around this place?" he asked brightly.

"I think we should wait for the Old Man now," Holly objected.

"Maybe, but not here. Father Winter—okay, the Old Man—might be a great guy, or he might not, but either way you don't want to meet him while you're trespassing in his private room, after trying to cook the books," Connor said, reasonably.

Holly brightened up. "Okay. Who knows, maybe some of the other reindeer are around here—he must have some extra ones, in case any of them on the team are sick or something. And they could fly us home!"

Connor nodded. "Sure. We might find something. Anyway, it's better than sitting here. So what do you think? Back out to the workshop? Or out into the courtyard, and try one of the other towers? If there was something like a stable, it might be out there."

"Okay," Holly said. She gave Connor a look that said *You're my big brother, and I'll follow you anywhere.* Yesterday, it would have irritated him, but now it made him feel strangely warm inside.

This time, the door of the Old Man's chamber swung wide open for them right away. Apparently you only had to knock when you were coming in. Connor peeked around the door, but none of the Nutcrackers were moving. After a moment, Holly followed him out.

While Connor was standing there trying to figure out if he really felt like trying to sneak past the Nutcrackers while fully visible, Holly tugged at his sleeve. "Connor," she said. "What about *that* door? What's in there?"

Connor turned around. He saw another door set in the wall of the gallery, between the door to the workshop and the one that led to the chamber of the List.

"That...wasn't there when we came in," he said.

Holly shrugged. "It's here now."

"Hard to argue with that. Well, let's check it out." Connor still mistrusted doors that appeared suddenly from nowhere, but it seemed like a better idea than trying to get past the Nutcrackers again.

They walked over to the door and studied it. Unlike most of the other doors they had seen, it actually had a knob, a shiny brass one set on the left. The door itself seemed to be made of plain wood. There was a symbol marked on the door in red. It showed an empty circle with a diagonal line across it. That was all.

"Wait," said Holly. "That's the sign that means not to do something, right?"

"Yeah," Connor said. "But it's empty. Usually there's something inside it, like a cigarette, say, and then it means 'don't smoke'. What does it mean if there's nothing inside?"

"Ummm...'don't do nothing'?" Holly guessed.

"Or maybe just 'don't'. But let's try it anyway, what have we got to lose?"

He turned the knob but the door wouldn't open. "Try the other way," Holly suggested. "Or pull on it."

Connor gave her a skeptical look, but when he pushed, and then pulled, the knob, the door popped open as if he'd released a spring. "That's weird," he said, peering at the latch mechanism. "How does that work?"

"Never mind," Holly said impatiently. "Let's go *in*."

But before Connor let Holly pass, he looked around for something to prop the door open. He didn't want to take a chance on this door deciding not to let them out. Luckily, when he'd knocked one of the Nutcrackers to pieces, its leg had wound up on the floor of the gallery. He dragged the leg over and shoved it against the door, and it held.

Cautiously, the two children stepped inside. Connor's first thought was that the room housed some kind of museum. There was a big open floor, and the walls were lined with some sort of exhibits, placed apart at a regular distance. Each was softly lit by a torch set in a wall sconce above, burning clearly with a steady flame.

"So what *is* this?" Connor stood in front of the first 'exhibit', his hands on his hips. It was a simple cube, resting on the floor, with nothing special about it except that it was striped with bright colors in a beach ball-type pattern.

Holly went to the next exhibit, a large ball with a rope attached to it. Dangling at the end of the rope was a handle, as if someone had taken a jump rope and shoved it inside the ball. When she picked it up, she saw that one end of the handle was hollowed out to form a sort of cup.

"Hey, I wouldn't touch anything, if I were you," Connor told her.

"There's no sign that says don't touch," Holly pointed out.

"There's no signs at *all*," Connor said, frustrated. "What, are we just supposed to know what all these things are?"

Then it came to Holly in a flash, and she laughed with delight. "I know where we are now. The Hall of Rejected... Snowthorn started to say it. It's the Hall of Rejected Toys!"

Connor looked puzzled. "Don't you see?" Holly appealed to him. "That first one, there..." She pointed to the cube. "It's a ball. Just a ball. But it's square, so it doesn't roll."

"Okay..."

"And this second one, it's a cup and ball," Holly went on. "You know, the little game we always used to get in our stockings, where you try and catch the ball in the cup? Only the ball is way too big..."

Connor chuckled, catching on. "I get it. This is like a lesson in 'How *not* to do it.' Or an intelligence test. That somebody failed. A *lot*," he added, looking at the long line of exhibits stretching down the wall.

The children skipped the next few, which consisted of lopsided tops and gliders that were elaborately designed, but obviously wouldn't fly. They halted in front of what looked like a game board, with a complicated apparatus set up on it.

"Hey, this is sort of like the one where you build a mouse trap," Connor said. "Do you remember that one?"

Holly nodded. "Sure. You always had to help me. It was fun, though. How does this one work?"

Connor bent over the board. "Well, let's see...it looks like this marble rolls here and falls down there, and then *this* springs up and tips over this basket, which launches this ball into the air and goes into the mouth of whatever *that* is, and then...I guess it begins all over again."

"Let's try it!"

They shared a quick grin. "Except," Connor said, "that this spinner looks like it's a little bit out of place..."

He made the adjustment, then dropped the marble in at the starting place. It looped around several times without stopping.

Holly watched, fascinated. "I don't think it's *ever* going to stop."

"Perpetual motion, maybe," Connor said thoughtfully. He pursed his lips. "But that's impossible. I think."

Just then the marble, instead of dropping into the open mouth of the frog-like creature at the other end of the course, ricocheted and hit Connor directly in the forehead. Holly dissolved in laughter. Connor managed to glare at her for two full seconds before he joined her.

After that, they followed the wall from exhibit to exhibit, laughing, playing with the ones that interested them. All of them were off in some way—for instance, there was a bubble wand that when you blew through it, made bubbles that dropped to the floor and bounced around instead of floating off and popping. But as they went on, the toys' flaws became more and more subtle, and it was a game in itself to figure out what was wrong with the game they were playing at the moment.

But mostly, they just played. It had been a long couple of years since Holly and Connor had done something together just for fun. But neither of them thought about that, or about having to get home, or their mother and father, or about anything else except what they were doing.

After a while, they didn't feel like playing any more, and just began to wander from one toy to another. Holly picked up one of them, a doll with a blank and featureless face which changed, after she'd picked it up, to look exactly like her. It talked, too, but only to echo the last part of whatever Holly said to it. She got bored with it after a few minutes and put it back down on its pedestal. Its face slowly faded again to a blank.

Connor got interested in something that looked like a futuristic ray gun. Instead of a trigger, it had a slider control with a plus sign at one end and a minus sign on the other. He experimented by pointing the gun at a one-legged metal robot that stood nearby, and setting the slider to the plus sign. Immediately the gun began to drag Connor over the floor toward the robot. When he moved the slider to the minus position, he was thrown backward and the gun went flying. He wasn't sure where it went, and didn't really feel like looking.

After that, he passed quite a few toys without being tempted, until he saw the sword. It stood there shining, hilt upright, set in a large stone like it was just waiting for King Arthur, or somebody like him, to come along and pull it out.

He took hold of the sword hilt, and just for that moment, there was nothing else in the universe that existed for him.

The sword emerged easily from the stone. Connor raised it and smiled to see the light reflect from the shining blade. Or was it just a reflection? For a moment, the sword itself seemed to glow with some powerful inner energy.

Then he heard a low growl from somewhere behind his back.

Swordplay

He spun around. A creature was lurching toward him. It looked vaguely human, but its eyes shone a dark red and twisted horns grew from its head. When it opened its mouth to growl again, Connor saw rows of sharp teeth.

Holly screamed. Instinctively he stepped toward the demon, keeping Holly behind him, whirling the sword up in a cut to the thing's neck. The sword cut through the demon's flesh like a hot knife through butter, and its head bounced on the floor.

A moment later, head and body had both disappeared. Connor stood holding the sword and staring at the spot where the demon had been. *Okay,* he thought. This *doesn't exactly fill me with holiday cheer. How's Holly doing?*

But when he turned to check on her, she just pointed over his shoulder, her eyes big as saucers. Connor whirled to see two more of the demons coming at him.

Connor dodged a slashing blow from one's claws, and chopped at the other's legs. The one he'd hit collapsed, howling, as Connor spun around and thrust the first one in what he hoped was the general vicinity of its heart. That demon, too, fell with a crash, and Connor struck off the other's head.

Once again, the bodies disappeared after a moment. Connor leaned on his sword, panting. The game was going through different levels, he realized. So the next one would be harder, and the next one, and the one after that...

And then, he thought, *usually you fail a level, sooner or later. It wouldn't be much of a game, otherwise.*

"Umm...over there..." said Holly in a small voice.

A few yards to his right, a giant appeared in the middle of the floor, bent nearly double under what Connor had to admit was probably, by its standards, a pretty low ceiling. It roared defiance at Connor and shambled toward him, hefting a huge club in its hand.

Connor, avoiding the first thunderous blow of the giant's club, managed to dodge between its legs, come out behind it, and slice off its club hand. While the giant stared stupidly at the stump, Connor slashed it behind the knee, and as it bowed down toward him, he was able, with a leap and an overhanded blow, to cut off its head too.

The giant's body shimmered and evaporated as Connor gulped air and looked around wildly for the next threat. At least, he thought, the sword could cut through anything. So far. He tried not to think about monsters made of stone or metal. Why borrow trouble?

In a couple of heartbeats, another creature exploded into being. This one looked like some kind of dinosaur, the two-legged kind. A predator. It hissed at him with three writhing, snakelike heads.

One head struck at Connor, fangs bared. He sidestepped and lopped it off, as easily as taking the head off a dandelion. Its blood was black, and smoked where it fell to the floor.

Hey, this isn't so hard, he thought. Maybe I've topped out on this game.

"*Connor...*" Holly hissed, her fingers digging into his arm.

The head that was on the floor disappeared. But from the stump of neck it had left, two more heads grew, pushing out of the flesh and rising up, with hissing roars, to sway beside the two that he hadn't touched.

Connor's heart sank. There was no way to beat this one, he realized. He clenched his teeth and brought the sword back up, waiting for the strike that would finish him.

"Oh, dear," said a voice from behind him. "I really think you'd better put the sword down."

Twelve

Connor risked one glance behind him. A woman stood there. The light shone from behind her, so he got just an impression of a grandmotherly sort of out-
line, and then he whipped back around to face the hydra. One of its heads struck again, and he twisted out of the way as it hissed in chagrin.

"Put the sword down?" he gasped over his shoulder. "You mean, like, *down* down? You've got to be kidding."

The woman sighed and came closer. "Let me show you."

She moved in front of him. He could see now that she had white hair, and was dressed in green. Connor tried to grab her shoulder. "Of all the crazy—"

One of the hydra's heads darted at her. She made no attempt to dodge. Its teeth met, or seemed to meet, in her wrist. The woman laughed and turned back to Connor, holding up her hand.

"See?" she said. "It can't hurt you. Just put the sword down."

Open-mouthed, Connor complied, backing over to the exhibit and thrusting the sword back into the stone, which opened like water to receive it. Immediately the hydra vanished with a soft popping noise.

"That's how you turn it off," the old woman explained.

Connor nodded. "Sure. Of course. Thanks for letting me know. Because when you're being attacked by huge *monsters*, the last thing anybody would ever *think* of is to let go of the only thing that's keeping them *alive!*" His voice kept rising, until he realized he was shouting at this woman. This old woman, who must be...who *couldn't* be...

She nodded, serenely. "Yes, that's the problem. You've put your finger on the design flaw in this one."

Connor gazed at her, breathing deeply. He wondered now how he could have thought she was old. Her hair was white, for sure, but there were no lines on her face. In fact, except for the hair, he would have thought she was a young woman. She wore a green robe, trimmed with white fur. It looked like she might have been getting ready to go to bed, tucked up for a long winter's nap.

Then, for just a second, she changed. Now Connor saw an bony hag in ragged clothes and broken shoes, clutching a broom like a witch.

Connor blinked and rubbed his eyes. When he looked back, she was once again the smiling, ageless woman he'd seen before.

"Who...are you?" he asked, and because that seemed a bit too rude, he added, not knowing what else to do, "...ma'am."

"Mother Winter, of course," Holly said, with complete certainty.

The woman smiled. "Anyone who has lived as long as I have has more than one name. Befana, or Doña Noel, or...oh, so many others. But since I'm at home, Mother Winter is just fine. That's one of my oldest names, and old names are like a good pair of slippers. They get more and more comfortable as the years go on."

Holly smiled at Mother Winter again. "I knew you would be here," she said simply. "And the Old—I mean, Father Winter—will be back soon, too, won't he?"

"He will," Mother Winter said, with an answering smile. "And then, Connor and Holly, you might have a bit of explaining to do."

"You know all about us," Holly said happily.

"Not *all* about you, but enough for now. You can tell me more, if you like, while we're waiting."

"Yeah, well, it wasn't our fault, getting caught by these...rejected toys," Connor said truculently. "Why do you keep dangerous things like that around?"

"It's for the elves," Mother Winter explained. "When the young ones start as apprentices, they go there to study, so they learn what not to do."

"But there are no signs or anything," Connor pressed. "You should be more careful with this stuff."

"Connor...there kind of *was* a sign," Holly pointed out.

"Oh. That," he muttered. "Okay...but still..."

Mother Winter raised her eyebrows. "We keep the toys in a palace floating in the air over the North Pole, in a closed room which, assuming you're not an elf, you can only find by chance. I think we weren't far wrong to think that not *very* many children would be put in danger."

"All right. Sorry." Connor held up his hands in a defensive gesture.

"All the same, I need to apologize too," Mother Winter went on. "I should have been down here sooner. But I was up in the towers, waking the owls, when I heard a noise down here."

"Waking the owls?" Holly asked.

"The owls stay awake all winter, while the elves are sleeping," Mother Winter said. "There are mice up in the towers, you see, and the owls hunt them."

"Do they...*eat* them?" Holly was half repelled and half fascinated.

Mother Winter nodded matter-of-factly. "They must, because there's a rooster sleeping at the top of the highest tower. If the mice make too much noise gnawing and scurrying around, they'll disturb him. And if that rooster wakes, and he begins to crow..."

"What would happen then?" Connor asked.

"Well," said Mother Winter. "Let's just say that a certain dawn would come much too soon, and things would be very different."

Connor shook his head in wonder. "I don't understand. Not that it matters, really." He looked into Mother Winter's beautiful face that wasn't either young or old. "I never dreamed I'd meet anyone like you...that is, I don't know whether I really...and all this stuff that's happened, I don't know what to..." He stopped, realizing that he wasn't making any sense.

"Believe?" Mother Winter gave him a sharp glance. "Oh, I see now. You spent some time with the Snow Fox, didn't you?"

Connor stared at her, surprised. "Yes. How did you know?"

"People like you usually wind up meeting him," she said cryptically. "Well, children, it might be just a little while longer, before my husband is back. Won't you come back into the study with me and have some refreshment in the meantime?"

Connor glanced at Holly. He still had some lingering doubts, but he could see that she was happy, with the luminous kind of happiness that comes from believing that lots of things are about to happen, and all of them will somehow make you happier still. Like…he searched for some comparison.

Of course, he thought. Just like a kid on Yule morning.

Holly followed after Mother Winter, and as he had been doing for so long, Connor followed her. She led them out to the gallery, with a faint *tsk* at the Nut-
cracker's ruined leg propping the door open, and back into the room where the List and the High Seat waited.

Holly stepped over the threshold and stopped short. Connor almost ran into her. He looked over her shoulder. "This...isn't the same room," he said.

Instead of a high chamber with a ceiling that reached up to the stars, they saw a snug, comfortable den. There was a huge fireplace full of piled logs resting on andirons with reindeers' heads. There were several large easy chairs arranged around the hearth, and on one wall, a floor-to-ceiling bookcase crammed with volumes in tattered binding. Opposite the bookcase was a big, old-fashioned rolltop desk with pigeonholes crammed with papers, and more papers littering the desk itself.

Holly and Connor stepped in hesitantly, feeling like children who had already stayed up too long, being called into the room where the grownups were waiting to send them to bed. Mother Winter went to the hearth and held her hand over the logs for a moment. Immediately a blaze started up, and in moments the most cheerful of fires was dancing there. The reindeer's antlers cast complicated shadows on the hearth, like the silhouettes of many-branched trees.

Mother Winter turned back to Connor and Holly. "Make yourselves at home, children," she said.

Holly tentatively moved toward the chair nearest the fire, but Mother Winter held up her hand in warning and shook her head.

"Better not sit in that one. You didn't like it much, a little while ago."

"But I didn't," Holly protested. "I never sat there."

"You did," Mother Winter said gently. "And you saw your mother and father, and then you fell."

"That's the High Seat?" Holly stared at it as if it were a snake coiling to strike. "Oh, Mother Winter...what I saw when I climbed up there..."

She didn't finish, but Mother Winter answered her unspoken question. "The High Seat looks out over time, as well as space. You might have seen things that are happening now, or things that have already come to pass.

It's hard even for my husband to tell the difference, sometimes."

Holly nodded, but not as if she found any real comfort in the answer. Connor looked at Mother Winter. "So this is…the *same* room, really?" he asked slowly.

She nodded. "You're seeing it now the way that we see it."

"But which one is real?"

"Well, we could talk for *quite* a long time about that," she said with a smile. "Let's just say that right now, what you see around you is real. More real, perhaps, than things you might see every day, down there in the world."

Holly looked around. "But that must mean the List is here somewhere. Where is it?"

Mother Winter pointed to the bookcase. "There it is."

"All those old books?" Connor walked over and studied the books. Scanning the rows, he couldn't see a trace of lettering on any of the spines. He noticed, though, that there was one gap where it looked like a volume was missing. "How do you tell them apart?" he asked.

"Oh, we have a system," Mother Winter assured him. "But don't worry about that right now. Here's a nice chair for you over here, and I'll take this one facing you."

The chair was so big it was almost like a loveseat. Holly and Connor both fit into it comfortably. A small coffee table stood before it, just within easy reach.

He let Holly snuggle up next to him. I'm staying close to her anyway, he thought. Until we find out if this is *really* a good place.

"Now, try some of the milk and cookies," Mother Winter beamed from the depths of her easy chair.

Connor looked at the table, and saw a plate of cookies, and two big glasses of milk, that hadn't been there a moment before. Holly picked up one of the glasses and took a drink, but Connor hesitated.

"Is there...well, any more grownup kind of drink here? Or maybe just water?" he asked.

"There's a drink that I and my husband have sometimes, of a winter's night," she answered. "But it would be much too strong for you, I'm afraid. As for water, *that* wouldn't really satisfy your thirst." Either Connor imagined it, or she gave him another sharp, meaningful glance as she said that. "Try the milk, it will do you good."

Connor took a brief sip. The milk *was* good. He had forgotten how good it could taste, and as he realized that, many other things he'd forgotten came flooding back to him: coming in from an afternoon's play to the smell of baking cookies filling the house...Holly in her high chair pretending to give her dolls a drink...his mother sharing biscotti dipped in coffee with his father, while he told the family stories about the missions that he'd flown all around the world...

I spent so much time hating being a kid, Connor thought. Wanting to grow up right away, like *now*. But sometimes...sometimes, it's okay to not be done with childhood, not quite yet.

"The cookies are even better, Connor," said Holly, with her mouth full.

They were. Some were chocolate, some purely sweet with butter and honey, and some tasted of spices he couldn't put a name to right away. He washed down each bite with long draughts of the milk. In a few minutes, during which there were only the sounds of eating and drinking (besides the fire's hiss and crackle, which, Connor thought, was only another kind of eating noise, after all), they had cleared the platter.

Somehow, the glasses they thought they'd already emptied still held one last sip of milk. The children sank back into the chair with sighs of contentment.

"That last cookie," Connor said. "The one shaped like a Yule tree. It tasted like...like..."

"Eggnog," said Mother Winter. "Those were eggnog cookies."

They had almost forgotten that she was there. "Oh," Holly said. "I'm sorry, we ate them all. We should have asked if you wanted one."

"You were hungry, and I'm not," she said with a smile. "But thank you."

Connor looked at her curiously. In the firelight, she looked a little older, though still hale and hearty. A thousand questions were clamoring in his mind. The one that came out wasn't what he had expected.

"Why do you dress in green?" he asked.

Holly glanced at him. Connor saw that she thought it was a very sensible question. "I've been wondering about that, too," she agreed.

"We always have," said Mother Winter. "Oh, sometimes I enjoy being Befana too, and then, of course, I wear black. But usually, it's green. People knew that, back—oh, a few hundred years ago. Later, some artists started making pictures of us in red. We didn't mind—it's always been one of the season's colors, thanks to the Holly—and the elves liked it. They're more concerned with keeping up with the times. You saw how they've brought new technology into the workshop. But my husband and I are a bit...well, I guess you could call us old-fashioned." She chuckled.

Holly opened her mouth to ask something else, but at that moment they heard a door closing, and the sound of footsteps approaching the study. Heavy, booted feet.

Mother Winter rose. "That will be him now."

The Old Man Himself

Connor and Holly looked toward the door, with bated breath. It seemed like a long time before it swung open, and at last they saw him.

Santa Claus...the Holly King...Father Winter...the Old Man himself.

Holly knew immediately that this was the right one, at last. Like Mother Winter, he was dressed all in green, in a heavy hooded coat trimmed with white fur. His beard was whiter still, bright as the new-fallen living snow she'd seen crossing the aurora bridge. He looked older than his wife did, and seemed grave and solemn at first, but his eyes twinkled at her under his shaggy brows.

But as with Mother Winter, Connor saw something quite different, just for a moment. A goat-man with horns and hooves came through the door, its long tongue lolling out, rattling chains as it came.

It was like a flash of his old visions. But then the Krampus disappeared and he saw Father Winter, just as Holly did.

Mother Winter went to him and they shared a kiss. Then he turned to the children. "Well," he said. "It's been a long journey for you, Holly and Connor. Welcome." His voice was just right, too—so deep the children could almost feel it in their bones, but bright with a sense of laughter always hovering around the edges.

While Connor was groping for the right words—or any words at all—Holly blurted out the first thing that came into her head. "You don't look as fat as I thought you would be," she said, and then, horrified, clapped a hand over her mouth.

Father Winter threw back his head and laughed. "I've heard that before, from children," he said. "Older people usually aren't so truthful."

"You mean," Holly said, forgetting her embarrassment, "that children *have* seen you before?"

Father Winter nodded. "Grownups too, sometimes. Though they don't always know who I am. Even children might meet me, and not realize. Think, Holly—have you ever seen me before?"

He smiled and put his hood up for a moment. His eyes gleamed out at her from the shadows, reflecting the dancing firelight.

"You were the prospector!" she cried.

"Prospector? You were that...polar bear, that changed into like, the old man standing in the river?" Immediately Connor felt like covering his own mouth, but instead he added lamely, "Um...I liked that. It was so *cool*."

"Come sit by the fire," Mother Winter urged him. "You must be cold."

"Just a bit," Father Winter admitted. "It's eighty-five below, up there. I'm letting the reindeer rest and warm up a while. We've gone ten thousand miles already, and the night's work is far from done."

He eased himself into the chair nearest the fire, with a sigh. Holly watched him closely. When he sat there, was he really seeing, somehow, not the cozy room and the fire, but instead the moon and the stars and the whole earth?

But as far as she could tell right now, he was looking only at her and Connor, with a smile of kindly interest.

He spoke to Holly first. "Well, Holly. You've come a long way. Would you like to come and sit in my lap for a while?"

Holly stood up hesitantly. "It's all right," Father Winter said, answering her unspoken thought, as Mother Winter had earlier. "Sitting here with me isn't at all the same thing as it is to sit in my chair alone."

Reassured, Holly climbed into Father Winter's lap. She still felt as if she were suddenly very high, as if she'd just climbed a mountain instead of only taking a step up into the chair.

But she felt warm and safe with the Old Man looking down at her. She smelled nutmeg and cinnamon, and something else she hadn't expected—a scent cool as a winter breeze, but at the same time, aromatic, and faintly medicinal. It reminded her of something from her mom's herb cupboard. Juniper berries, she thought. That was it.

Tell Me What You Want

Connor waited, feeling, again, as if he were much younger, waiting in line at the store to talk to Santa. Except that had been a time of pleasurable anticipation, and now it felt more like facing the music. He glanced over at Mother Winter, but she had taken out a skein of wool and a pair of needles and was knitting.

Father Winter looked down at Holly with a smile. "This is the time when most little girls would tell me what they want for Yule."

"Well...first I want to ask you some things. Is that okay?"

"Yes," he said. "It's all right, though I may not be able to answer every question you have."

She wriggled in a bit closer. There were bits of melting snow on Father Winter's coat, but she didn't mind. "What were you doing," she asked, "down there in the river?"

"I was working on the List," he answered, seriously.

"Oh. Wasn't it supposed to be finished already?"

"I'm always at work on it. And it will never be finished. Not, anyway, until more time has passed than you can imagine."

"But those fish..." Holly paused, puzzled. "What did that have to do with the List? And why did they turn to gold?"

He chuckled. "Your second question isn't the right one to ask. You should ask, why did only *some* of them turn to gold? Why not all of them?"

"Well," said Holly obediently, "why not?"

"For the same reason that people don't always choose to be good. Not even if they suspect that someone, somewhere, might be keeping a List. That's all I can tell you now. Maybe you can ask me again, when the world is older. The important thing is, I've been finding out what kind of metal you and your brother are made of."

Her brow furrowed. "What metal?"

"Oh, there's gold there," Father Winter mused. "Mixed with a few other things, of course. But what I pay attention to is the gold."

Holly was feeling sleepy all of a sudden, and couldn't quite follow what Father Winter was saying. She yawned. Then she remembered something. "Snowthorn," she said. "I wanted to tell you about Snowthorn."

Connor saw that Mother Winter had already finished what she had been working on—a scarf with a pattern of red reindeer jumping over white stars, on a green background—and was beginning another.

"You're *fast*," he said.

"Thousands of years' practice," Mother Winter answered comfortably, without looking up from her work.

"What about Snowthorn?" Father Winter asked Holly. He seemed to be trying not to smile.

"Well...it wasn't his fault. I talked him into taking me here. So he shouldn't get into trouble. And maybe he could get one of those R and B jobs, you know, even if...he *might* not have any brownie points left at all, and maybe I had something to do with it?"

She looked up at Father Winter appealingly. He waited for a moment. "Is that all?" he asked gently. Holly nodded.

Father Winter sighed. "You have to realize that Snowthorn has been...well, let's say a bit thoughtless, for a long time. After all, he'd already used up nearly all his elf points, before you even met him."

Holly's eyes filled with tears. "But...now he has nothing left and...it's because of me! I made him take me to the North Pole because I was naughty...and th-then he had to use more of his magic to help me when I was naughty *again*...and I didn't know, and I'm sorry! I really am!"

Father Winter held her as she sobbed, and waited for her to work her way through to sniffles again. Then he said, "No. You didn't know. I'll see what can be done for Snowthorn, Holly. I promise to look into his case myself.

"But I doubt that you really made him do anything. He liked you. So he wanted to stay with you and help you however he could. That's the truth, no matter what he said."

"He complained a lot," Holly said, with a sudden giggle.

"He had some reason," Father Winter said gravely. "You *were* rather naughty, you know."

Holly hung her head. "I know. I mean, I know that it said so, on the List. But I don't really understand. All I was trying to do was help Connor."

"Yes. But changing the List wasn't the way to do that. You were trying to make Connor nice by giving him what he wanted. But getting what they want, or what they think they want, hardly ever turns a naughty person into a nice one. Remember Rule Three. You can't make someone else be good. They have to decide for themselves."

"I see now," Holly said slowly. "I'll try to remember that."

She was quiet for a while. Father Winter smiled at her. "Is there something else you want to ask?"

"Well..." Holly said. "Rule Four. That still just doesn't seem fair. *Why* are there no guarantees?"

Father Winter nodded gravely. "It's a hard thing to understand, Holly. But you can't think just of yourself making a wish, as if you were alone in the world. This world, and every world, are full of people who are making wishes too, and making mistakes, or even doing things purposely that are wrong. And the world has laws. People are always running up against them and trying to get around them, but they don't go away.

"So when anyone asks me to grant a wish, I need to fit it in with everything that is happening and all that must happen."

Holly had no words to answer. She still didn't understand, not really. But she remembered Snowthorn saying, *You will,* and had a strange feeling that he'd been right. Someday, she would know.

And for now, that was enough.

"It's almost Connor's turn now, Holly. So no more questions. Tell me what you want for Yule."

"But...I was naughty. Do I still get to ask?"

"Yes," said Father Winter. His voice was solemn, but Holly thought she saw his lips twitch, under the beard, in a small smile. "You still get to ask."

"Well, then..." Holly hid her face in his beard, soft as clouds, for a moment, then gathered her courage and looked up again. "I don't know if it's still naughty, but I have to ask that you forgive Connor. What I did was bad, but he came here just because of me. Only because of me, to keep me safe. And when I climbed up to your High Seat and fell, he was there to catch me."

"Hmmm," Father Winter said, stroking his beard. "Let me think about that."

"Did I break Rule Three again?" asked Holly plaintively, peering up at him.

"Not this time," said Father Winter gently. "But isn't there anything that you want to ask for yourself? Last chance."

Holly didn't hesitate this time. "I want my daddy to be all right, Father Winter. I want him to come home. And if you don't..." She gulped, then went on. "If you don't help him, I'm afraid he never will."

"I'll do what I can, Holly," Father Winter said. "But you have to know that there are some things—"

"Don't say it!" Holly wailed. "Not you, too!"

"I was going to say," Father Winter went on, raising an eyebrow, "that there are certain things that can be a *little* tricky to arrange. But I promise that I'll do everything I can."

"Rule Four," Holly muttered, looking crestfallen. "I know."

"I heard someone say once that rules are made to be broken," Father Winter said, with a wink. "Now, climb down and go have some more milk, and have a talk with Mother Winter. It's Connor's turn now."

Not Entirely an Accident

Holly gave Father Winter a quick hug and kiss, and was at Mother Winter's side in a moment. She laid down the second scarf she'd been knitting, finished now, and smiled at Holly. Connor got up out of his chair, but stood shifting from foot to foot, feeling awkward. *Me, sitting in his lap? Not a cute picture*, he told himself.

"Well, Connor, you're a little big for my lap," Father Winter said, echoing his thoughts. "So why don't you sit back down over there, and we'll just have a talk. Can you tell me what *you* want for Yule?"

Connor looked down. "The first thing is," he said, apparently talking to his own feet, "that Holly doesn't really know what happened. I told her, but...I might have told it a little differently. Anyway, I got here because I picked up Snowthorn's Wishing Cap by mistake."

"I wouldn't be too sure about that," Father Winter said.

"What do you mean?" Connor stared at him.

"Well, just that it might not be entirely an accident that you weren't able to climb in the window, and tripped over the cap in the first place."

Connor thought about that for a minute. He tried to understand the whole chain of events that needed to take place just to get him in that place at that moment, but he couldn't grasp it. "You mean," he asked slowly, "that there isn't any such thing as an accident?"

"Oh, I wouldn't go quite that far," Father Winter chuckled. "You and Holly winding up in the Hall of Rejected Toys was an accident, though luckily not a bad one. But I'm forgetting my manners—I shouldn't interrupt. Please go on."

"Anyway, with the Wishing Cap, I thought I could save Holly, and be a hero, without it costing me anything. Without having to even *do* anything, because I would wish that none of it ever happened. But even so, I still wanted to show off." Connor nearly blushed, thinking of how he'd tried to wish his gang up to his camp. "It didn't work, of course. And *then* I had a stupid accident, and I lost the cap. Some hero."

"That wasn't exactly an accident, either," Father Winter said. "As you found out, you can't make wishes that take away other people's free will. That would go against Rule Three. And as for wishing away Time itself, and making something as if it had never been—well, not even I can do that.

"Anyway, North Wind saw what you were trying to do. Her heart's in the right place, but she can be a bit rough at times, and she has no patience with naughtiness. She blew the cap out of your reach so that—"

The Old Man stopped himself and smiled. "Sorry, there I go again. I'm supposed to be listening to you. Keep right on, Connor, don't mind me."

"So that was why I was following Holly," Connor went on. "I really didn't know what else to do, and I had nowhere to go. And as for saving her..." He stopped and looked over at Holly, who was chatting happily with Mother Winter. "I was just in the right place at the right time, that's all. But Holly—the only reason she came here was to help me. And I would have fallen if it wasn't for her—before, when we were crossing the bridge. It was only following her, thinking of her, that kept me alive.

"So—" Connor drew a deep breath. "I'm not doing this very well, but what I want to ask his, that Holly should get what she wants for Yule. It's not fair that she should be down on the List as naughty because of me, because of what she tried to do for me."

Father Winter nodded. "All right. But I must say that Rule Three seems to be an especially difficult one, for people in your family. So I'm going to ask you again, just as I asked Holly. What do you want for yourself?"

Connor closed his eyes a moment, remembering the nightmare he'd seen floating outside the palace: his father on the mountainside, being buried by an avalanche, over and over again. "Just to have my dad back," he said at last.

"But I thought you were angry at your father," Father Winter said, raising his bushy eyebrows. "I thought you were busy doing all the bad things you could think of, just to show how little you cared about him."

"How...how did you know about what I was feeling?" For a moment Connor flashed back to the Snow Fox and his talk of stolen dreams.

"It's been a very long time, Connor," Father Winter said, a faint note of weariness coming into his voice, "since people have thought of new ways to be naughty. Or even new ways to justify it. But about your father..."

He rose and strode over to the desk, put on a pair of spectacles that had been resting on a shelf, and rummaged about, pulling one piece of paper after another out of the pigeonholes. "Ah," he said. "Here it is."

He turned back to Connor, holding out a letter. Connor felt a shock. He recognized the handwriting. "Both you and Holly asked me, first, to give the other one what he or she wanted," Father Winter said. "Since it turns out that you both want the same thing, I don't need to decide which of your wishes I try to grant. To make things even easier, I have a letter here from—well, let's just say someone very close to both of you—and *she* is asking me for the same thing, too."

"So it wasn't just a dream," said Connor, half to himself. "But how did you get it so quickly?"

"Your dream, the one you had in the Snow Fox's den, drifted all the way up here," Father Winter smiled. "And your mother's letter was part of it. Don't think about it too much," he advised, as Connor shook his head helplessly. "I don't have any quarrel with Time or Space, myself, but I can't say I always understand them. The important thing is that your mother also asked me for another thing, something that I *can* promise. To bring you, Holly and Connor, back to your home."

Holly and Connor looked at each other. Connor thought of his bed, carefully made, smooth as newfallen snow. Holly thought of seeing her mother's haggard face from the High Seat.

And both felt a wave of homesickness.

"I'm ready, Father Winter," Holly said, after flinging her arms around Mother Winter and giving her a kiss too.

"Um...so am I," said Connor awkwardly, not sure if he was expected to do the hugging thing. He hadn't even hugged his mother in a year or so, though just at the moment, that was beginning to seem a bit sad. Then he suddenly remembered something else. "But one thing first," he said.

He fished in his jacket pocket and pulled out the small book he'd picked up from the floor of his house the day before. He held it out to Father Winter. "I think this is yours, sir. It's the part of the List that Snowthorn was supposed to bring. I picked it up and tried to look at it. I'm sorry."

Father Winter took it and nodded his thanks. He turned to the bookcase and fit the book into the gap in the rows of ranked volumes. For a moment Connor had a flash of double vision. At one and the same time he saw Father Winter sliding the book into its place, and also touching the small book to the cover of the huge tome that they'd seen before, which seemed to absorb it and grow slightly thicker.

"Then the List is—finished?" Holly asked, in awe.

"For now," Father Winter said. "And for now, it's time to say goodbye."

Mother Winter stood up, beaming, and wound one of the scarves around Holly's neck, and the other around Connor's. She had a third ready, as well, which she handed to Father Winter. "For the journey," she said. "The night is deep, and the upper air will be still colder."

The children shivered, remembering. Holly hugged Mother Winter. "Thank you," she said. "For everything. Will we ever see you again?"

It was Father Winter who answered. "It's not often that children come to us, Holly," he said. "And I go only where I'm most needed. So it may be a while."

"But not so very long, I think," said Mother Winter softly in her ear.

Connor hugged Mother Winter awkwardly, and the children went out with Father Winter into the star-filled night. They passed the Nutcrackers, who seemed harmless now, looking like clowns with their garishly painted faces. They went past the tree that stood with stars caught in its dark branches, and the sleigh stood there shining before them, with the reindeer lifting their heads to gaze curiously at the children.

"I should tell you," Father Winter said, "no one who rides in my sleigh ever remembers it. You'll fall asleep when you step in."

"Will we fall down?" Holly asked.

"Don't worry. I'll lay you down gently. When you wake up, you'll be home."

"Sir," Connor ventured, "will we...will we think this was all just a dream?"

Father Winter smiled. "You'll think whatever you choose. Your memories are your own."

Holly, behind Connor, whispered in his ear, "He put that third scarf away in his pocket. Who is *that* for?"

But just then Father Winter reached out his hand, and Connor took it and stepped up into the sleigh. So he could never remember if he'd actually tried to answer Holly's question.

Something About the Dawn

Still, there was one memory Connor carried out of the frozen darkness. It was the memory of a dream. It seemed true to him, but he could never quite be sure. After all, how can you dream about the place where all dreams go?

He saw the cozy room they'd just left, empty now except for Mother Winter sitting by the glowing fire. She was still working, sewing something now, but he couldn't quite see what it was she was making—maybe just a soft, white blanket, big enough for the whole world to pull over itself and settle down to sleep.

Then there were footsteps at the door, and she put her work aside. As she did, a single feather drifted down to the floor like a snowflake.

"Dawn was nearly breaking, in that part of the world," Father Winter said, as the door closed behind him. "Time may slow down, but even for me, she never quite stands still."

"Hey, watch it," a voice complained from behind him. "You nearly shut my tail in the door."

The Snow Fox came into the study after Father Winter, looked around, nodded at Mother Winter, and promptly curled up by the fire. Well, Connor thought, that *proves* that this is a dream.

Father Winter lowered himself slowly down into his easy chair again. "So," he said to the Fox. "Busy night?"

"Not compared to yours." The Snow Fox yawned. "A little boring, actually, after Connor left. How did that whole quest thing work out for him, anyway?"

"Well, I think," Father Winter said softly. "Very well."

"Well, personally I think you went too far, this time," Mother Winter told the Fox. "The way you were making him see the palace. A sleigh full of coal? Snowmen with fangs? Really!"

"Artistic license," said the Snow Fox complacently. "It kept him going, didn't it? Would he have kept following his sister and been there to save her, much less found out what he really wanted, if he thought she was just taking a little vacation at Club Elf?"

Was I just another sucker, then? Connor wondered. He was a little surprised to find that the thought didn't bother him. He no longer felt that being smart was all that mattered.

"It's always a risk," Father Winter said. "You have a few others who are still on the way, I think?" he asked the Snow Fox.

"One or two who'll probably be wandering around invisible until next year's Eve at least," the Fox admitted. "I can't help it, I'm a persuasive guy."

"And what about those wolves?" Father Winter raised his eyebrows.

"Hey, I'm not taking the blame for *them*. If they had anything on the ball, they would have made it here *years* before they got trapped in those animal shapes." The Fox chuckled. "Oh, even the Pack will get through to the next level. Eventually. But they've still got a decade of howling at the moon to go, or I'm a pixie."

Father Winter snapped his fingers. "Speaking of pixies, that reminds me. Snowthorn still needs to stand first watch. Someone has to go and wake him up."

The Snow Fox scrambled to his feet. "No problem. I'll do it." The door opened a crack for him, and he padded out with an evil chuckle.

"Gently, now," Father Winter called after him. "Do you think he'll be surprised?" he asked Mother Winter, when the Fox had gone.

"In the best way," she smiled. "And what about Duck Egg? Did you remember her?"

Father Winter nodded. "Her people will have good hunting until the spring, and plenty of ivory to carve. I wish…"

Connor thought that it was strange to hear Father Winter, who made wishes come true for other people, wish for something himself. Mother Winter looked steadily at her husband and waited.

"I wish," he said finally, "that no one ever lost their way. And that everyone always knew what they really wanted. And that I could always give it to them."

She came softly over and held him, laying her head on his shoulder. Father and Mother Winter stayed that way for a long time, while the fire quietly murmured to itself. It was saying something about the dawn, Connor thought, the dawn that was still far, far away, but always getting closer, crossing Time and Space to bring light to the world.

Connor would have liked to know if Father Winter's wish was granted, and who—or what—could possibly do that.

But he never found out.

Because, of course, it was only a dream.

Thirteen

Let It Snow

When Connor woke up, he was lying on something cold and hard. *Father Winter's sleigh isn't all that comfortable,* he thought. *But what can you expect from a guy who mostly carries freight, not passengers?*

Then his eyes snapped open and he saw that he was sitting, with Holly curled up beside him, on the old wrought-iron bench on their own front porch. It wasn't yet dawn, but the sky was beginning to grow pale in the east.

Holly woke up at the same time, and stretched, looking around in a casual sort of way. Then she suddenly realized where they were, and leaped off the bench, jumping up and down.

"Connor! Father Winter did it! We're back!" She threw herself at him and gave him a hug that was more like a football tackle.

"Okay, okay," Connor said, returning her hug. "It's great. But look, we've got to think fast. We need a story."

Holly gave him a blank look. "A story?"

"Right. They'll ask us a lot of questions, so we need to agree on at least the main points," Connor said rapidly. "So here's what we tell them. There was—let's see, this old fat guy who came and grabbed you out of the yard. I saw his car pulling away and I jumped on the bumper. He took you to this abandoned house on the edge of town and chained you up in the basement. Hmm, I guess we'd better say he caught me, too, while I was trying to get in, and chained me up with you. Then—"

"I think," said Holly, "we should just tell her the truth. About Father Winter and the elves. And Duck Egg's igloo."

Looking at her grave face, Connor felt laughter begin to build up inside of him, and finally it exploded, almost painfully, like water bursting a dam. "Sure," he gasped. "Of course. What was I thinking of? I must be crazy."

It must be, he told himself, the last lingering effects of the ice water the Snow Fox had offered him. Well, he'd never touch the stuff again. Milk and cookies beat it all hollow.

The door swung open and their mom stood there, blinking away sleep. "I thought I heard..." she began.

Then the children both hit her from opposite sides, and she almost stumbled backward, but managed to stay upright. "Connor?

Holly?" She held them blindly, sobbing while she tightened her grip, until it felt like she would never let them go.

And that was a good feeling.

"Come in," she finally managed to choke out. "Come in, come in."

They wound up in the living room in front of the tree, which was fully decorated now and blazing with lights. They sat on the couch together, Holly and Connor still in their coats and scarves since their mother didn't want to let them out of her sight for even a moment.

"But what *happened*?" she asked at last. She'd asked that before, in the middle of laughing and crying, but this time it sounded like she actually expected an answer, and was willing to wait until she got one.

"It's a long story," Connor began diplomatically, but Holly upstaged him. "We went to the North Pole, mommy!" she said excitedly. "An elf took me! And Connor came too because he found a magic wishing cap, and we crossed a bridge floating way up in the air, and met Father and Mother Winter, and—"

"All right," her mom said, with a confused smile. "Don't tell me now. Tell me, um, later, when you've had a chance to rest, and have something to eat. You're both okay? Really okay?"

For the third or fourth time, she felt over their arms and legs and shoulders, looking for broken bones. This time she rested her hand on their foreheads, too.

"We're not sick or crazy, Mom," Connor chuckled. "But yeah, we'll tell you later. I *did* say it's a long story."

"Okay." For the first time, she noticed how they were dressed. "Holly...Connor—where did you get those parkas? And those scarves?" Then she waved her hand, dismissing her own question. "A long story. I know. Look, why don't you guys get out of these things, and I'll call Charlie. He's been out looking for you, I don't think he's been able to sleep much, either."

"Mom," Connor said. "What about Dad? Have you heard anything?"

Her smile vanished for a moment. "No word yet."

She went out and they heard her on the kitchen phone while they were hanging their coats and scarves on the hall tree. "Charlie, thank the Goddess. You're not going to believe this, but they're back. Connor and Holly. They just showed up on the doorstep! Yes, just now..."

Connor and Holly shared a grin. Then Holly looked out the side window, next to the door, and gave a squeal of delight. "Look, Connor! It's snowing!"

Connor looked out too. "You're right. It's like we never left the North Pole."

"It's different here! Mom! Mom! It's snowing! Snowing on Yule!" Holly called, bouncing up and down in transports of delight.

Connor smiled. It was certainly pretty, the first dawn light spilling through the clouds while the large flakes spiraled lazily down. If the sun comes out while it's still falling, he wondered, could there be a rainbow? What would you call that, a snowbow? This seemed like the day it could happen, if ever.

Then, for just a second, he saw it—a curtain of red and green fire, blazing across the sky. It was a bit like the Northern Lights, but Connor was pretty sure that nobody ever saw them this far south. Especially in broad daylight.

He rubbed his eyes and gazed out again. The lights were gone, but the sun was still shining, and the snow kept on falling. Then he saw something else: a tall man in a dirty parka limping down the street, hesitantly, looking around as if he didn't know, or couldn't believe, just where he was.

Must be one of those homeless guys, Connor thought, with a faint pang of sympathy.

All the Colors of the Rainbow

Then his eyes widened as the man turned in at their own gate. His limped a little faster as he came up to the porch. Holly saw him too, and before he could even knock, she had flung the door wide open.

"Daddy—?" She almost wasn't sure. A cold wind swirled around him, like a breath of the Arctic. His face looked older, somehow. He had the beginnings of a beard, with white hairs standing out against the black.

But when he looked at Holly, she saw that his eyes were her father's.

"Holly," he said then, in a hoarse voice. "I wasn't sure if I would ever see you again..."

He folded her in his arms. Connor stood there, feeling paralyzed. His father turned to smile at him too. "Connor," he said, his voice still rough. "Son. I can't tell you how...how..."

His father swayed and nearly fell then. Connor was at his side in a moment, helping him to keep standing and come inside the house, and his mother was there too, trying to help too, though mostly she got in the way and it was nearly a fresh miracle that they made it into the living room.

When they could all breathe again, and his mom had gotten something to drink for all of them, they sat together, with only the tree lights on, but sunlight strengthening around them all the time, streaming in from the windows, while the glittering snow continued to fall.

Their mom nestled closer to their dad, ran her finger gently across his knee. "Your poor leg," she said. "What happened? And why didn't anybody tell us that you were found, that you were coming home?"

Connor's dad chuckled. "I wanted it to be a surprise. Well, that too, but mostly I wanted you to hear it from me first. It's—well, kind of a strange story.

"It started with the climbers who fell going up the glacier—you heard about that. Another plane flew over with me. We'd found all but one of the climbers when the avalanche hit. The whole ravine was buried. The other pilot took back the people we'd rescued, since a couple of them needed to get to a hospital. And I...well, I stayed. For a little while. There wasn't much hope, but I couldn't leave just yet."

He grinned. "It wasn't long before I couldn't leave, period. The snowstorm hit and visibility went down to nothing. I didn't give up looking for the last climber, but before I saw any sign of him, I ran into a rock wall. I'm sorry about that. He had a family who won't see him coming home again."

Their mom hugged him tightly, and it was a moment before he could go on.

"I was knocked out, and I had to burrow out of the snow when I finally woke up. But I was lucky—no concussion, just a few cuts and bruises. After a while of trying to move downslope, I stumbled into an ice cave. They can be dangerous, of course, but right then I needed shelter, any shelter. Once I was in, I should have stayed put, but something made me start to explore."

"That must be what I saw, in the high seat," Holly said to Connor. He nodded.

"You'll have to tell me what that means, later," their dad said. "Anyway, it was a big cave, and the ice turned all the colors of the rainbow in my light. It was just so quiet after the roaring of the avalanche, and the winds…it was like I was hypnotized, I just had to keep going on and on, climbing over boulders and finding new passages. It was like tunneling into the heart of a giant diamond.

"I'd gone fairly deep in when all of a sudden, it looked like the cave might be collapsing. There was no way to get out other than retracing my steps. I turned around quickly—too quickly. I caught my foot in a crack in the ice, and fell. That's when I twisted my leg, too. It didn't look like I had much hope of getting out, but then..."

"Then?" Connor prompted when his dad paused.

"Well, this is going to sound a bit crazy, but...I saw somebody. Somebody else was in that cave. Except, there couldn't have been."

"Altitude sickness?" their mom asked.

He shrugged. "I just got a glimpse, like a shadow. It was somebody really short, I could tell that. I thought...well, of the kinds of things that people see on the mountain sometimes. Ghosts, maybe, or goblins, or dwarves. Something like that."

Holly caught Connor's eye and winked.

"I *know* how it sounds, but we've all heard these stories. People who see phantom climbers and follow them to safety. Anyway, I followed this...person, and it turned out there was another exit from the cave. A lot closer. Once I got out, I found that the snow had stopped. I couldn't quite tell where I was, and there was no short guy anymore. Or not that I could see. But there were footprints. Footprints in the snow, leading down the mountain, and I followed them.

"A thousand feet down or so, around the tree line, I met some park rangers coming up after me. They had a paramedic look me over, and then one of them gave me a ride back.

"And here I am."

After a while their mom disappeared into the kitchen to put together a good, solid breakfast, suitable for returning Arctic travelers. She didn't really disappear, though. She kept looking out every few minutes, making sure everyone was staying put.

Holly just climbed up into her father's lap and snuggled there.

"You're a little like him, now," she said, looking up at her father's face, with its stubble that was black and white and gray, like the sky when a storm was just beginning. "Father Winter, I mean."

"Not much," Connor's dad chuckled. "My magic isn't working. Here it's Yule and I've brought nothing for my family."

"Yes, you have," Connor said, a little shyly.

His father turned to him. "Connor, lad," he said seriously, "I have to tell you this. I'm not that good at being a father, not really. All I knew about was my own childhood. My father and I weren't close. The best times for me were when he just left me alone, and I convinced myself that was fine with me. But I don't think it's really what I wanted or needed. And it's not what I want for you and me."

"Me neither," Connor said around the lump in his throat. "And I'm sorry...I haven't been the best son, either. I mean..."

"Well, then," his father said gently. "We'll just have to start over again, won't we? I'll be around more now. I don't think I'll be flying again. Not for a while."

Connor wasn't sure exactly how that made him feel. He wanted to be with his dad, yes. But he didn't really want him to stop flying. Not anymore.

"But when you're ready to fly over that mountain again," he told his dad, "We'll do it together."

His dad couldn't speak, but he nodded. Connor swallowed hard. He leaned his head on his dad's shoulder, and his dad ran his hand through Connor's hair. That would have made him angry once, being treated like a little kid. But this time, he felt something like he had when drinking the magic ice water in the Snow Fox's den—everything was so luminously clear, as if he were seeing and knowing the world for the first time. The difference was that now he felt a great and growing warmth, inside and outside.

The rest of the day was a blur of happiness for both Connor and Holly. But there were two moments that stood out clearly from the rest.

One was when they finally got around to taking down the stockings. One thing in Connor's dream had been wrong—his mom *had* gone ahead and filled all the stockings, even though at that point, she had no idea anyone would be home on Yule morning. But still, it seemed there were a few...extras.

Connor got a silver sword pendant on a leather thong. When he put it around his neck, the sword started glowing, just like the real one in the Hall of Rejected Toys. Holly found a small, wind-up Nutcracker in her stocking. Connor wasn't sure how she would feel about that, but she was delighted, winding it up over and over to watch it walk around waving its tiny sword.

Their dad pulled out a scarf, with a design of reindeers and stars. He immediately wound it around his neck. Their mom kept staring at it, then looking over at Connor. He pretended to be really interested in Holly's Nutcracker, which she'd put down under the tree. Actually he *was* interested, because he saw Grimalkin, who had been sniffing at the Nutcracker, back off quickly when it poked its sword at his nose—without anyone winding it up first.

Later, when they started opening the presents, and their mom brought out milk and cookies nearly as good as Mother Winter's had been, Holly saw an envelope sitting on one of the tree branches. It was addressed to her. It wasn't her mother's handwriting, so she brought it over to Connor and they opened it together.

There was a letter inside. It was from Snowthorn.

Dear Holly, he wrote. *I just had to let you know. Somebody woke me up to take my shift, told me to take a look at my card, and I nearly...well, let's just say the rumors of my retirement were greatly exaggerated. Somehow, I'm back up to a thousand elf points—and I'm finally getting that job in R&D! The others will be jealous when they all wake up in the spring, and there's a certain pixie who I'll be...well, never mind.*

Anyway, I just met the Old Man at last, and he says it's all because of you and your brother. I guess that whole thing with the List worked out, because I sneaked a peek, and you and Connor both have Nice next to your names now. In gold letters!

Got to go now. I just wanted to say thank you. And Merry Yule!

"So you did it after all," Connor said to Holly. "You changed the List."

Holly shook her head. "You don't get it, Connor," she said. "But I love you." She hugged him tightly, and he hugged her back, surprised at how good it felt.

"But I do get it," he told her. "We didn't really change the List. Nobody can. It was us who changed. It was us."

Holly hugged Connor again and kissed his cheek.

Then she turned away, standing by the window to watch each snowflake take fire for an instant as it fell. She remembered Rule Four, but this time without sadness or anger.

Okay, she thought. *So there are no guarantees. But that's all right, because sometimes...sometimes...*

She didn't realize she'd said that aloud until Connor finished her thought. "Sometimes," he said softly, "there are miracles."

ERIC TANAFON

I live in New England with my family. I've never traveled to the Arctic, but I had fun looking at webcam videos from the North Pole while writing this story.

Please consider leaving a review on Amazon and/or Goodreads. I'm happy to hear what you liked about the story, as well as what you didn't. Thanks!

I'm also the author of Robin Hood: Wolf's Head and The Road to Hel (Sean's Saga Book 1), available in both print and Kindle editions. The Well of Time, the next installment of Sean's Saga, is due out in 2018. By special arrangement, Sean has also created his own Pinterest board.

I'm also on Goodreads, and please visit my blog at www.etanafon.com and my Amazon author page.

Made in the USA
Las Vegas, NV
13 December 2023